Mama
gets
Hitched

OTHER BOOKS BY DEBORAH SHARP

Mama Does Time
Mama Rides Shotgun

FORTHCOMING BY DEBORAH SHARP

Mama Sees Stars

Mama
gets
Hitched

A Mace Bauer Mystery

DEBORAH SHARP

MIDNIGHT INK
WOODBURY, MINNESOTA

First Edition
First Printing, 2010

Book design and format by Donna Burch
Cover design by Lisa Novak
Cover illustration © Rick Lovell
Editing by Connie Hill

Midnight Ink, an imprint of Llewellyn Worldwide Ltd.

Library of Congress Cataloging-in-Publication Data

Sharp, Deborah, 1954–
  Mama gets hitched : a Mace Bauer mystery / by Deborah Sharp. — 1st
ed.
      p.   cm.
  ISBN 978-0-7387-1922-1
1. Bauer, Mace (Fictitious character)—Fiction.   2. Mothers and daughters—
Fiction. 3. Florida—Fiction. I. Title.
  PS3619.H35645M364 2010
  813'.6—dc22   2010004386

Midnight Ink
A Division of Llewellyn Worldwide Ltd.
2143 Wooddale Drive
Woodbury, MN 55125-2989
www.midnightinkbooks.com

Printed in the United States of America

DEDICATION

To Charlene and Nancy, who love me despite the
cranberry-colored taffeta with humongous bows
I made them wear as bridesmaids;
and to Abbie, our fourth sister of the heart.

ACKNOWLEDGMENTS

I owe a debt to friends and family members who've invited me to their weddings—in some cases, multiple times. All your ceremonies were in excellent taste. I never witnessed a single tacky moment, or anything remotely resembling the fictional mayhem, not to mention murder, that mars Mama's Special Day. On the other hand, there had to be some payback for making me shoehorn my bridesmaid-self into that strapless Scarlett O'Hara number. (You know who you are, Miss Bride!)

As always, I want to thank the world's greatest husband, Kerry Sanders, for unfailing love; and the world's greatest mama, Marion Sharp, for inspiration.

I'm grateful to my fabulous agent, Whitney Lee, and to the talented staff at Midnight Ink. Connie Hill's editing prowess saves me; Courtney Colton spreads the news about my books; and Lisa Novak's genius makes the cover designs pop.

Thanks to Deborah "Dab" Holt, who bid in a charity auction for the chance to have a character named after her in *Mama Gets Hitched*. Always a good girl, she confessed she wanted her character to be bad. I pray she didn't get more than she bargained for.

Thanks, again, to the town of Okeechobee, Florida, the real-life inspiration for fictional Himmarshee.

Finally, I'm indebted to those I've named, to anyone I missed, and especially to you, for reading.

ONE

SMALL, SILVER-TRIMMED CIRCLES OF tulle covered the tabletop. Mama held up what looked like two identical pieces of the fabric, one in each hand.

"Don't tell me you can't see the difference, Mace." She thrust the first circle under my nose. "*This* is celadon." She shook it for emphasis. The fluorescent lights of the VFW hall gave the green tulle a dull gleam. "And *this*," she waved the second circle within inches of my eyes, "is honeydew."

I batted away her hand. "Like I told you, Mama, they look exactly the same. Light green."

She rolled her eyes and sighed heavily, as if she couldn't stand to deal for one more minute with poor dumb trash who couldn't tell the difference between subtle shadings of tulle. I decided I'd had just about enough of her Bridezilla routine.

"Wouldn't you say you're going a little nuts, Mama? Does it really matter whether every square centimeter of tulle is dyed exactly the same shade as the next? All this whoop-de-doo is kind of tacky, anyway. After all, this *is* your fifth trip down the aisle."

Mama looked wounded. "You know I've never had a real wedding, Mace. I eloped with your daddy. And when I got married after he died … well, you know all about Husband No. 2. After that nightmare, I thought I might jinx my third try by making a big to-do. Turned out that one didn't take either, big wedding or small. And then No. 4 and I met on that cruise and decided to have the ship's captain tie the knot."

I remembered. My sisters and I were horrified when Mama came home with a new husband, twenty years her junior. We also got souvenirs that said *My Mother Went to Cancun and All I Got Was This Lousy T-shirt.*

"Poor No. 4," Mama said. "He didn't seem as good a choice on dry land as he had on the high seas. Maybe I shouldn't have mixed champagne with Dramamine. Anyway, Mace, Sally is the first man I've really loved since your daddy. I want this wedding to be perfect."

Mama was marrying Salvatore Provenza—Sally—in less than a week. Under the pressure of pulling off the Ceremony of the Century in Himmarshee, Florida, she'd mutated into someone my sisters and I barely recognized. She was driving us crazy, which wasn't the unusual part. She's always done that. But we'd never seen Mama so obsessed over the inconsequential.

Here's a woman who nearly landed in prison after a corpse turned up in her turquoise convertible. Then, she found an old beau keeled over dead in his Cow Hunter Chili. She's tangled with a gator, and was nearly trampled to death during a week-long

2

horse ride through Florida's cattle country. And that's just what Mama's survived in the past year.

Now, tulle had her in a tizzy. I was ready to head out into the swamp to escape. And my sisters, Maddie and Marty, were almost willing to brave the gators and the snakes to come with me. But I knew I had to give her the customary daughterly pep talk.

"Take a deep breath, Mama," I recited. "Everything's going to be fine. The wedding will be incredible. You'll be the prettiest bride ever."

Mama perked up. She rarely misses a Sunday at Abundant Forgiveness, Love and Charity Chapel. But she must have skipped over that part in the Bible about vanity being a sin. She's tiny, with perfect features in an unlined face. Almost sixty-three, she's still beautiful. And she never tires of being reminded of that fact.

"I'm sorry, Mace." She ran her hands through her platinum-hued hair. "It's all these details. And, of course, That Woman. I'm telling you, honey, she's getting on my last nerve!"

"That Woman" could mean only one person: C'ndee Ciancio, Sal's cousin-in-law from his first marriage. C'ndee had swooped down from New Jersey a month ago, bragging about her wedding-planning expertise, and bulldozing her way into helping Mama. Mama went along, mainly because C'ndee was kin to Sal, and Mama loved Sal.

"Where is she, anyway?" I asked.

Glancing at her watch, Mama frowned. "Running almost twenty minutes late, just like Ronnie Hodges. We were supposed to meet him here at nine a.m. sharp to go over the catering and the *hors d'oeuvres*. I had to steer C'ndee off melon balls wrapped in something called 'prosciutto.' That might fly in Hackensack, I told her, but not in Himmarshee. We're just a little country town. We like things simple."

Simple? Like a *Gone with the Wind*–themed wedding, complete with crinolines and bridesmaids' parasols for my sisters and me? But I wasn't about to start the debate again about those hideous dresses. Like the South and the Civil War, I'd already lost that fight.

Mama returned her attention to the tulle, scrutinizing the circles like a jeweler examining diamonds. I looked out the window. Low, gray clouds had leaked rain all morning, making for a dreary Monday.

"Looks like we're getting an early jump on the rainy season. It's barely June," I said.

"Good thing," Mama said. "It's been so dry, the trees are bribing the dogs."

The rain-slicked parking lot was deserted out front. Water droplets formed and fell from the red flowers of a jatropha branch that brushed against the window. I said a silent prayer the weekend would bring better weather for Saturday's wedding.

Inside, it was all too obvious the VFW had served lots of meals at last night's spaghetti dinner. A ground-beef-and-garlic-scented cloud hung in the air. We'd have to remember to light some of Mama's aromatherapy candles in the hall before the ceremony.

Just then, the side door burst open. C'ndee rushed in, breathless, smelling of rain and White Diamonds perfume. Everything about her was big: A mass of dark, curly hair. Blood-red lips. Generous curves, emphasized by a clingy top, short skirt, and perilously high heels.

Mama looked pointedly at her watch. C'ndee pretended not to see.

"Let me tell you, there aren't enough hours in the day!" She collapsed onto a chair next to Mama. "I found you some to-die-for bridesmaids' gifts, Rosalee."

She plopped a girly looking shopping bag on the table, next to an appointment book and a huge leather purse with more metal studs than a hardware store. "You'll absolutely love them."

"We'll see." Mama folded her arms over her chest.

I just hoped C'ndee hadn't bought us animal-print thong underwear. I'd gotten an unfortunate glance at a leopard pair she wore, when she leaned over in a pair of tight hip-huggers. The undies rode up, the slacks rode down, and I learned more than I wanted to about C'ndee's taste in lingerie.

"Where'd you park, C'ndee?" I asked. "I didn't see you pull in out front."

"There's a big, muddy puddle out there. I parked in back, where it's drier."

I hadn't thought to look in the back when I dropped Mama at the front door, and then waded in from a parking space in ankle-deep water. In the boots I wear for work at Himmarshee Park, I'm not as fussy about getting wet as I might be if I wore shoes like C'ndee's. They gave her "toe cleavage," and probably cost two weeks of my salary.

I could see Mama eyeing the sack on the table with curiosity. I pushed back my chair.

"I'm going to look in the kitchen, see if maybe Ronnie slipped in from the back parking lot, too," I said.

Mama was already tearing at tissue paper as I walked away. C'ndee, meanwhile, lifted the two tulle swatches from the table.

"Oh, my Gawd!" she cried. "These shades are completely different! This is awful, Rosalee!"

Turning, I caught Mama's look of vindication. Then I continued through heavy swinging doors from the dining room into the VFW's kitchen. The lights were off. Weak sunlight peeked through the sole window, a tiny slit near the ceiling. On this gray day, it barely illuminated a corner of the big room. I felt along the wall on each side of the swinging doors.

No light switches. I picked my way carefully into the dark space.

The farther I moved from the little window, the darker the kitchen got. I could just make out the shape of a big stove, and spaghetti pots stacked on tall wire shelves. My eyes were on the shelves when I felt something slick under my boot. I hoped whoever had used the kitchen last had picked up the big stuff. I didn't want to sprawl into grease or sauce or whatever that was on the floor.

A sliver of light shone at the far end of the kitchen, a crack of sunlight under a back door. I inched toward it, hands out to either side to catch me, or anything I might be about to run into.

Finally, I rounded a countertop and reached the door. Feeling for the switches, I flipped on all three. The kitchen gleamed. I felt bad about maligning the cooking crew. I could see extra care had been taken in scrubbing everything clean.

Which made that nasty spot I'd stepped in by the stove seem all the more strange.

Suddenly, I didn't want to find out what was on the floor. I'd walked into something I wished I hadn't a few times before. I hesitated, wondering if I should call Carlos Martinez, my on-again-off-again police-detective boyfriend. Things hadn't gone so well the last time we talked. Plus, how silly would I seem if what had felt slick and scary in the dark was only a puddle of cooking oil?

I retraced my steps around the corner, toward the hulking stove. It was just on the other side where I'd slipped. I swallowed. My mouth was suddenly dry. Slowly, I rounded the big stove and looked down.

A man lay motionless on the floor. His left arm was caught under his body. The right was splayed above his head as if he were reaching out for something—or someone. I recognized brown hair going gray and the tattoo of a tiger on his muscled forearm. Ronnie Hodges.

Blood soaked his white T-shirt, and pooled onto the floor around his body. At the far edge of the dark puddle, a print from a heavy work boot was just my size.

TWO

O<small>NE OF THE SWINGING</small> doors eased open. Mama poked her head into the kitchen.

"Mace, honey? Did you get lost in there? I hope you're making us coffee."

I held up a hand. "Don't come in, Mama. I'm afraid I have some bad news about Ronnie."

She ignored me, as usual, taking a step inside. "Did he call your cell-o-phone and say he won't be able to make it?"

Taking a last look at the body on the floor, I said, "Well, he won't be able to make it, that's for sure."

I hurried out the doors to stop Mama from tromping into a crime scene. At the same time, I found my cell phone in my pocket and hit the speed dial for Carlos. Looks like we'd be "on again," at least for the purposes of another murder investigation.

As his number rang, I was steering Mama back across the dining room. C'ndee still sat at the table, busily separating circles of tulle into two piles.

"¡*Hola, niña!*" Carlos answered, and I could almost see the smile on his face. "Long time no talk."

For a second, I was pleasantly surprised at how happy he sounded to hear from me. Then I remembered why I was calling, and made my tone appropriately grave. "You need to get over here, Carlos," I said. "I just found a body on the floor of the kitchen at the Veterans of Foreign War hall."

Mama's eyes went wide. C'ndee stopped sorting fabric.

"Your phone must be breaking up. I thought you said ... "

"A body," I filled in. "You heard me right."

Mama clutched at her throat with one hand and at my wrist with the other. "Is it Ronnie?" she said in a small voice.

I nodded yes, shushing her with a finger to my lips.

"It's the caterer Mama hired to do her wedding," I said into the phone. "She was supposed to meet him here this morning. When he got to be a half-hour late, I went looking for him. And Carlos? You better bring the crime scene investigator. A big kitchen knife looks to be missing from a hanging rack. And there's an awful lot of blood."

———

Mama, C'ndee, and I sat, shell-shocked, at a round table for eight in the dining room. We were waiting for the police and ambulance to arrive, though I was absolutely certain Ronnie was beyond emergency medical assistance.

All of us were rattled. C'ndee hadn't said a word since I came out of the kitchen. She kept glancing at the closed doors and twisting a gaudy charm bracelet on her left wrist.

"Who'd have wanted to kill Ronnie, Mace?" Mama finally asked. "Do you think it was a robbery?"

"I don't know what to think at this point, Mama."

"I want to see his body."

"Mama, I can tell you for sure he's dead. I checked for a pulse. There was none. He was already cold, and waxy-looking. And there was so much blood."

"He was my neighbor," she said to C'ndee. "We weren't close, but Ronnie and Alice go to my church, Abundant Forgiveness. Well, Alice does anyway. Ronnie's not so big on church services, but he never misses a prayer breakfast. The man sure does love to eat." She paused, laughter dying on her lips. "*Loved* to eat," she corrected herself.

Mama was rambling, like she does when she's nervous. But I knew she'd return to wanting to see for herself that Ronnie was dead.

"I'm sorry, Mama," I said, "but you can't go waltzing around in there. Carlos would have a fit. It's bad enough I tracked through the blood on the floor. The place is a mess. And they don't need any more random visitors in there to account for."

"Well, then," she said, "the least we can do is say a prayer for Ronnie."

"I agree," C'ndee said.

Coming from her, that surprised me. I wouldn't have pegged C'ndee as the godly type. The three of us bowed our heads and joined hands at the table.

"Dear Lord, welcome Ronnie into heaven," Mama prayed. "Let him dwell at your side in eternal peace until the day comes when all of your children will be reunited in your love."

"Ahh-me…" I started to say, when I felt Mama squeeze my hand and continue.

"And, please Lord, remember I'm getting married this coming Saturday…"

I opened one eye and glared out of it at Mama. She snapped her eyelids shut.

"…please give us strength and guidance to complete all these details," she went on, "such as deciding how we're supposed to fill the stomachs of our one hundred and fifty guests."

"Mama!" I hissed.

"In Jesus' name, we pray…"

"Amen!" I added, before she could put in a plug for sunny weather and ask God to keep Uncle Teddy sober through the whole reception.

"Amen," C'ndee echoed softly, as she crossed herself. She glanced again toward the kitchen. Her scarlet lipstick looked even redder now that her face was so pale. Maybe that tough Noo Joisey image was a façade. She seemed more shaken than we did at the idea of a man lying dead in the next room. Then again, Mama and I'd had some experience in the past year finding bodies.

When C'ndee spoke, her normally strident voice was a whisper. "Do you think Ronnie crossed the wrong people?"

Mama and I looked at her blankly.

"Back home, if someone pisses off the *wrong people*," she wriggled her fingers in quote marks, "they wind up in concrete boots."

Mama, exasperated, said, "Just say what you want to say, C'ndee. My stars and garters! I thought all you Yankees were supposed to be direct!"

"Sleeping with the fishes," C'ndee clarified.

Ah-ha.

"That's not how things work in Himmarshee," I told her. "We're just an itty-bitty town. The Mafia wouldn't bother running things down here."

C'ndee raised her palms in a shrug, a gesture right out of *The Sopranos*. "I'm just askin'. That's all I'm sayin.'" She looked toward the kitchen again. "You know, I could really use some coffee."

"Well, you can't go in there to find some."

"I know, Mace. I'm not stupid." A flash of irritation surfaced. "I meant I'd be glad to run to that diner and pick up enough for everybody. I'll bring some back for the cops, too."

I started to protest her going, but then realized coffee might be what all of us could use. I couldn't leave, since I'd found Ronnie's body. Besides, if I left Mama alone with C'ndee at the VFW, Mama might kill her. And since Carlos was the Himmarshee Police Department's only homicide detective, having to handle two murders in one morning might stretch him a bit thin.

"Fine," I told C'ndee. "But hurry back. Detective Martinez might want to talk to you, too."

She'd only been gone a few minutes when Carlos rushed through the door. Outside, I saw what looked like the entire department, including the police chief, arriving in three squad cars behind an ambulance.

My stomach fluttered at the sight of Carlos, just like always. It hardly seemed right to be thinking about how fine he looked, with poor Ronnie's body growing colder in the next room. But I couldn't help myself. The man was as gorgeous as a Spanish prince. Dark skin, black eyes, broad chest tapering to a waist without an ounce of fat. I knew how firm and muscular his body felt under that button-down dress shirt and blue-striped tie. I might have blushed, or licked the drool from my lips. Instead, I thought about Ronnie's fate, and felt my features form into a more suitable expression.

All business, Carlos nodded brusquely at Mama and me. "Where is he?"

I pointed to the closed kitchen doors.

"Poor Ronnie," Mama said. "This is just awful."

"Yeah, you two have a knack for being in the wrong place at the wrong time. I didn't know when I left Miami that Himmarshee would end up taking its place as Florida's murder capital."

Before either of us could jump to the defense of our normally tranquil hometown, we heard a hubbub erupting in the parking lot outside.

"Let me through! Somebody said there'd been a knife fight. Who got hurt? Mama! Are you in there? Are you all right?"

The voice, accustomed to silencing an auditorium of Himmarshee middle-schoolers, belonged to my red-headed sister, Maddie.

"I'm fine, honey," Mama yelled.

I went to the window and slid it open. "The fight was already over when Mama and I got here," I said through the screen. "Ronnie Hodges is dead."

Maddie's hand flew to her throat, just as Mama's had done earlier. Their gestures were the same, but their looks couldn't be more different. Maddie towered over Mama, who barely reaches five feet in heels. And while Maddie may be the oldest sister, I never tire of reminding her that I'm still the tallest, at five-foot-ten.

Marty, the youngest, rushed across the rapidly filling parking lot. Her blond hair bounced in a braid from one slender shoulder to the other. Breathing hard, blue eyes filled with fear, she peered into the VFW window. "Are y'all okay? We were so worried, Mace! Maddie even jumped out of my car while it was still moving." She jabbed an elbow at our big sister. "I just about ran you over!"

That poke passed as criticism from Marty. Petite and pretty like Mama, our librarian sister was normally as gentle as a baby lamb. I'm somewhere between the two of them: Not as sweet as Marty; not as scary as Maddie.

"We're okay," I said. "Ronnie isn't."

I filled them in. Maddie looked sad; Marty shuddered when I described the murder scene.

"Has anyone told his wife?" she asked.

Carlos came to the window just in time to overhear Marty's question. "No telling what she's heard by now. I'm still amazed at how news travels in a small town. That's not to say it's always accurate."

The Himmarshee Hotline was surely humming. It wouldn't be long before half the town arrived to check out the crime scene.

Carlos had his cop face on. "Mace, I need you to come back in and tell me exactly what you saw, and when. And then I'd like you to translate for your mother." He nodded to the table where Mama still sat. "She's obviously upset, since the man was a neighbor. But she keeps going off on tangents. Something about food for a hundred and fifty and some kind of tool."

"Tulle," I said. "It's a fabric. You tie it around three candied almonds as a wedding favor. But believe me, Carlos, you really don't want to know."

14

THREE

A BATTERED WHITE PLYMOUTH screeched into the VFW parking lot. Even after the driver parked half onto the grass and shut off the ignition, the engine continued to knock. A wild-eyed woman flung open the car door. She leaped out, eyes scanning the growing crowd.

"Uh-oh," I said to my sisters, who still stood outside the open window. "Heads up. Here comes Ronnie's wife. She's probably heard something, and she's fearing the worst."

The three of us straightened, waiting to see what Alice would do. You could almost see the terror rising in her eyes as she checked each face, failing to see her husband's familiar features. I've always been single, but both my sisters are married: Maddie for twenty years; Marty for more than ten. I imagined they were running through in their minds how it would feel as a wife to be on the receiving end of the official confirmation Alice Hodges was about to get. I didn't need to have a husband to know it would feel awful.

As I watched from inside the window, Marty started toward Alice.

"Honey, why don't you let me take you inside? It looks like the skies are going to open up again at any moment out here. No sense in getting wet."

Marty's voice was kind and soothing. I was glad she got to Alice first before Maddie steamrolled her.

"Where's my husband?" Alice asked, her voice laced with anxiety. "Where's Ronnie?"

"Let's go in." Marty spoke calmly and slowly, as if to a child. Maddie followed our little sister's lead, approaching quietly from Alice's other side. She didn't say a word, which is rare for Maddie, just took one of Alice's arms while Marty held on to the other.

I looked around for an officer. The policemen—and one woman—who'd come in behind Carlos were busy starting to shoo people from the lot. The chief was out by the street, talking to the *Himmarshee Times*. Yellow crime scene tape was going up. I don't think anyone official noticed my sisters escorting a middle-aged woman in a faded housedress and sensible shoes. She didn't register as the wife of the murder victim inside the VFW.

"Mama," I called over to the table where Carlos had asked her to wait. "Run over to the kitchen and tell Carlos Alice Hodges just got here. Somebody needs to come take care of her."

I knew first aid, since we've had our share of emergencies at Himmarshee Park. If Alice were to collapse or go into shock, I'd know what to do. But Carlos would want to talk to her. By the time a young policewoman stopped my sisters at the front entrance, Mama had found Carlos. He strode across the rental hall to the door.

"It's okay. Let them through," he said to the policewoman.

She stepped aside, and Maddie and Marty entered the dining room. Alice walked, white-faced and fearful, between them.

"Are you in charge?" she asked Carlos, and then her words tumbled out without waiting for his answer. "I got a phone call. Someone said there'd been a murder. My husband was here early this morning, preparing for an appointment. I haven't been able to reach him on his cell phone. I've told him and told him not to go off and leave it lying on the front seat of his car." She stopped talking, took a couple of shallow breaths. "What good is a cell phone if you never have it with you? I've told him…" Growing softer, her voice finally petered out.

Carlos nodded at me, and then to a chair at a nearby table. I pulled it over. He introduced himself and invited Alice to sit. I moved back to the window, giving them privacy.

"I don't want to sit down." Alice's voice rose in anger. "I want to talk to my husband."

Marty gently eased her into the seat, and Maddie applied a little pressure to her shoulder to keep her there.

"I'm sorry to have to tell you this," Carlos said, and he did look sorry, all knitted brows and sympathetic eyes. "There's been an accident."

An accident? Only if Ronnie had a career I hadn't known about as a knife-throwing circus contortionist.

"Mrs. Hodges, your husband is dead."

Alice recoiled from Carlos' words as if he'd slapped her. "That can't be. I just made him oatmeal this morning." She passed a hand over her eyes, as if fixing in her mind the image of Ronnie eating breakfast. "Are you sure it's him?"

17

"Yes, ma'am," Carlos said. "He had his wallet on him with ID, and several people have confirmed his identity."

Alice shook her head, limp gray hair falling into her face. Her hands were busy, kneading the hem of her dress. Marty leaned over and brushed a few strands of hair from Alice's eyes. Maddie gave her shoulder an awkward pat. Carlos watched. His dark, intelligent eyes registered Alice's every sound, every twitch.

Mama walked silently to my side. "That poor woman," she whispered. "I can never see a new widow without thinking of that day in the hospital, twenty-one years ago, when they told me your daddy was dead."

That's something you don't forget. I still remember Maddie, Marty, and me standing in the street, watching Daddy disappear in an ambulance after his heart attack. That was the last time we saw him alive.

"Honey, Alice looks like she can use a drink. The manager got here to unlock the bar and office so the police can look around. Why don't we go see if we can find her a drop of sherry?" Mama paused. "Maybe something stronger."

I glanced toward Alice, who was now struggling to rise from the chair. Stooping down next to her, Marty spoke softly, urgently. Maddie clamped a principal's grip on her shoulder. Alice's eyes were dry, and blazing with anger.

"I want to see him! You can't keep me from seeing him!" she said to Carlos. "Just let me in there for a minute. I need to make sure it's Ronnie."

Alice was flying through those five famous stages of grief in record time. We'd already seen denial and anger. Now, she was bargaining. All that was left was depression and acceptance.

"I'm not sure Alice will take a drink," I said to Mama. "I think she's a teetotaler."

"Desperate times, Mace."

In short order, we found the manager and some brandy. Mama took a little nip for herself, and then got a fresh glass and the bottle, and we headed back to the dining room.

"I expect Alice will do fine after the awful shock wears off," Mama said. "She's a bit of a cold fish, to tell you the truth."

"Mama! That's a horrible thing to say. That booze must have loosened your tongue."

"It's not booze, Mace. It's only brandy. And I'm just stating a fact. She's a good woman, but that marriage has had its problems."

"Like most marriages," I said.

Mama, the expert, waved her hand dismissively.

"The two of them were as different as corn and beets," she said. "Alice never missed a Sunday at church. Ronnie would rather watch football. After he got hurt at the feed store, he'd taken an interest in getting in shape. Lately, he'd really spiffed himself up. And Alice … well, you saw Alice. I don't think a tube of lipstick ever touched those lips. She'd sooner gamble on a Sunday than step foot into Hair Today, Dyed Tomorrow, even though we could work wonders for her at the salon."

"Mama, not everyone wants to go around looking like a painted parakeet."

I looked meaningfully at her lemon-sherbet colored pantsuit, orange-green-and-yellow floral scarf, and platinum hair. Her lips gleamed with her favorite shade, Apricot Ice.

In return, she raised a perfectly-plucked eyebrow at my ensemble: boots, jeans, and a T-shirt I'd found hanging on the bathroom doorknob that morning. It probably should have gone in the wash instead.

"I'd rather look like a parakeet than a ragged old possum you've dragged out of some newcomer's attic, Mace. I'll never understand why you don't make more with all the physical blessings God gave you."

"Here we go again," I muttered, as we rounded the corner into the dining room.

What we saw next silenced both of us at once. Alice moaned, and rocked back and forth on the chair, her arms wrapped tight around her upper body. When she saw Mama, she let out the emotion it seemed had been trapped inside her chest.

"He's dead, Rosalee! My Ronnie's dead." Her cry turned into a scream.

Mama rushed to her, and Alice just about collapsed on top of her, sobbing. It looked like she'd jumped right ahead to acceptance of the fact that Ronnie had been murdered. As Mama handed me the brandy bottle so she could comfort her grieving neighbor, our eyes met. I didn't have to say a word. Mama and I both knew what I was thinking.

Alice didn't look like such a cold fish now.

FOUR

"Okay, people, there's nuthin' to see." A Bronx honk blared from outside. "Nuthin' to see here, people. Do like the officers say, now. Move along."

I looked out the window and saw Mama's fiancé inserting himself into the scene. His towering size, his voice, the sheer force of his personality—all these things made people do the bidding of Sal Provenza without asking questions. And that was saying something today, since he looked ridiculous in orange-and-green plaid golf knickers and a color-coordinated beret. A little orange pompom jiggled on the crown of the cap with every step he took.

Leaving my sisters and Mama inside with Alice Hodges, I went out to the parking lot to join Sal. The sun had broken through the rain clouds. It wasn't even noon, and already it was hot.

As soon as Sal spotted me, he immediately stopped shepherding curious townsfolk. Worry knitted the brow below his jaunty plaid cap.

"Your mudder's not in there is she, Mace?"

"She is, but she's fine. Shaken up, like all of us," I said. "Didn't Mama tell you she had an appointment here this morning with your caterer?"

Avoiding my gaze, he tugged at the collar of his blindingly green knit shirt. Then he pulled a cigar case from the top pocket. He extracted a cigar. Tapped it. Took his time snipping off the end.

"Didn't she?" I prodded.

He lit the cigar, puffed, and then finally looked me in the eye. "I couldn't say, Mace. The fact of the matter is, I've stopped listening when your mudder talks about the wedding. I think she's gone a little overboard."

Overboard? Mama had plunged deep into the nuptial sea and forced the rest of us in with her. Without life jackets.

"Tell me about it," I said.

I filled Sal in on the morning's events, though he already knew most of the basics.

"How'd you find out about the murder?"

"Pro shop," he answered. "Everybody at Himmarshee Links was talking about it."

It was a relief to know Sal had been out at the new golf course community south of town. At least there was some excuse for that outfit. I'd been there, once. I'd never seen so many men who were old enough to know better dressed in colors you'd never find in nature.

"Your cousin was here earlier," I told him.

His face darkened. He took two nervous puffs. "How were the two of them getting along?"

"Well, there was no fistfight."

"That's encouraging." He exhaled.

I waved my hand in front of my face.

"Sorry, Mace." Sal lowered the cigar, angling his three-hundred-pound heft to block the smoke from blowing my way. "Just thinking about Rosalee and C'ndee together in the same room makes me antsy. They've both got pretty strong personalities."

Mention of C'ndee made me wonder if she'd disappeared. She'd left at least an hour before for coffee, and there'd been no sign of her since. Gladys' Diner was only a couple of miles from the VFW hall. Where was she?

Just as I was about to ask Sal to tell me more about his cousin from the North, a cherry red Mustang roared up the street. C'ndee was behind the convertible's wheel—hair flying, sunlight glinting on a pair of over-sized, gold-framed, designer sunglasses. She parked outside the crime scene tape, and began unloading cartons of take-out coffee. She fluffed her hair, thrust out her chest, and carried a cup in each hand to the closest cop she saw. A male, of course, a new hire I didn't recognize.

She said a few words, and then handed him both cups. Smiling, she leaned in close, and then pointed over toward Sal and me. They talked a bit more, C'ndee raking a seductive hand through her big hair. He gave back one of the cups, which she opened for him. I knew she had him when he took a sip and smiled at her.

I was like an anthropologist, observing human flirting rituals I'd heard rumored, but couldn't replicate. If you have a question about the wing-waving courtship of the anhinga, however, I'm your girl.

"That woman had better watch herself." Mama had sidled up to me. "She might just come on to the wrong man."

Sal grabbed her in a bear hug. "I'm so glad to see you, Rosie! Now, be nice."

"Honey, I'm a Southern gal. I'm always nice."

Tossing a last sultry look over her shoulder at the young cop, C'ndee grabbed two cartons of coffee cups, ducked under the tape, and sashayed toward us across the parking lot.

"My gawd!" She pushed one of the cardboard, four-cup holders into my hands without asking. "I thought I'd *never* get out of that diner. Must everyone tell the check-out girl every detail of their lives? 'How's your daughter, Donna? Still off at college?'" C'ndee affected an overdone down-South accent.

"'Oh, she's fine, honey. Having a little trouble with English lit, and of course she's packed on a few pounds. The Freshman Fifteen, they call it. And she's dating a boy we absolutely cannot stand. He's from New York...'

"Aaaargh! How do you people *ever* get anything done?"

As if the flashy convertible wasn't enough in a town full of pickups, C'ndee's impatience for niceties nailed her as an outsider. In Himmarshee, everybody knows—and cares—about everybody's business.

"Well, we could stand out here and yammer all day. Or, we could get a few of those coffees inside," Mama said pointedly. "Carlos could definitely use one, what with all the goings-on and the grief pouring off Alice."

"How is she?" C'ndee's voice was filled with concern that appeared surprisingly genuine.

"About like you'd expect." Mama's face was grim. "It's an awful shock."

We were all silent for a moment. Finally, Sal said, "Well, why don't we go pass out some of these cups, C'ndee? They'll appreciate the coffee."

"It'll have to do," C'ndee said. "You can't get a good cup down here. Not like up North. It's not even imported."

"As far as I know, all coffee is imported, C'ndee. It doesn't grow in the United States," I pointed out.

She ignored me. "I'm just sayin' it'd *never* fly in New Jersey."

C'ndee strutted away, with Sal on her heels. Mama whispered, "Speaking of flying in New Jersey, where'd That Woman park the broom she flew south on?"

"Hush," I whispered back. "She did offer to go get all those coffees."

"Humph," Mama said.

I added three sugars and sipped. The coffee tasted great to me. As we watched the two of them passing out cups, I thought about all that had happened this morning. Mama was quiet, too.

"Maybe C'ndee will grow on us," I finally said. "Remember how long it took us to warm up to Sal?"

She nodded. "And now he's going to be your new step-daddy."

"Hopefully, the last in our long line of step-daddies."

Returning, Sal stuck his big head in between Mama and me. "You know what they say, girls: Fifth time's the charm."

"I believe the saying is 'third time,'" C'ndee butted in.

Mama's back was to both of them. She stuck her finger in her mouth and crossed her eyes. *Gag me.* Very mature. I hid my smile behind the rim of my cup.

And then in a flash, Mama's face became serious. I turned to see Marty leading Alice out the front door of the VFW. Her arm was around Alice's thick waist. A foot taller, Alice leaned onto Marty for support.

A murmur passed through the crowd. Those in the know were likely telling those who weren't that Alice was Himmarshee's newest widow. I heard a few gasps. As the two women inched toward Marty's car, Sal shook his head sadly, the golf beret's pom-pom bobbing. Mama grabbed my hand and squeezed. C'ndee, uncharacteristically, cast her eyes to the pavement.

Marty got Alice settled in the passenger seat, buckled her in, and then moved to the driver's side. She motioned to us over the roof, the universal hand signal for *I'll call you.* I glanced at Alice, and saw her staring out the car window at our little group. I gave her a small wave. No response.

Marty got in, fastened her own belt, looked for her keys, and then started the engine. Through it all, Alice's intense stare never wavered. I looked at Maddie to see if she noticed the odd look. She gave me a half-nod, and a shrug. As Marty backed out and drove past, Alice twisted herself around to continue to stare. C'ndee lifted her gaze for just a moment, but long enough for the two women's eyes to lock.

C'ndee quickly ducked her head again. But not so quick that I didn't notice her face turn as red as her Mustang convertible under the heat of Alice's glare.

FIVE

"So, TELL ME AGAIN what we have to do?" Maddie asked.

We were in my Jeep, on our way to the golf course community where Sal played. I'd gotten an emergency call from a newcomer who'd been taken with the notion of country living, until the country came to call.

"Some lady has a snake in her laundry room," I explained. "She wants me to come get it out."

After being cleared by Carlos to leave the VFW, I offered Maddie a ride back to work. The deal was she'd tag along with me first. The posh new development at the county's south end was bringing in new people with Northern accents, city attitudes, and lots of money to spend.

We used the fifteen-minute ride to hash over details about Ronnie's murder.

"Suppose it was a teenager, looking to rob the place for money to buy drugs." Maddie said. "What if it was one of my former students?"

Drugs were becoming a scourge for the young people of Himmarshee. Like a lot of rural kids, they were turning out of boredom to some pretty scary stuff. Methamphetamine and crack were a far cry from the pot and booze we'd fooled around with as teens.

"I don't know, Maddie. Drug addicts prefer the path of least resistance. It's not easy to kill a man Ronnie's size with a knife. You'd have to really be motivated."

"Something personal, then?"

I shrugged. "Hope not. That seems worse somehow."

I started searching along U.S. Highway 441 for the turnoff to Himmarshee Links. We passed a cattle ranch with a For Sale sign tacked onto a barbed-wire fence. "Will Sub-Divide," it said, which wasn't a good omen for the agricultural way of life in middle Florida.

"I'm not fond of snakes," Maddie announced. "I'm staying in the Jeep."

"Suit yourself."

My sister shuddered. "I hate to agree with Mama, but climbing into small spaces after critters the way you do … it's an unseemly job for a woman, Mace."

"Excuse me?" I looked at her sideways. "That pothole in the road must have jolted us clear back to 1950."

We were coming up on the grand entrance for Himmarshee Links, all red brick pillars and geometrically trimmed hedges. Would it have killed them to plant something native? Some saw palmetto, or marlberry for the birds?

Maddie said, "You know that's not the way I mean it, Mace. You're free to do any job you want. It's just that this one is kind of icky, isn't it?"

"Icky? You've been spending too much time with your seventh-grade girls. You're starting to sound like a twelve-year-old."

I punched on the radio. The country station was playing Carrie Underwood's "All-American Girl."

"Besides, Maddie, trapping's only part-time. It brings in a few bucks to add to my pay from Himmarshee Park."

The manicured fairways of the golf course stretched out on both sides as we drove into the subdivision. Stopping to wait for a golf cart to cross the road ahead, I tracked a flash of brightly colored sportswear on the driver's side. Before, when this land was wild, I'd watched the wings of birds in flight and the white tail flags of leaping deer.

"Remember all the animals we'd spot out here when we were kids, Maddie?"

"No." Maddie changed the radio to her favorite, Dr. Laura. "That was you communing with the woodland creatures, Mace. I've always been partial to civilization."

A tasteful wooden road sign pointed the way to the golf course's clubhouse ahead.

"You want to stop by the eighteenth hole? See if you can wrestle another nuisance gator out of a water hazard?"

I looked over to see if Maddie was making fun of me.

"What?" she asked, eyes all innocent.

"Just that you called me Gator Gert for two months after that job. And making those mating grunts every time you saw me got real old, too."

"Sorry, Mace. I couldn't resist. Truth is, we were proud of you. There aren't too many women alligator trappers in Florida ..."

"Our cousin's the official trapper. I just helped."

"The point is you're skilled. Which came in pretty handy last summer when Mama got herself into that mess with the murder."

I glanced at Maddie again. She looked serious.

"I mean it, Sister. I hate to think what would have happened to Mama if you hadn't been there."

"We're not going to hug now, are we?"

"Not a chance." Maddie grinned. "Speaking of Mama, I hope she doesn't get herself into trouble again. She *was* there when Ronnie's body was found."

"Yeah, but I'm the one who found him, and I can vouch for her whereabouts."

Maddie's hero Dr. Laura was belittling a caller. I punched the button back to the country station. Joe Nichols sang "It Ain't No Crime."

"I'm not sure exactly where Carlos and I stand these days. But I'm pretty sure he knows Mama and I wouldn't conspire to murder her neighbor."

"Speaking of Carlos, what's up with you two, anyway? We're all sick to death of you going back and forth, forth and back. Y'all need to either go, or get off the pot."

"Elegantly put, Maddie."

"I thought he'd be your date to the wedding. Now Mama tells me you asked her to invite him separately. Why'd you do that?"

"Quiet. I'm looking for the address."

She snorted, meaning she wouldn't give up.

"Okay, fine. I didn't want the added pressure of being a couple at the wedding. All sorts of expectations go with that. What if we break up for good? Carlos will be in all the wedding pictures."

Maddie was silent for a moment. "That's ridiculous, Mace. Given Mama's track record, even the groom could be out of the picture before the wedding album is bound. You're making excuses. Lame ones, too."

I slammed on the brakes. "Dammit, I passed it. I told you I needed to concentrate."

Backing up, I scanned addresses. You could tell the leisure pursuits of the residents by their mailbox designs: some were shaped like largemouth bass; the others looked like golf balls perched on tees. I passed two bass before I came to a ball.

"Looks like we're here." I pulled into a circular driveway, parking behind a silver Lexus.

"Don't think you're getting off that easy, Mace. Once you've made this cul-de-sac safe from rampaging snakes, we *will* talk about your sorry love life."

I got out, slamming the Jeep's door. Maddie had to know I'd sooner face the snake.

———

A blonde of indeterminate age answered my knock. She took a step back when she saw my get-up. I held a forty-inch rod with a hooked end, and snake tongs with a rubber-coated jaw. My leather gloves were lined with Kevlar; extra long cuffs shielded my wrists and forearms.

It was probably just a yellow rat snake or an Eastern garter, which I could have plucked out by hand and plopped into a pillowcase. But it didn't hurt to be prepared if the specimen was more lethal. Besides, the customers felt they got their money's worth when I showed up looking ready for war.

"Are you the snake woman?"

"Guess so," I answered.

"Thank God you're here! I nearly had a heart attack when I went in to get my clothes out of the dryer." She smoothed her already perfect hair, bobbed precisely to the chin. "No one told us when we bought here the place was crawling with snakes."

I wanted to ask where she expected them to go after the developers plowed up the snakes' homes and plopped down tract housing. Instead, I said, "Well, the good news about snakes is they keep the rat population down."

She gave me a funny look. Hard to tell if it was a grin or a grimace with all the Botox in her face.

I figured I'd better make some polite conversation, work on my customer relations. I nodded toward the Lexus. "Nice car. Do you like it?"

"It's getting ruined with all these bad roads down here."

"Yep, you don't see too many fancy cars in these parts." An image of C'ndee's snazzy red Mustang flitted through my mind.

"Funny, I just saw another Lexus early this morning, at Gladys' Diner in town. Deep green. First one I've seen down here." She patted her non-existent stomach and gave me what could have been a guilty look. "I'm hooked on that little spot's pancakes and sausage."

She motioned me into the living room. It was as blinding as a blizzard—white leather sofa, plush white carpet, a decorator's collection of white reeds in a ceramic floor vase. I hoped the mud from the puddle in the VFW parking lot—not to mention Ronnie's blood from the kitchen—wasn't still stuck in the tread of my boots.

We passed down a long hallway. Family photos in white frames hung in neat groupings on the walls. Kids with good teeth and resort tans posed with surfboards, tennis rackets, or snow skis. They grew up as we progressed, until the last few pictures showed them cradling young children of their own.

So the blonde, with her stylish Capri pants and pale pink toenail polish, was a grandmother. Funny, she didn't look a bit like Maw-Maw, who'd had a comfortable, generous lap, and gray hair tucked up into a granny bun.

"It's in there." With a shudder, she pointed a pink fingernail at a closed door off the hallway. "Be careful."

As I opened the door, the blonde plastered herself against the opposite wall, side-stepping down the hall. I thought about making a fake rattling sound, to really convince her I was earning my fee, but decided against it. I didn't want her to faint right there on the floor.

I closed the door behind me and stepped to the dryer.

A beautiful corn snake, orangey-brown with black-bordered reddish blotches, was coiled near the vent. He'd probably been enjoying the serpent's version of a dry heat sauna.

"Don't worry, fella, I'm not gonna hurt you." I whispered, since it wouldn't do to let the client know I'm friendly with the enemy. "We're gonna find you a nice, new home."

I leaned toward the snake, my hook at the ready.

SIX

THE BLOND NEWCOMER FOLLOWED me down the driveway and pressed some rolled-up bills into my hand. "There's a little something extra, for you being so brave!"

I smiled modestly, glancing at Maddie just in time to see her roll her eyes.

Once we were back on the highway, my sister turned in her seat to the rear of the Jeep. Lifting the air-holed lid off a plastic pail, she peeked inside at the snake.

"Oh, c'mon, Mace." She snorted. "You took that poor woman's money for this? It's still a baby!"

"Not technically, Maddie. Two feet is definitely an adult."

"So that works out to, what? Forty dollars a foot?"

"Fifty. Not including the tip."

"You're shameless, Sister!"

"Hey, she had a problem, I was the solution. That's business. Besides, that gal with her white slacks and manicured nails is not about to go crawling around after a snake. To her, it's worth what she paid, maybe more, to not have to do it herself."

"So you're really performing a public service."

"That's right."

"Yeah, and Donald Trump just wants the best for all those people he fires on TV. Be sure to take that creature in the pail far away from my house. And, by the way, Moneybags, you're buying the pizza for Mama's house tonight."

Maddie and I passed the ranch for sale again on our way back to town. Cattle herded together in stands of sabal palms, seeking shade from the midday sun. I envied them, in a way. They had no concept of the future, no foreboding about the development creeping inland from the coasts, threatening to ruin the ranches-and-rodeo lifestyle that makes Himmarshee unique.

"Look at that sign," I said to Maddie. "It's a shame, huh?"

"Sure is," she said. "Looks like they're aiming to build a new housing development when what we could really use is a Super Walmart."

I looked at her.

"What?" Maddie said.

"Are you sure we're sisters?"

"Shopping is not a sin, Mace. And, yes, I'm sure. I remember Mama saying you were growing in her tummy, and then Daddy and her bringing you home from the hospital. Everyone said how adorable you were with those big blue eyes and that shock of black hair."

I worked my fingers through my hair. It was still black, whipped by the wind through the windows into some shocking snarls.

"My reign as the center of the universe was over." Maddie shook her head sadly. "And I wasn't even four."

"You need to get over that sibling rivalry, Sister. It was thirty-two years ago."

She sniffled, playing it up. "Early traumas aren't easily forgotten."

Then her face turned grave. "Speaking of trauma, I didn't even ask you how you felt about finding Ronnie this morning. That must have been horrible."

An image of Mama's neighbor and all that blood forced itself into my mind. I gazed ahead at the road, keeping my eyes focused on the center yellow line.

"Yeah," I finally said. "It was hard. And I felt so sorry for Alice, too. I'm glad Carlos wouldn't let her see Ronnie. She should remember her husband the way he was."

The radio was playing a commercial for the Home on the Range Feed Supply and Clothing Emporium. I switched to a station giving the weather forecast. High humidity, temperatures in the 90s, and we were barely into June. Welcome to middle Florida, where the nearest ocean breeze is sixty miles away.

"What do you suppose that weird look meant that Alice gave C'ndee?" I asked.

Maddie was punching up Dr. Laura's station again, even though it was my Jeep, and she knew how I felt about that show. She lifted a shoulder in a shrug.

"Don't know. C'ndee's from New Jersey. Maybe Alice doesn't like her on principle."

"No, it was more than that. It was like Alice knew her, and she wanted C'ndee to *know* she knew her. It was like she was sending some kind of signal."

"Maybe it was disapproval," Maddie said. "Alice is pretty modest, and did you see that skirt C'ndee had on?"

"Oh, yeah. And you know what Aunt Ida would have said about that skirt…" I began.

She finished, " 'Girl, go put on something decent! We can see clear to the Promised Land.' "

We'd almost made it to Maddie's school when she turned off the radio and brought up the topic I thought I'd been lucky enough to avoid.

"You didn't think I'd forget, did you? I'm a school principal. I can remember the names of two hundred students by heart."

I squirmed around in the driver's seat. But it was no use trying to get comfortable. The comfort zone my sister was violating wasn't physical. It was emotional.

"Well?" she repeated. "What's your problem with Carlos? After you patched things up on the Cracker Trail Ride, the man moved back here from Miami. But every time y'all get close to having something real, you find a reason to pick a fight or back off. I can't believe you even asked him to give you some space. What a cliché, Mace."

I could feel her eyes boring into me. My own gaze never left the road.

"He's going to get tired of your hot-and-cold bit. And you're not getting any younger. By the time you hit your mid-thirties, the bloom's off the rose."

I'm not vain, but I couldn't resist a peek at myself in the rear-view mirror. Startling blue eyes looked back at me, my best feature, I've been told. But were those crow's feet beginning to branch out around the corners? The Florida sun is no friend of fair skin.

Maddie pinched my arm. "Stop admiring yourself. You're going to run us into a ditch. You're just as pretty as ever. Men's heads still turn at your figure, even though you're usually hiding what you've got in those awful clothes. My point is it doesn't last forever. Do you want to be a wrinkled old crone, living alone in your house in the woods, with a bunch of animals you treat like your kids?"

I remembered a homeless woman we'd seen once in downtown Fort Pierce. Dressed in several layers of mismatched clothes and muttering to herself, she was pushing a black carriage. A little dog sat inside, wearing a baby's bonnet tied with a bow under the chin.

"No," I said. "But maybe the reason I'm not ready to take it to the next level with Carlos is that he's not ready either."

"What do you mean?"

"He smothers me. And I know it's because he hasn't gotten over the awful way he lost his wife. I can't live with someone who's constantly afraid some kind of harm is going to come to me. I feel like I can't breathe with the way he always needs to protect me."

"Wanting to protect someone is not normally a bad thing, Mace."

"It is when it's motivated by guilt. The last time we were together, he woke up from a nightmare just drenched in sweat. His heart was pounding so hard, I could feel the vibration on my side of the bed."

"Was he dreaming about his wife?"

I nodded.

I could barely get the image out of my head of how I found Ronnie. How must it be for Carlos, to replay the same murder scene over and over? Except in his case, the body lying bloodied on the floor was that of his beloved, pregnant wife.

SEVEN

MAMA'S CRAZY POMERANIAN THREW himself against the front door, yowling as if I were an ax murderer come to slaughter the innocents inside.

"Hush, Teensy!" Mama's command echoed from the kitchen. It worked just as well as usual. He ratcheted up, in both volume and intensity. I feared the dog might give himself a stroke, which would definitely take the fun out of our regular, gals-only Beginning of the Week Pizza Party.

"Will somebody come and get this dog?" I yelled through the window. "My hands are full of food."

I knew that last part would bring Maddie running.

"Teensy!" My sister bellowed, using her scariest principal voice. The dog gave a final yip, and skedaddled back to the kitchen and Mama's protection.

Opening the door, Maddie frowned. "What took you so long?"

"Good evening to you, too, Sister. Oh, no, that's all right. You don't have to thank me for going to get the pizza. For paying, either." I performed a little bow. "It's my pleasure. I exist to serve you."

"Stop it, you two," Marty called from the kitchen. "Did you get my cheese pizza, Mace?"

"You mean the meatless pizza you have *every* Monday night? No, Marty. It came to me suddenly as I was standing at the counter: Maybe Marty quit being a vegetarian. So, I ordered you the carnivore special. Hope that's all right."

"Sarcasm is an unattractive trait for a lady," Mama shouted.

"So is yelling from the kitchen, Mama."

I sidestepped Maddie and walked into the kitchen just in time to hear Mama whisper across the dinette to my little sister, "We'll just have to ignore Mace's sour mood, honey. She's probably got her monthly visitor."

"Too much information, Mama," Maddie said, as she followed me in.

She put out her hands for the two boxes. "Let me take those. And, have I mentioned how eternally grateful we are that you bought the pizza? I know that poor newcomer's hundred dollars must have been burning a hole in your pocket."

Mama shouted, "A hundred dollars!" which startled Teensy, and began a whole new round of barking, along with a discussion of supply and demand and the principles of capitalism.

Just kidding about that last part. It started Mama and Maddie on the topic of what a bad person I am for taking advantage of nature-wary rich folk who can't tell a rat snake from a rattlesnake.

"Can we just eat, please?" Marty finally said. "All this arguing is making my head hurt."

We all hushed up, quick. Marty suffers terrible migraines. Sometimes, they're bad enough to send her to bed in a darkened room for a full day. None of us wanted to be to blame for one of those headaches.

Maddie opened the pizza boxes and started divvying up the slices onto the good china.

"You know what I always say, girls: Life's too short to eat off paper plates." Mama topped off hers and Marty's glasses from a cold box of Rambling Rosé wine.

I grabbed a Budweiser from the fridge, and got Maddie a glass of tap water with ice. Teensy circled the table, looking for the easiest mark. He bypassed Maddie and me for Mama, who plucked a pepperoni slice from her pizza and slipped it to him under her chair.

"That's why that dog begs, Mama," I said. "You've taught him all he needs to do is stand there and look pitiful."

Mimicking Teensy, Maddie turned soulful, starving dog eyes on us. Marty and I laughed. "I've seen that same expression," I said. "That's how Mama looks when one of us is eating butterscotch pie. No wonder she loves that dog so much. He's just like her when it comes to mooching hand-outs."

Mama scooped Teensy off the floor and into her lap. A shower of white dog hair fell onto her blueberry-colored pantsuit. "Come up here, you darlin' dog." She nuzzled his neck. "You're Mama's little baby, aren't you? You'd never criticize or make fun of me, would you?"

The dog licked her face. When Mama kissed him on the mouth, I nearly lost the bite of pizza I'd just swallowed.

"Mama, are you still planning on having Teensy be your ring bearer?" Marty asked the question in a careful, neutral tone.

We'd all tried to talk Mama out of that plan. But she wouldn't be dissuaded, not even when we told her it wasn't very *Gone with the Wind* to have a Pomeranian prance down the aisle with wedding rings tied to a satin pillow secured to his back like a miniature saddle.

"Teensy's a member of the family, girls," she'd announced, and that was that.

She'd even bought him a little vest and bowtie in celadon-colored satin to match the ring pillow. I could hardly wait for the wedding pictures.

"Of course I'm having him carry our rings, Marty." Mama held up Teensy for our inspection. A few stray hairs floated onto my pizza slice.

"Look how adorable Mama's little darlin' is! Besides, Betty at the salon already helped me find him the cutest little top hat from that Wide World of the Web. Those people with the Internet are going to put a rush shipment on it, so it'll be here in time for the wedding."

And here I'd thought the ceremony couldn't get any tackier.

"Now, don't forget, girls," she continued, "our final fitting for the dresses is Wednesday morning. And then the shower is Thursday night at Betty's. She says she has all kinds of fun games planned."

My stomach formed a hard knot around the beer and pizza. I loathed bridal showers, with their organized gaiety. Mama had invited most of the female population of Himmarshee. There'd be enough estrogen in the place to make me start smiling at babies and weeping at sad movies. Most of the invited guests would probably show, too. Everybody wanted to see how a woman about to embark on her fifth marriage would manage to blush when she opened the gift wrapping on yet another sexy negligee.

I was just about to point out that Mama seemed to be going a bit over the top, considering this wasn't the first, or even the fourth, time she'd tied the knot, when a sound from outside stopped the words in my throat.

"Shhhh." I held up my hand. "Did y'all hear that?"

Maddie cocked her head, her pizza stalled in midair. Marty brushed a lock of blond hair behind an ear, as if to listen harder. Mama put Teensy, now barking and squirming, on the floor. The dog flew toward the living room, his nails scrabbling across peach-colored tile. He launched himself against the front window like a cartoon dog, howling at whatever was outside.

"I don't hear anything but that ridiculous animal," Maddie said.

"It sounded like a scream," I said. "I think it came from Alice and Ronnie's house."

Within moments, there was a loud pounding at Mama's front door. A woman's frantic voice called from the porch. "Let me in, Rosalee."

We jumped up from the table. "That's Alice," Mama said, as we rushed to the living room.

"It's awful." The tremor in Alice's voice came right through the front window. "Dead. Bloody. Somebody left it on my front porch."

When I opened the door, Maddie grabbed a hold of Alice. She was white and trembling; her eyes glazed. I hoped she wasn't going to pass out.

"Get her onto the couch," I told Maddie, who did so without argument.

"Who would do such a thing?" Alice muttered the words, not really focusing on any one of us. "Especially now."

Once Alice was seated, Marty asked her, "What is it? How can we help?"

"I can't talk about it. I don't want to see it again." Alice's hands tugged at the fabric of the same faded housedress she'd worn that morning at the VFW. "The stench. It's horrible. Would you go over and get rid of it for me?

"Well, what ..." Mama began, but I put a restraining hand on her arm.

Whatever was dead on Alice's front porch clearly had her in a state. With everything she'd been through, the least we could do was take care of this without a lot of back-and-forth and fuss.

"Mama, why don't you pour Alice a little drop of that wine you and Marty had? We'll go on over there and see what we can do."

Maddie got a cast-iron frying pan from the stove top. Marty grabbed a heavy cane from the umbrella stand in the hallway. We started for the door.

"Mace?"

Alice's voice, a bit stronger now, stopped us. I turned around. The color was returning to her face. She took a tiny sip from the wine glass Mama poured.

"I don't think you'll need those weapons," she said. "But you better take a shovel and a big trash bag. It's not pretty."

———

We crept toward Alice's house, hugging the picket fence that runs along the property line between the two yards. An orange jasmine bush bloomed out front, snowy white flowers glowing in the moonlight. A scent as sweet as orange soda perfumed the air.

As we got closer to Alice's, a different odor prevailed. Rusty, like dried blood, and fetid, like rotting meat. I heard the buzz of flies before I saw them. Within seconds, Marty and Maddie heard them, too.

"That doesn't sound good." Marty nodded toward Alice's house.

"Well, she did say something was dead," I said.

As we approached, I shone a flashlight onto the porch, near the front door, and toward the far railings.

"What is it, Mace?" Maddie and her cast-iron pan were right beside me, so close I felt her breath on my cheek. I got a faint whiff of the grease Mama uses to season the heavy pan, which was preferable to that other smell that hung in the air.

"I don't know yet, Maddie. I need to get closer to see it. And watch out with that pan. You could knock somebody out."

"Isn't that the idea?" she said, lowering it just a little.

At the bottom step, we stopped. The thing that Alice saw was a dark mass in the shadows at the corner of her porch, placed between a white wicker footstool and a pot of geraniums. Flies circled and landed, illuminated in the beam of my flashlight.

"Can you see it yet, Mace?" Marty hid behind me, her hand a tight fist balling up the back of my T-shirt.

"Marty, honey, let go." I pulled at the shirt's hem until she loosened her grip. "I'm going up to take a closer look."

My sisters linked arms, planting themselves on the concrete walkway. I climbed three steps, and started across the wooden porch. Potted plants vibrated with my footsteps. The flies took off, buzzing as if in annoyance.

"Be careful, Mace," Maddie whispered.

Rivulets of nervous sweat pooled at the small of my back. My flashlight flickered, and then died. I stopped, pounding it against my thigh until it lit again. I continued across the porch.

Covering my nose with the sleeve of my shirt, I drew close and aimed the light. Cloudy black eyes stared lifelessly. Two yellowed tusks curved upward. The flies were back, a moving blanket over coarse bristles and leathery skin.

"It's a wild hog," I announced. "Or was."

Marty gasped. "Oh, the poor thing! Is it dead, Mace?"

"I'd say so, Marty. There's nothing here but the head."

I stooped to examine the creature's neck in the light. The spinal cord had been cleanly severed.

"We better call Carlos," I said over my shoulder. "Looks like whoever took off this critter's head knew how to use a big knife."

EIGHT

Mama's house smelled of carnations and lavender, scents she recommends when stress is a problem. Aromatherapy was a definite improvement over the stinking mess on Alice's porch. But how well would it work for Alice? Finding out your husband was murdered, and then discovering the decapitated head of a wild boar on your front porch is probably more stress than can be soothed by sniffing at the essential oils of herbs and flowers.

"How's Alice, Mama?" Marty asked.

"About as well as can be expected." Mama plopped a handful of ice cubes in her warm wine, which had been forgotten a couple of hours earlier along with our pizza when Alice pounded on the front door.

Next door, the police activity was slowing down. Teensy had barked himself out with the comings and goings at Alice's. My sisters and I had returned to Mama's, where she'd been taking care of her devastated neighbor.

"I burned some candles, and then drew a nice hot bath for her with a few drops of chamomile oil. That seemed to work, along with a sleeping pill I had left over from when I was going through my divorce to No. 4."

I looked from the kitchen entry down the darkened hallway to a closed door at the end.

"So she's in Maddie's old room?" I asked.

"The Rose Room, yes," Mama corrected me.

After the three of us girls moved out, she redecorated our rooms in floral colors and gave each a fanciful, English-garden title. Rose. Buttercup. Violet. I suppose it could have been worse. She could have saddled us instead of our bedrooms with those flowery sounding names.

Maddie rummaged through Mama's freezer, probably looking for something sweet.

"Grab me a couple of ice cubes, will you, Sister?" Marty held up her wine glass with one hand, lifting the lid on her cheese-pizza box with the other.

"Humph!" issued from the freezer.

Though muffled, it was Maddie's snort of disapproval. I should know. I've heard it enough.

"What's wrong?" I asked her.

She turned around, holding Mama's old-fashioned plastic ice bin upside down. She gave it a couple of hard shakes, raising an eyebrow at our mother.

"Now, I wonder who used the last piece of ice?" Maddie said.

Mama sipped her now-chilly wine, overflowing with cubes clinking against the glass.

"I said, I wonder…" Maddie only got those few words out before Mama interrupted.

"So sue me for helping myself to the ice in my own freezer, Maddie. Just open another tray. Don't make a federal case out of it."

"All I'm saying is the last person to use it should replenish it. It's a rule."

"I wasn't aware my freezer falls under the ruling authority of the principal's office at Himmarshee Middle. And if you're looking around in there for the ice cream, Teensy and I ate it after I got Alice into bed. Besides, you know what they say about dessert, Maddie: A minute on the lips, a lifetime on the hips."

I held up my hands like a referee before Maddie could snipe back at Mama for that jab about her size-16 shape.

"Enough!" I hissed, trying to keep my voice low so as not to wake Alice. "You two are really something, you know? After everything that's happened today to that poor woman in Maddie's room…"

"The Rose Room," Mama said with a pout.

"Whatever. You both need to keep in mind what's important. And it's not empty ice bins or a tiny bit of fat on somebody's butt."

"Amen, Mace." Marty clinked her glass against my bottle of warm beer.

"I'm big boned," Maddie grumbled under her breath.

There was silence at the table for the next few moments. Without a word, Maddie cracked open a fresh tray of ice, filled the bin, and added a couple of cubes to Marty's glass.

"It's been an awful day," Mama finally said, looking chastened. "Sorry, girls."

"Me, too," Maddie echoed.

I expected tears at any moment from Marty. Instead, a low knock sounded at Mama's front door. Teensy barked twice and started toward the living room. But even Mama's manic dog seemed to have less energy than he'd had at the start of the night.

"Mace?" The voice through the door was masculine, with the slightest trace of a Spanish accent. My breath quickened, like always when I hear Carlos speak my name. "Is anyone still up?"

Maddie reached over and straightened my hair. Mama handed me the tube of lipstick she always keeps in her pocket. Marty got up, loaded two slices of cold pizza onto a plate, and slipped it into the microwave.

"Be sure you invite him to come in and have some dinner with you," she whispered. "Tell him you know how hard he's been working, and how you just thought he might be hungry."

"That's right, Mace." Maddie nodded. "Men are always hungry. And for God's sake, dab on a little something of Mama's before you go out there. You should smell sweeter than that awful thing on Alice's porch."

The Committee to Fix Mace's Love Life had swung into full operation. The three charter members weren't about to let little details like a murder investigation or a butchered hog get in the way of their mission.

"Don't forget to smile, honey." Mama bared her own teeth in case I needed a demonstration.

"Just be yourself," Marty said.

"Oh, Lord." Maddie rolled her eyes. "Don't tell her that."

Mama dug in her pocket again and pulled out a tiny bottle of almond oil mixed with secret scents. "There's ylang-ylang flower in this."

Carlos rapped a little harder. Teensy gave a half-hearted yip.

I'd been about to knock away Mama's hand, but when she held out the open bottle, it did smell good. Musky, yet sweet. I let her swipe a bit of the scent on my neck.

As I finally ran to get the door, I heard Mama whisper to my sisters: "It's an aphrodisiac."

NINE

THE OLD SWING ON Mama's front porch squeaked as Carlos and I pushed with our feet against the wood railing. Leftover pizza crusts sat on a plate on the floor. We each had a cold bottle of beer.

"I really appreciate the food, Mace." He clinked his Bud bottle against mine. "I missed dinner."

"No problem." I added a silent thank-you to my little sister, much wiser than I am in the ways of men. "Crazy day, huh?"

"Yeah. You could say that." He swigged from the bottle. "I don't know what's in the water here, but things aren't quite as peaceful as I thought they'd be when I moved up from Miami."

I held my tongue. We'd gone around on this topic before, like other topics. I usually ended up getting mad about Carlos' notion that Himmarshee was some kind of bizarro-world version of Mayberry. Truth is, bad things happen anywhere. It just so happened in the last year or so our little town had experienced more than its share of bad things. And since Mama had managed to stumble right into a couple of them, my sisters and I had become necessarily familiar with murder investigations, not to mention with Carlos as the investigator.

"Do you think the hog's head is related to Ronnie's murder?" I asked him.

This was the first chance I had to ask questions. He'd had no time earlier; and then I let him eat. Maddie, Marty, and I had hung around for more than an hour in front of Alice's with a few of the other neighbors. We'd watched the authorities come and go, and speculated about what the butchered animal might mean. But talk was all it was. Nobody really knew anything.

Carlos sipped his beer thoughtfully before he answered. "It seems like a pretty strange coincidence if the two things aren't related. Better safe than sorry, which is why I asked for the scene to be processed as if it's part of the homicide investigation."

I would have followed up, but I was a bit distracted. From my angle, I could see into Mama's front window. My sisters lurked behind the curtain like Mutt and Jeff. I couldn't see Mama, but I was fairly certain she was eavesdropping right behind them, probably holding that ridiculous dog. I wanted to say something scandalous just to see what they'd do.

Carlos, you look good enough to eat. Why don't we forget our differences, rip off our clothes, and do the wild thing right here on Mama's front porch swing?

But, of course, I didn't say that. I called through the window instead. "Maddie, Marty, why don't y'all come on out here?"

The curtain moved. I heard quick steps inside, and an annoyed growl from Teensy. Then, Maddie's voice drifted through the house from the kitchen. "What's that, Mace? Did you want another beer?"

"We've barely started these. But sure, why don't you bring them out? Put 'em on the ring pillow. Let's have Mama's little dog practice toting them on his back."

More running around inside. Now Mama's voice came from her bedroom, which opens onto the opposite side of the porch.

"Mace, honey, you'll have to speak up. I can't hear you from way inside here. Did you say something about Teensy?"

I got up, opened the front door and hissed into the living room: "I said, it's a good thing poor Alice took a sleeping pill with the three of you shouting and stomping around. Now, come on out on the porch and Carlos will fill us in on what he can."

In no time, Maddie, Marty, and Mama squished themselves together on a white wicker love seat across from the swing. Unable to help herself, Mama motioned me to move closer to Carlos. He caught her signal and looked amused, which was fairly humiliating.

Now, hands folded in their laps, they looked at Carlos expectantly. Three teacher's pets in the classroom's front row. He cleared his throat.

"You know I can't talk about much. It's an ongoing investigation."

Their faces fell, like the teacher just chose somebody else to help take attendance.

He relented. "I can tell you the medical examiner will check the knife wounds on Ronnie's body against the hog's head to see if the same weapon was used."

"I knew it!" Mama said. "It's just like on *CSI*."

Carlos smiled. "Well, not exactly. There's a lot of dramatic license on TV and in the movies. And don't get me started on murder mystery books."

He spent the next few minutes trying to establish what we heard from Alice's house and when we heard it. Of course, we couldn't agree on the answers to those crucial questions.

"Teensy would have barked if he heard anything before Alice screamed," Mama insisted.

"Are you kidding? A serial killer could have been hiding with a hatchet in the next room and your dog wouldn't have given a whit," I said. "Don't you remember? I'd just come in with the pizza and Teensy's whole being was focused on getting a bite off somebody's slice."

"No, ma'am." Mama shook her head firmly. "I do not remember that. Teensy knows better than to beg from the table."

Even Marty snorted at that. "Sure, Mama. And you never steal food off my plate before I'm done either."

"All right, all right." Maddie, in the middle, put a hand on each of their knees. "We can all agree that Teensy—and Mama—are easily distracted by food."

"Ring. Ring." I held out a pretend phone to Maddie. "The black kettle wants to talk to you, Pot."

She narrowed her eyes at me. "Is that a crack about my weight?"

I was just about to say if the feedbag fits . . . when I noticed that familiar vein at Carlos' temple beginning to pulse. He was trying to hold something in, but I knew he wouldn't be able to.

"Would everybody just shut up?"

Mama gasped. Carlos had used the S-word, a sin in her book. She'd always made us say *hush* instead. "Only low-class types and Yankees tell people to shut up," Mama used to lecture us. Since Carlos was originally from Cuba, which is farther south than us, it was clear which of those two camps his shutup-saying self fell into.

To his credit, he took one look at Mama's frozen face and realized his verbal boo-boo.

"Sorry, Rosalee." He wore that contrite look he'd been brushing up on since he moved to Himmarshee. "I just wish you four wouldn't bicker so much. It reminds me of the first night I met you. Sometimes I wish I'd tossed you all into jail and thrown away the key."

Crossing my arms over my chest, I felt a frown coming on.

"Here's a shovel, Carlos," Maddie said. "Go ahead and dig yourself in deeper."

Carlos naming Mama as a murder suspect was still a sore subject with me. Not to mention the fact he was insulting our family dynamics. Anybody with two eyes can see we love each other, even though we pick a little.

"Too bad you had to be content with just violating Mama's rights," I said. "Imagine sending a senior citizen, a Sunday school teacher, to the slammer."

"I wish you wouldn't call me a senior citizen, Mace."

I ignored Mama's pout. "You're lucky any of us forgave you, Carlos."

"Oh yeah, I'm lucky all right..."

"Stop it!" Marty said, and both Carlos and I were taken aback. "I think Carlos was right earlier when he said there's something strange in the water up here."

"So y'all *were* listening in..." I started.

"Oh, for God's sake, Mace. Shut up!" Marty's voice was soft, which made her rude use of the S-word no less shocking.

Mama blinked. Maddie's mouth opened and closed without her uttering a single word. My face burned. Even Carlos didn't seem to know how to react.

Marty leaned over and tried to pat my knee, but I jerked my leg away. "Sorry to say it so plainly, honey, but somebody needs to tell you to quit looking at every word anybody says as the start to a fight."

I felt akin to that hog on Alice's porch. Decapitated by the sharp, uncharacteristic criticism from my normally sweet sister. I sipped at my beer and stewed. Everyone else was quiet, too.

Finally, Mama could stand the tension no longer. "Let's all count our blessings, girls. Imagine if any one of us were Ronnie, or his poor widow, Alice."

I did as she said, adding a silent vow that I'd also try to be less of an argumentative jerk.

Out of the blue, Maddie said, "Maybe that hog's head is linked to the Mafia."

Mama tapped her lip with an index finger, thinking. "Wasn't there something like that in a movie? I remember a pig's head in a man's bed."

"A horse head," Carlos said. "From the first *Godfather*."

"With Marlon Brando as Don Corleone," Maddie added. She was Himmarshee's movie expert, on account of her daughter being in college in California, studying film. "The don sent the horse's head as a message. Maybe this is the same thing."

Tucking her hair behind her ears, Marty stared at Maddie. "A Mafia don? In Himmarshee? That seems a little far-fetched, Sister."

"May I remind you of Jim Albert and his murder last summer, Marty? Not that I'm trying to start an argument." I smiled when I said it, but I was still smarting a little.

Carlos said, "Jim Albert's criminal enterprise was set in place a long time before he came down here." His eyes got a far-away, thoughtful look. I had the urge to take my thumb and smooth the wrinkle in his brow, and maybe follow that with a little something with my tongue.

Maybe Carlos was right about the water. I was angry one minute, aroused the next. Either I was getting some kind of weird hormones from the faucet, or the shock of finding Ronnie's body had upset me more than I let on.

"What are you thinking?" I asked him.

"Just that Maddie might be right."

My big sister beamed.

"Not about a Mafia godfather," he said. "But maybe about a message."

An image of Ronnie's corpse popped into my brain, all jumbled up with the blood-crusted head of the pig.

"What would the message be?" I asked. "This is what happens when you squeal?"

TEN

THE NEON SIGN FOR the Booze 'n' Breeze lit up the dark road ahead, a red-and-purple beacon for the thirsty motorist. It reminded me I could use a six-pack for the fridge at home. I put on my blinker, slowed, and turned into the drive-thru lane. As I did, my Jeep's headlights flashed on an ancient Toyota parked next to the little store's dumpster.

Two things made the car stick out in Himmarshee: It was a compact, whereas most of the locals drive trucks; and it had some unusual bumper stickers for a town that likes to call itself the buckle in the cattle belt of Florida.

Meat is Murder, the right rear bumper scolded. *Fur: Brush It, Don't Wear It*, said the left side.

I was surprised nobody had plastered over those sentiments with a more common sticker seen in these parts: *Beef: It's What's for Dinner.*

I motored up slowly to the cashier. The Booze 'n' Breeze is a barn-like, wide-open building with a road right through the middle. Stock is arranged on either side. The whole idea is that drivers can mosey through and tank up without ever getting out of their cars.

I recognized the blond dreadlocks on the head bent over a book propped on top of the cash register. When I got closer, I saw the title on the book's spine: *Animal Liberation*.

"Hey, Linda-Ann," I said. "Doing a little light reading?"

She looked up, eyes sleepy beneath two small silver hoops, one piercing each eyebrow. "Hey, Mace. My boyfriend gave me this." She lifted the book so I could see it. "Trevor says after I read it, I'll understand how we exploit and abuse animals every day."

An impressionable girl and an activist boyfriend. Now there's an original concept.

"Have you read it?" she asked me.

"Can't say that I have," I said. "When you finish it, why don't you give me a synopsis?"

"Say what?" She stuck the end of a dreadlock in her mouth and sucked on it.

"A summary."

She nodded, brushing the hair across her lip. "I'll try, but it's about ten times harder than anything I've ever read. I hope I can get through it, not to mention understand enough of it to give you that..." She paused.

"Synopsis."

"Right," she said, smiling. "Now, what can I get for you?"

I told her to hand over a six pack of Heineken, and to make sure they weren't warm ones.

Watching her return to the register and place the beer on the counter made me think of an old joke. "Hey, what's a redneck's idea of a seven-course meal?"

"A possum and a six-pack." She rolled her eyes. "I've only heard that one about two hundred times, Mace. I think I was still at Himmarshee Middle School the first time I heard it. How is old Mad Hen Wilson anyway?"

That was how the students at my sister's school referred to her behind her back. Little did they know that Maddie, Madison Wilson, actually embraced the nickname.

"Doin' fine," I said. "Keeping the kids on their toes."

"Yeah, I'll bet." She put the beer into a plastic bag. "Anything else?"

My eyes roamed over the offerings: chips, candy, milk, eggs, enough liquor for the next three spring breaks in Daytona Beach.

"Still thinking," I said.

"Take your time. Hardly anybody stops in this late at night. I like the company, to tell you the truth."

A drive-thru in Okeechobee County had been hit recently by an armed robber. The cashier wasn't hurt, but it had all the clerks nervous in the neighboring counties.

"You remember that murder from last summer?" she asked me.

Of course I did. The victim had been Linda-Ann's boss. And Mama was briefly the prime suspect. I nodded.

"Whatever happened to that good-looking cowboy who came in here the day I met you? The one you used to like. Did y'all ever get back together?"

Jeb Ennis. I felt a shiver of desire at the thought of him. I guess with a first love that never really goes away.

"He's back on the rodeo circuit," I said. "I don't think Jeb and I were cut out to be a couple."

I wondered if the fit was better for Carlos and me.

"I was just asking because I have a serious boyfriend now." She looked down, studying the tip of one of her dreadlocks. "He's my first one, if you know what I mean."

Judging by the blush on her pretty face, I knew exactly what she meant.

"Trevor has changed the way I look at everything," she gushed. "He's in graduate school. And he's incredibly smart. Trevor says I'm intelligent, too. He says I just have to learn to apply myself."

She gazed at the thick book on the counter. She didn't seem all that eager to apply herself to it.

"Just be careful, Linda-Ann." I knew I was about to sound like an old fogey who can't understand young love, but I couldn't help myself. "It's all right if both of you agree to make some compromises. But you should never let a man change you too much. When you try to be somebody else to make a man happy, you lose who you really are."

She chewed methodically on the end of her hair. I couldn't tell if she was pondering what I said, or just passing the minutes until closing time. I glanced at the big clock on the wall. Ten minutes to midnight. I was beat. It'd been a long day.

"I guess that'll do it," I said.

"So, you're done thinking? Should I just ring up the beer?"

I was just about to tell her yes when I remembered the display of beef jerky that used to sit right on the counter at driver eye level. The spicy maple flavor was addictive.

"What happened to that jerky y'all used to sell?"

Her hair-chewing speed increased. "I moved them to the back. Trevor says eating animal products is like eating our own brothers and sisters. I promised him I'd only sell them if somebody really, really, really wanted them."

I thought about it for a moment. Between Maddie, Teensy, and Carlos, I barely got any pizza earlier. My stomach growled. I pictured the sorry state of my fridge at home: A jar of salsa which I was certain had grown mold; an apple so old its skin was wrinkled; and a stale chocolate bunny leftover from Easter with both ears eaten off.

A horn honked behind me. I looked in the rearview, saw a blowsy woman with big hair impatiently waving me on.

"Ohmigod, that's Dab Holt!" Linda-Ann rolled her eyes. "Must be out of booze for those parties she throws down at the lake. I'm not going to look, but tell me: Does she have one of those young guys she's always running around with?"

I peeked in the mirror again; gave the woman a friendly wave. "Nope she's alone."

"Not for long, I guarantee you."

My stomach grumbled. "Why don't you run and grab me a handful of that jerky? I'll take three of the spicy sweet ones, two with cracked pepper; and one with garlic."

"Do you really, really…"

"Yes," I interrupted. "I really, really, REALLY want them."

ELEVEN

THE AROMA OF BISCUITS and sausage gravy enveloped me like a high-calorie blanket as I opened the door at Gladys' Diner. I spotted Mama at our favorite breakfast table, the one next to the calendar from Gotcha Bait & Tackle. C'ndee was at the table, too, sitting in Mama's usual seat. I would have liked to have seen the tug-of-war for that spot, from which Mama could normally see—and be seen by—everyone in the diner.

"Yoo-hoo, Mace! Over here, honey!"

I gave her a wave, mainly to stop her from flapping her arms and shouting loud enough to raise the dead in the cemetery next to the Baptist church off State Road 70.

Mama's dreaded wedding book lay open between C'ndee and her on the table. The huge tome contained everything from the seating chart for the VFW reception, to the ice-cream colored fabric swatches for our bridesmaid gowns. If we were going to discuss the ruffles yet again on those *Gone with the Wind* parasols, I knew

I'd better get some coffee. Taking a seat, I signaled to Charlene, the waitress, to pour me a cup.

Coffee pot in hand, she leaned over The Book and stared at a picture Mama had clipped from a magazine of a dashing young man modeling Sal's white wedding suit. "Isn't it exciting, Mace?" Charlene's eyes shone. "Not many gals get to be the bridesmaids at their own mama's marriage."

With good reason, I thought.

"Mace isn't like most gals, Charlene. She doesn't like weddings," Mama explained. "I guess they remind her of the fact that she's thirty-two and not even close to getting hitched. She has a boy-friend, in a fashion. But you know what I always say: No man's gonna buy the cow when he can get the milk for free."

My cousin Henry picked just that moment to join us. "Mooooove over, would you, Mace? I'd like to sit down. And would you pass that creamer over this way? The one with the free milk?"

"Very funny, Henry." I punched him in the arm. "You're a laugh riot, as usual."

He didn't hit back because his attention was now riveted on C'ndee. She was bursting from the V-neck of her tight, off-the-shoulder, red paisley top. Matching hair combs, glittering with rhinestones, swept her mass of black curls off her face into waves that cascaded onto her bare shoulders.

"I don't believe we've had the pleasure," Henry said, fairly licking his chops.

"How's your wife, Audra, Henry? And those fine young children?" I smiled sweetly.

C'ndee extended a hand across the table as my cousin took a chair. Her scarlet nails gleamed under the wagon-wheel lamp that hung from the ceiling.

After introductions were made and everyone got straight how everybody else was related, Charlene returned to the table. She dropped off a plate of hot biscuits beside Mama, and took our orders. Then Mama and C'ndee got down to business.

"I don't know, C'ndee. I still think we should just go in there with scissors and trim this last row of ruffles off. See how that would accentuate the graceful curve of the parasol?"

She turned The Book so C'ndee could see the parasol, held by a smiling Southern belle in crinolines. Dress and umbrella matched, a sickening shade of lime-sherbet green. God help me, that one was my costume.

"So, Henry," I stole a biscuit off the plate Mama hadn't offered to share, "what do you hear about Ronnie Hodges?"

My cousin's the best-known attorney in Himmarshee. This isn't saying much, since we can count the number of attorneys in town on one hand. But he does have a pretty good pipeline to the police department and courthouse. If there had been any kind of development in the investigation into Ronnie's death, Henry would know. His face turned grave.

"It's a mystery to me how someone could do that. That was one awful murder," he said. "Poor Ronnie."

The scene from the VFW kitchen flickered into my mind. Putting the biscuit down, I glanced at C'ndee and Mama. They'd gotten quiet, too.

C'ndee rose and pushed back her chair. I noticed her hand shaking as she reached for a gigantic silver purse on the chair next to her. "I'm going to visit the little girl's room."

Mama and I traded a look as she walked away. Henry was concentrating on the view of her behind in tight white slacks, like two baby possums tussling in a pillowcase.

"Even if you weren't married, cousin, that's too much woman for you," I said.

"A man can dream, can't he?" He turned to Mama. "Aunt Rosalee, I thought you told me you couldn't stand That Woman. How come she's helping you with the wedding?"

Mama sighed. "I really didn't have much choice, Henry. First off, she's kin to Sal through his late wife. That's a family tie I have to honor. Plus, no matter how I feel about her, Sal is fond of C'ndee."

"What man wouldn't be?" Henry said.

"Careful, cousin. You're drooling on the biscuits."

"And second," Mama raised two fingers, "Ronnie's murder left me in a bad spot."

"Not as bad as the spot it left Ronnie in," I said.

"Hush, Mace! I know how that sounds to say it. But it's the truth. I have a hundred and fifty hungry guests coming to the VFW on Saturday, and no one to feed them. C'ndee's helping me get all that organized, pulling together the food suppliers and serving people Ronnie used for catering. She seems to know all about this kind of thing. She says her family was in the restaurant business back in New Jersey."

Mama clamped her lips shut. C'ndee was returning. I noticed a customer at another table was getting up to leave just as she approached. She blew by the woman, nearly knocking her down, instead of stepping aside to let her into the narrow aisle. Mama winced at C'ndee's civility breach.

"Yankees!" she tsked-tsked in my ear.

"My Gawd!" C'ndee exhaled as she sat down. "The floral scent was so thick in that bathroom I nearly choked to death. What is it with you people down here with perfumed rooms and potpourri? I even smelled a big bowl of it on the counter at the gas station the other day. What are you trying to cover up? Don't Southerners bathe regularly? Is it a lack of running water?"

Her voice carried like the horn of a semitruck on the New Jersey Turnpike. Several diners turned to stare. The woman she'd nearly trampled looked especially offended.

Mama's smile was like ice. "C'ndee, honey." Syrup dripped off the word "honey." "Didn't your mama ever teach you that if you don't have something nice to say, you shouldn't say anything at all?"

"No, Rosalee. *Honey.*" Something that wasn't sweet oozed off the word. "We always spoke our minds and worried about the consequences later. Being truthful was more important than faking nice in my family."

They glared at each other over The Book. I hoped the heat didn't singe the pages. Or, if it did, it burned up the one with the picture of that lime-colored gown and stupid parasol.

"Now, what's this I heard about family, Aunt C'ndee?"

A good-looking guy with an Ivy League voice stood beside the table, smiling down at us. His teeth were as white as his polo sport shirt, worn with the collar casually turned up. He looked like he was ready to head to his private club for an afternoon of squash.

C'ndee's dark mood brightened in an instant. "Anthony!" she called, rising to embrace him in a smothering, two-armed hug.

"This is my nephew, everyone. Tony Ciancio." She rotated him by degrees so he could face each of us. I was heartened to see he looked embarrassed at being spun like a game show prize.

"It's nice to meet you, ma'am." Greeting Mama first, he demonstrated that he, at least, had good manners. "I've heard that wedding of yours is going to rival a Broadway show. I don't doubt it, because you're as pretty as any leading lady."

Mama rewarded him with a flutter of her eyelashes.

"And you must be Mace." He turned to me, green eyes lively in a chiseled, sailboat-tan face. "I'm looking forward to visiting Himmarshee Park. I hear you have a great nature path. People say that the wading birds and those huge cypress trees are something to see."

He had me at "nature path."

Tony stuck out a hand to Henry, who stood up as the two men shook. I could see my cousin's sharp eyes assessing this outsider from the North. With his corny jokes, his football-star-gone-beefy paunch, and his rumpled suits, Henry liked to play the country bumpkin. But he'd graduated top of his class from the University of Pennsylvania Law School. Henry Bauer, Esquire, is no dummy.

Tony met Henry's gaze head-on; confident, yet not aggressive. "I'm looking forward to seeing the Brahmans play at Himmarshee High," he said. "I understand they have a pretty good chance at a state title this year."

A delighted grin spread across my cousin's face. He pumped Tony's hand, and then clapped him on the back. "Their chances are excellent, my friend. Excellent!"

Charlene came back just then with our food. She looked around for a place to put down her big tray, crowded with heavy plates. Tony jumped to clear away water glasses and coffee cups from an adjoining table.

"Let me give you some room." He flashed a blindingly white smile. Charlene, in full swoon, nearly lost her tray.

It was hard to believe C'ndee and Anthony Ciancio ever sat at the same family table. He must have gotten her share when they were passing around charm and courtesy.

Food safely delivered, Charlene's eyes drank in Tony's long, lean build. Apparently, she was one thirsty waitress. "Are you that male model in Rosalee's wedding book? The one in the white suit?"

He shot his aunt a puzzled look. She patted his cheek twice, doubly affectionate, I guess.

"Tony's not a model. But he's gorgeous enough, even after driving south all night," C'ndee said. "He's here on business, actually. We're looking at some opportunities to expand in the area."

Mama and I each raised an eyebrow. In the month since she'd steamrolled into our lives, this was the first we'd heard about C'ndee starting a business in Florida. I'm sure Mama was calculating how geographically distant that definition of "in the area" might be.

"Is that right?" Henry clapped Tony's back again. "What are y'all planning to do?" Tony hesitated for just a moment, seeming to weigh how much to say. "We want to do a full-service, event-planning business."

All of us looked at him blankly.

"Like bringing in demolition derby and monster-truck events?" Charlene asked.

C'ndee looked horrified.

"More like special-occasion events," Tony said. "We'd do everything from décor to food."

Henry and I looked at each other over the rims of our coffee cups. He zeroed in like the attorney he was: "Is a wedding the kind of special occasion you'll handle?"

Tony nodded.

"Looks like you arrived in the nick of time, then," I said, my tone as neutral as a judge.

TWELVE

BETTY TAYLOR WAS BUSY at Hair Today, Dyed Tomorrow, combing out a permanent for the wife of the president of the local branch of First Florida Bank. She grinned above a head full of unnaturally dark curls as Mama and I came in, bells jangling on the beauty parlor's door.

"Mornin' ladies." She punctuated her greeting with a hurricane-force blast of hair spray. Coughing, First Florida's First Lady squeezed her eyes shut.

"I see you're working, Betty. How 'bout I come back for our consult some other time?"

"Oh, no you don't, Mace. I think you'd rather go to the dentist than come to my shop. Sit down over there, next to that hairdryer." She pointed her purple comb to a far corner. "I've got to finish here and then I have one quick cut to do. We can talk about your hair then."

Mama reached up on tiptoes to grab a handful of my hair. "I'm thinking something with lots of curls, Betty."

"Ow, that hurts!"

"But it has to look nice with the girls' bonnets." She let go of my hair, her hand making a hat-shaped arc above my head.

Bonnets? Lord deliver me.

"Aren't the parasols enough, Mama?"

"In for an inch, in for a mile, Mace. You can't be half a Southern belle."

Mama had been promoting fancy hairdos for the wedding. Of course I'd been resisting. Betty was supposed to persuade me to go along today by showing me sample styles in some kind of beauty book.

"Don't worry, Mace," Betty said. "I'm a professional. You'll look gorgeous."

I glanced at the bank president's wife, who looked like a poodle in earrings.

Muttering darkly, I grabbed a *People* magazine and took a seat to wait. Mama bustled around the shop, straightening up and lighting her aromatherapy candles.

"Hey, y'all!" A voice came from the supply closet in the back.

"Hey, D'Vora," Mama and I chorused.

Betty's twenty-something beautician trainee, D'Vora had made a big boo-boo last summer involving peroxide, an overly long cell phone call, and Mama's platinum dye job. But all Mama's hair grew back; and she'd forgiven D'Vora for the mishap.

Now, I looked up from an article on Angelina Jolie's brood to see D'Vora emerging from the closet, juggling several bottles of shampoo and conditioner. I wondered which ones were responsible for the smells at Hair Today: green apples, tropical fruits, and citrus, all overlaid with the ammonia-like odor of permanent solution. Add in Mama's aromatherapy candles and the lingering cloud of hair spray, and the shop was an allergist's nightmare.

As D'Vora began restocking shelves, I saw she was wearing her customary, jazzed-up uniform: painted-on purple pants and too-small smock, zipper revealing her cleavage. Appliquéd flowers and lilac-colored butterflies along the neckline further accentuated her chest.

Like C'ndee, D'Vora was a fan of the "If you've got it, flaunt it" school of fashion. They shared that, along with the fanciful use of apostrophes in their self-created first names.

"I saw y'all through the window at Gladys' this morning," D'Vora said to Mama, who'd stepped in to help her shelve the hair products.

"You should have joined us, honey."

"She was running late, as usual." Betty shot D'Vora a sharp look as she rang up the bank president's wife.

"Sorry, Betty," D'Vora recited by rote. "Anyways, who was that gorgeous guy at your table?"

Mama supplied the details on Anthony Ciancio as I leafed through *People*. What is it about Hollywood that makes celebrities go crazy? The star of a kids' show arrested for porn. A pop singer out in public with no undies. A famous actor caught in a racist rant. I tuned in to the beauty shop chat again.

"I should have known that guy was related to C'ndee," D'Vora was saying. "She's so glamorous!"

"That's a nice word for it," Mama said dryly. "But I have to admit, I do like that nephew. Maybe he can be a backup beau for Mace, once she screws things up completely with Carlos."

"Hello? I'm sitting right here!" I said from behind my *People*.

Mama clapped a hand over her mouth. My presence in the shop was so unnatural, I'm sure she'd forgotten I was there.

Ignoring her editorial comments on my love life, I said, "I'll give you the fact Tony is charming..."

"And gorgeous," D'Vora chimed in from near the shelves.

"Right," I agreed. "But doesn't it seem a little strange he and his aunt have those plans for a new catering business? I mean, Ronnie Hodges isn't even in the ground yet."

Betty was already snipping at the wet hair of her next appointment, a woman I didn't recognize. Scissors flying, she added her two cents' worth. "Everybody can agree it was horrible what happened to Ronnie, girls. But you have to strike while the iron is hot. That's the business world."

None of us had anything to add to that. The break in the conversation gave me time to think, not for the first time, that I was happy I worked mostly in the animal world.

Expertly navigating the lull, Mama steered the talk to her favorite topic, my marital prospects. "Betty, you've got to do something extra special with Mace's hair for Saturday. Weddings are fertile fields for romance. Maybe Carlos will pop the question once he sees Sally and me tying the knot."

All of a sudden, I was fed up. The dresses. The hair. Mama's constant meddling. Not to mention the assumption that Carlos was the one dragging his feet. I slammed my *People* onto the purple chair beside me.

"Let's put aside for the moment that seeing you get married for the FIFTH time might have just the opposite effect on Carlos, Mama. And on me. Have you given a bit of thought to the fact I might want to be certain things are right between us before I run off to the altar? I mean, I don't want a long string of ruined marriages, like some women I could mention."

Mama's hand flew to her throat. She looked at me like I'd put my boot to her three-tier, buttercream-frosted wedding cake. No one else said a word. All of us knew which woman in the shop had a history of ruined marriages. I felt my face getting hot. My stomach churned around a leaden ball of biscuits and sausage gravy. Funny how you dream of saying just what you want to say, but it never feels as good as you think it will once it comes out.

The customer in Betty's chair stepped into the strained silence and saved me. "I didn't mean to eavesdrop earlier," she said quietly. "But I heard y'all talking about C'ndee Ciancio, and I wondered if you knew she'd been staying at Darryl's Fish Camp, out by the lake."

Mama and I both burst out laughing at the same time, which felt good. Almost normal.

"C'ndee? At a fish camp? That's like hearing Madonna's been dishing up chili dogs at the Dairy Queen," I said.

"Well, she was. I know, because I'm renting one of the cottages out there. Just until I find something better."

I took in her cheap tennis shoes and bad teeth, and remembered how she'd told Betty she'd take just a haircut today: No shampoo, no blow dry, and no color. She had the look of hard times, and it'd probably be a good long while before she found "something better" than that rundown cottage at the fish camp.

"C'ndee could have been out there. Stranger things have happened, Mace." Mama's tone to me was snippy, but she smiled encouragingly at Betty's customer. "What's your name, honey?"

"Luanne. The only reason I mention C'ndee is because she's gone now, and a lot of us wondered what happened to her." She looked around, like she expected C'ndee to be lurking in the closet, listening in. Lowering her voice to a whisper, she said, "She really did a number on Darryl Dietz, the guy who owns the camp. He's been mean as a striped snake and drunk ever since she left." She paused. "Well, he's always mean. But he's been drunker than usual."

"So C'ndee—Jersey accent, flashy clothes, cherry red Mustang—was going out with this Darryl?" I asked.

Luanne nodded, her newly trimmed hair a pretty frame for her worn face. "Darryl walked out on his wife and everything. The same wife he's now trying to crawl back to since C'ndee disappeared."

D'Vora nodded. "Oh, I've been there, Luanne. After I found out my no-account husband was cheating, I smashed the headlights on his truck and tossed his sorry butt out of the trailer. He can beg all he wants. He ain't coming back, and neither is that stupid Rottweiler of his. Both him and Bear are as dumb as dirt."

Betty pointed her scissors at us: "Can't trust a cheater."

"Amen to that," Mama said. "Or a liar."

Our spat was forgotten now, in the face of this fresh gossip.

"Cheating with C'ndee wasn't the worst of it with Darryl," Luanne whispered. "He's beat on his wife more times than I can count."

I didn't know Darryl, but I could picture him, having visited more than my share of fish camps in my rowdier days. I thought about his wronged wife, and for some reason Alice Hodges' face popped into my head. But, try as I might, I couldn't conjure up an image of C'ndee running around with a guy with cheap beer on his breath and fish-gut stains on his shirt.

"What happened?" I asked Luanne. "Why'd C'ndee break it off?"

"We all heard she took up with somebody new. She left Darryl for another guy. He lives up here, in Himmarshee."

THIRTEEN

SOMEBODY AT DARRYL'S FISH camp was a fan of classic rock. Guns N' Roses blasted loud enough to spook the cormorants off their perches on the boat docks. Maidencane grass vibrated on the canal banks. Cypress branches trembled, even though there was barely a breath of wind. "Welcome to the Jungle," indeed.

Luanne hadn't known who C'ndee took up with after she dumped Darryl. And, of course, that's what all of us wanted to know. A little voice niggled at my brain, telling me that information might be important.

I left Hair Today, Dyed Tomorrow, and decided to poke around at the camp to see what I could learn. Between that or looking at hair in a picture book, it was no contest. Anyway, I'd pretty much given in to Mama's will on the wedding. I'd likely regret that when I saw what hairstyle she'd chosen from that book.

My Jeep bounced over a rutted driveway into an open yard circled by a dozen or so ramshackle cabins. A rusted-out muscle car sat up on concrete blocks, hood popped. The stadium-volume rock came from a boom box on a lawn chair next to the car. A big guy in jean overalls and no shirt held a wrench and bobbed his head to the beat. By the looks of the ancient car and the size of him, he might have more luck just adding some tires and pushing the old heap wherever he wanted to go.

I gave a short toot on my horn, just in case there were dogs. Of course they might be deaf, considering the Guns N' Roses. Sure enough, a coonhound rose from one of the crooked wooden porches and loped, barking, toward the Jeep. Mr. Overalls lifted his head from the engine block and whistled to call the dog. I was surprised he was so young, mid-twenties maybe. Vintage hard rock must be enjoying a renaissance. Mercifully, he hit the volume button on the boom box just as Axl Rose entered full scream.

I drove up to the decrepit car and spoke from my window. "Camaro, huh? What year?"

He ran a hand over the fender, which seemed to be more grey body filler than actual metal. "Sixty-nine," he said. "Found her in a sugarcane field over near Clewiston."

I took another look at the car and resisted the urge to ask him if he was crazy. "Well, good luck." I said instead. "Is the dog okay with me getting out?"

"Sure," he said. "Slash only goes after what I tell him to."

That was reassuring, I supposed. Climbing slowly from the Jeep, I offered a closed fist to the hound so he could sniff at me. I guarantee I smelled better than the dog did. I scratched a little behind his ears, until he seemed satisfied I wasn't there to do harm to Overalls. As if I could. The guy had at least a hundred pounds and six or seven inches on me. Losing interest, the dog walked back through the dirt yard to Cabin No. 7. He settled himself in the shade next to the door, and went back to sleep.

"Nothin' a coon dog loves more than a front porch." I leaned against the Jeep's fender, and smiled at Overalls. He didn't smile back.

"What can I do for you?"

Right to the point. I followed his lead.

"Have you seen Darryl, the guy who owns this place?"

He jerked his head toward the docks. "There's a fish-cleaning table back yonder, under them cypress trees. That's probably where he's at."

I thanked him.

"Enjoy," he said, cranking up the music again.

I smelled dead fish and cigarette smoke before I spotted Darryl. He stood at a high wooden table, which was washed by a faucet. As he cleaned his catch, he tossed heads and innards into the dark water of the lake-access canal below. He was bent over the task, but I could see the strong line of his jaw, and a thick head of tar-black hair. As he worked his knife, sinewy muscle stood out across his arms and broad shoulders. I got a pretty good look at his build, because he wasn't wearing a shirt. Just filthy jean cut-offs and bare feet covered in the mucky sediment that plagues the natural sand bottom of Lake Okeechobee.

Darryl looked like a creature right out of the swamp.

I thought I'd been pretty quiet coming up. But his head lifted for just a moment, like an animal getting a scent in the wild. He didn't turn around, and the knife never stopped, but he knew I was there.

"Yew lookin' for me?" His voice was pure Florida redneck.

"Depends," I said. "Are you Darryl?"

He nodded, still cutting. The sun reflected off the silver blade of his long knife. *Slice. Glint. Slice. Glint. Slice. Glint.* I waited, expecting he'd turn around to talk to me, but he didn't. So I walked a little closer and situated myself alongside the fish table. When he tossed a handful of gills and guts from a black crappie right next to my boots, I spoke up.

"I wondered if I could ask you a few questions."

He shrugged. *Slice. Glint.*

"I'm a friend of C'ndee Ciancio's."

The knife paused for just an instant. He quickly recovered his rhythm.

"I know you two were going around together."

"So? What's it to yew?" *Slice. Glint.*

He had me there. I wasn't sure why I was so interested in C'ndee's love life. I just knew I was. I'd learned in the last year or so to pay close attention to things that don't seem to add up.

"Her friends have been kind of worried about her behavior." I prayed the Lord wouldn't strike me down for lying, though I couldn't imagine He took much interest in a low-down snake like Darryl Dietz. "We're trying to find out who she's seeing," I continued, "because we want to make sure she hasn't hooked up with somebody dangerous."

The knife went still. For the first time, he raised his face to me. I had to admit he was handsome, in the same way you can admire the beauty of a rattlesnake while still knowing its bite can kill you.

"I wouldn't worry too much about C'ndee if I was yew. That's one girl who can take care of herself. I'd worry about the poor guy she took up with instead."

"Why's that?" I asked.

The smile he gave me was as cold as the ice in the chest full of fish at his feet. As I waited for him to answer, an osprey's plaintive *scree* sounded from a tall pine. The breeze sighed a bit, rustling a Confederate flag on a pole. Axl Rose crooned "Out Ta Get Me."

"Well?" I prodded.

He picked up the burning cigarette that had been balanced on the table's edge. With a hand covered in fish blood, he drew it to his mouth and took a drag nearly to the filter. Then, he flicked the butt into the dark water and silently bent his head again over his mess of fish.

Slice. Glint. Slice. Glint.

I started to rephrase my question. I managed, "Who ..."

"You're a nosy bitch, yew know that?" His hiss was low and menacing, like a rattler before it strikes. "We got ways out here to deal with people who don't know their place. Now, I'm gonna ask yew nice to take all your questions and shove 'em. And then get the hell off of my land."

Slice. Glint.

He didn't have to tell me twice. I think what convinced me was that final, violent jerk of the knife, all the way from tail fin to head. I hurried to my Jeep and lit out of there, but the rutted driveway would let me go only so fast.

In the rearview mirror, I noticed Overalls fooling with a boat in a slip near the fish-cleaning table. How long had he been there? Then, I saw Darryl step from the dock into the yard to watch me go. His black eyes were hypnotic, holding my gaze without a blink. Heart pounding, I had to wait for traffic to pass before I could pull out onto the paved road. Behind me, Darryl propped a foot up on a tree stump. His eyes moved to the knife in his hand, and so did mine.

My last image of the camp was Darryl testing the sharpness of that silver blade by shaving a hair off his bare leg.

FOURTEEN

BARRELING ALONG US HIGHWAY 441, I'd put five miles between me and the fish camp before I finally felt my grip begin to loosen on the Jeep's steering wheel. I was holding on like I expected Darryl to vault into the driver's seat and yank me out with those blood-stained hands.

That was one creepy dude, for sure.

What had C'ndee Ciancio been thinking? I can understand occasional slumming. Bad boys can be exciting. Plus, let's face facts: One of my exes showed up shirtless on *Cops*. It's kind of hard for me to criticize another woman's flawed taste in men.

But Darryl? He seemed to go beyond dangerous to deranged.

I searched through my purse on the passenger seat for my cell phone. I needed to call my boss. Nothing like hearing all the afternoon tasks that awaited me at work to banish the image of Darryl and that knife.

Slice, glint. Slice, glint.

I hit the speed dial for the park office. The cultured purr on the other end of the phone was reassuringly Rhonda, my way-too-gorgeous-for-government-work supervisor. Not only did she carry herself like an elegant African queen, she was smart, too. I always told her she was wasting her time shuffling schedules and pushing papers at a nature park in middle Florida. She could have been a model-turned-mega-industry, like Tyra Banks. But Rhonda had moved home to Himmarshee from New York to help care for her ailing grandmother. She wound up as the boss for the county's parks.

"How are plans coming for the big day, Mace?"

She'd been great about arranging my shifts to accommodate my obligations to The Wedding of the Century.

"Don't get me started," I said. "Suffice to say the ring-bearer's a yappy dog in a top hat, my dress makes me look like a lime pop with a parasol, and Mama can't serve enough booze to make anybody forget this is the fifth time she's tied the sacred knot of matrimony."

"That bad, huh?" Rhonda chuckled. "Listen, no pressure, but I just wanted to check if you're still doing that sunset nature walk tomorrow. I've had a few calls about it, so I know there's some interest. I can handle it if you can't."

Damn. I'd completely forgotten. I was about to beg off, but I didn't want to take advantage of Rhonda. She wasn't really the nature-loving type; and I might need another favor before the week was out.

"Absolutely," I said. "I'll be there early enough to feed the critters and then do the walk."

There was a pause from Rhonda's end. "About the animals, Mace... Ollie nearly ate a raccoon that found its way to the bank of the gator pond today. Some church school kids who were at the park on a field trip were awfully upset. Their teacher complained about nightmares."

As Rhonda spoke, I watched a big truck gaining on me in the rearview mirror. It always surprises me how fast people drive on this narrow stretch of the road that rings Lake Okeechobee.

"Did you hear me, Mace? Can't you do something to make sure none of the other animals have access to Ollie's pond?"

"Gators eat raccoons, Rhonda. That's nature. We're a nature park." I glanced at the mirror again. The driver's face was shadowed by the brim of a beat-up straw hat. Was the truck going to pass me or run me over?

"I'm aware it's nature, Mace. But it may be just a little too much reality for young kids to witness. And suppose there was a toddler down there on the bank instead of that raccoon? Oh my god, that would be horrible. Not to mention the liability."

I didn't answer. Now the truck was right on my bumper, flashing its lights.

"We might have to talk about getting rid of Ollie, Mace."

The truck's horn blasted. I couldn't hold this conversation right now with Rhonda, not with some moron about to race up my tailpipe. "I hear what you're saying, Boss. Let's talk about it when I get in, okay?"

I rang off quickly, dropped the phone on the seat, and gave my full attention to the truck behind me. I'd had a bad experience last summer, when I was run off the highway into a roadside canal.

That night, I'd been caught by surprise. Now, I wasn't about to let the same thing happen again. I began tapping my brakes, signaling to the driver to back the hell off.

Slowing, he leaned out the window and gestured for me to pull over. When he did, a slant of sunlight revealed his face. It was the big man in overalls from the fish camp. A knot of fear formed in my chest. I sped up; he did, too. I slowed to a crawl; so did he. We were miles from anything. A deep canal ran close by my side of the road. Huge trucks rumbled past in the other lane, hauling sugarcane or sod.

I could keep going, and take the chance he'd bump me off the highway. Maybe I wouldn't be as lucky this time. Or, I could stop and see what he wanted. I eased off on the gas and reached for the tire iron I learned to keep hidden under the seat.

He slowed as I did, pulling off on the narrow, grassy shoulder. The water was so near, I could smell the mud and the grassy scent of hydrilla floating on the canal's surface. Easing open my door, I kept my eyes on the rearview as he hefted his bulk out of the truck. His hands hung by his sides; no weapons. Then again, those overall pockets were so big, he might be carrying a cannon and I wouldn't see it. My fist clenched around the metal rod, which I'd brought to a ready position on the seat.

As he approached, I flew out of the Jeep, waving my tire iron. A look of utter surprise flitted across his face.

"Don't come another step closer. My other hand's on the phone in my pocket, ready to speed dial 911." I cursed the fact I'd actually left my cell on the seat where it fell. I prayed my voice didn't sound as shaky as I felt.

He raised his hands, palms showing in a gesture of submission. "Whoa, ma'am. I don't mean you no harm. I just want to talk to you."

I lowered the tire iron a half-inch. "You weren't exactly chatty earlier."

"I couldn't talk at the camp. That bastard Darryl keeps an eye on everything that goes on there. He's my stepfather."

I immediately felt a surge of sympathy for Overalls. Looking at him now, I realized he was no older than Maddie's college-girl daughter. "What's your name?"

"Rabe, ma'am," he said.

"Dietz?" I asked.

He spit on the ground. "Hell, no. Darryl married my mama, but I still have my daddy's name. Adams. All Darryl ever gave me was black-and-blue beatings."

I dropped the tire iron a bit lower, feeling faintly ridiculous.

"Sorry I scared you," Rabe said. "I was just trying to get your attention. I heard you asking Darryl about that woman, C'ndee."

Now I realized why Rabe had been at the boat dock: He was watching; listening. Kids who grow up in a home with alcoholism and abuse learn those skills early.

"What about C'ndee?" I said.

"I heard the two of them fighting before she cleared out of camp. If you're worried about her, you might have cause. Darryl's a real violent man. I watched him beat Mama for years, and she'd always go back to him. He used to do me the same way, until I finally got big enough to knock him stupid."

I thought about Rabe as a boy, cowering on a narrow bed in one of those rundown little cabins. It about broke my heart.

"Thanks for coming after me," I told him. "I hope it doesn't get you in trouble with Darryl."

"Naw," he said. "Him and me give each other a wide berth these days. And Mama says she's finally done with him, too. I just wanted you to know he gets crazy jealous. If that C'ndee is your friend, you should keep an eye out for her. No telling what Darryl will do."

He jiggled the keys to the truck in his hand, looking thoughtful. "I once saw him take after Mama with his belt, just because he *thought* she looked at another man. And he did even worse one time in a bar. Some guy bought Mama a drink, friendly-like, and Darryl just about beat in his skull for his trouble. The ambulance came and everything."

His face got a distant look, like he was replaying those events from the past. I thought of one more thing I wanted to know about the present.

"You said you heard Darryl and C'ndee fighting. What about?"

"She was breaking it off. She told him it'd been fun, but she found somebody new."

Fun? I shuddered at the thought. "How'd he take it?"

"'Bout like you'd expect. He cussed a blue streak and kicked one of the cabin doors right off its hinges. Slash lit out and hid under one of the cars for a full day. Darryl never touched C'ndee, though." Rabe's eyes looked far away again. "He would have, given time."

"Did C'ndee tell Darryl who she was dating?"

He rubbed a hand through the sparse beard on his chin. "Not by name, no. But she did throw it in Darryl's face that the guy was a successful businessman in Himmarshee. She said he owned a catering business."

FIFTEEN

THE JEEP'S TIRES HUMMED as I drove over the little wooden bridge at the entrance to Himmarshee Park. All usually felt right with the world when I heard that sound. But today a lot felt wrong in our little town.

Ronnie was dead, a fact I couldn't forget because I kept seeing a filmstrip in my head. Darryl Dietz could have had a motive to kill him, based on what the stepson told me. And where did C'ndee fit in the equation? Had she just been playing with Darryl, or was it something more? And why hadn't she let on how very well she knew Himmarshee's only caterer?

A leafy tree canopy shaded the narrow lane. It was like driving into a green cave, with the dim coolness doing its best to soothe my mind. Alongside the winding road to the parking lot, butterflies flitted in the yellow tickseed that grew in sunny patches. I turned off the radio and tuned in to the outdoors. Frogs croaked in Himmarshee Creek. A pileated woodpecker *rat-a-tat-tatted* on a dead pine. A gator bellowed from the distant swamp. I started to feel some of the stress leaving my body, like a reptile shedding skin.

My heartbeat quickened as I rounded a turn into the parking lot. A white, late-model sedan sat under the shade of a sabal palm. It was an unmarked police car. Carlos' car. We'd gotten along pretty well at Mama's last night. Maybe we could reconnect, enter a more lasting up in our up-and-down relationship. There's always hope, right?

Within minutes, I was out of my Jeep and on the nature path to the park office. Drawing near, I saw him through the big windows that look out onto a hardwood hammock, thick with gnarled oaks and black tupelo. He was laughing at something Rhonda had said. I paused in the shade of a hickory tree, wanting to watch him for just a moment in an unguarded state. It seemed like the two of us were always walking on tippy-toes around each other.

He sipped a small cup of take-out coffee, which reminded me of the first night I met him in the lobby of the Himmarshee Police Department. I remember being bowled over by his looks—black hair, skin the color of buttery caramel, dark eyes that hid plenty of secrets. I'd had all I could do back then to stay mad at him for hauling Mama's butt into jail.

And now? He still looked as yummy as a buttered biscuit. But I didn't have trouble any more staying mad at him. And I'm not sure why, or what that means. Sometimes, I try to make sense of human behavior by looking to the animal world. Maybe I'm just not cut out to be a Sandhill crane, which chooses its partner for life.

As I opened the door, Carlos smiled and held up a large-sized cup: "I brought *café con leche* for you and Rhonda."

He'd been beside himself with happiness when he discovered a Cuban restaurant—more of a gas station with a tiny food counter—on the outskirts of Himmarshee. They only served breakfast and a couple of lunch specials. But the *café Cubano* flowed all day, giving Carlos the fix he needed. Sipping the super-sweet, high-octane brew seemed to make him feel more at home in Himmarshee.

I took the cup he offered. "You the man!"

Cuban crack, he called it, and the stuff *was* addictive. I drank mine mixed with three-quarters steamed milk. Carlos' poison was the traditional *cafecito*, a tiny, sugared shot of pure caffeine.

My boss picked up her cup from her desk and lifted it toward us. "Here's to a summer without hurricanes."

"Here's to the two most beautiful women I know," he responded.

With Rhonda's dark skin, I couldn't tell if she was blushing. Probably not. Unlike me, she'd surely heard tons of such toasts before. They both looked at me, waiting.

"Uhmmm," I said eloquent as always. "Here's to finding Ronnie's killer."

And to murdering the moment. Carlos' face hardened.

"Yeah, we're working on that, Mace. It only happened yesterday."

"I didn't mean it that way."

I tried to shovel out of the hole I'd dug. "I wasn't criticizing."

"That's how it sounded," he said.

"Sorry you're so sensitive."

"Now, that's what I love." Carlos glared. "An apology that's actually an accusation."

Rhonda averted her eyes, staring at the phone on her desk. I'm sure she was willing it to ring and rescue her. When did Carlos and I become one of those couples who embarrass everyone by bickering in public?

I reached out to touch his arm, but he sidestepped me. "Let's start over again," I offered.

His face was still stony; but a relieved look flickered across Rhonda's features.

"Thank you for the coffee, Carlos." I grinned at him. "You are really, really, really, *really* the man!"

A tiny smile chipped at the granite in his jaw.

"And I am sorry," I continued. "It's just that Ronnie's been on my mind because of what I found out today at a fish camp at the southern end of Lake Okeechobee."

Carlos lifted an eyebrow.

Here's where I had to tie on those toe-walking shoes again. He hated it when I went off investigating. But there was no way I couldn't share with him what I'd learned. Rhonda's hand hovered over a stack of maintenance requests as she waited to see what I'd say next. No sense in making Carlos doubly mad, spilling information about a possible suspect with her listening in.

"Why don't we go outside?" I said to him. "It's nice and cool in the breezeway, and I'll buy us something sweet from the vending machine to go with the coffee."

Carlos gestured for me to lead the way.

"Okay if I take a few minutes, boss? When I come back, I'll see if I can't get a track hoe out here to dig another pond for the little critters to drink from. One without an alligator in it."

Rhonda lifted her hand, shooing us toward the door. "I know you'll take care of it, Mace. And, Carlos, *gracias por el café con leche*." Her Spanish accent was as perfect as everything else about her.

We settled onto a wooden bench with our snacks—a package of lemon cookies for me; a gooey cinnamon bun for Carlos. And then I told him what I'd discovered about C'ndee and about Darryl.

"What'd the knife look like?"

"Long and thin, like a filet knife. Big, but not big enough to behead that hog. As for killing Ronnie? I don't know much about what kind of blade you'd need to knife somebody to death."

Carlos' face was grim. "You'd be surprised at the kind of damage any knife can do if you hit the right spot." He took a swallow of his coffee. "How'd this Darryl act?"

I wasn't about to let on how frightened I'd felt. Carlos would just get angry.

"Like a sorry-ass redneck, showing off with a scary knife."

He peered into my eyes. "Did he threaten you, Mace?"

I didn't want to outright lie, especially when the truth might reveal a pattern of behavior.

"Yes," I admitted.

"¡*Coño*!" I don't know why you do things like that, Mace. Going out there alone? Do you have a death wish?"

"No." I studied the toes of my work boots.

"Well that's the way it looks to me. You're not a police officer. It's not your business to run around asking questions, especially to someone who might turn out to be a killer."

He chomped off a hunk of the cinnamon bun, probably wishing it were my head.

I tried to make my voice neutral, not antagonistic. "It kind of *is* my business, Carlos."

"Yeah, why's that?"

"Well, Ronnie was catering Mama's wedding..."

He interrupted, "Not that stupid wedding again!"

I felt myself getting huffy on Mama's behalf. I may have agreed her wedding was ridiculously over-the-top, but Carlos still shouldn't call it stupid.

"I'm just saying that makes us involved, whether we want to be or not. And now that I know C'ndee was involved with Darryl, and then with Ronnie, and now she's catering Mama's wedding..."

"What?" he said.

I couldn't believe what was about to come out of my mouth. "It's just that I don't want anything else to happen to ruin Mama's Special Day."

He scowled at me.

"I'm not talking about the wedding flowers being a little wilted, or the appetizers coming out cold. I mean, I don't want anybody else to get hurt. We both know Mama manages to wind up in the middle of things. Suppose she comes to harm? You know it's happened before."

It didn't escape me that I sounded as paranoid about Mama as he did about me. I guess seeing someone you care about survive some close calls will do that to a person.

The angry lines in his face softened. He took another, smaller, bite of the bun. Chewed thoughtfully. Finished his coffee.

"I'll grant you, your mother manages to get herself into some serious messes. That still doesn't give you the right to meddle in a murder investigation. You shouldn't be sticking your nose into things that aren't your business."

It was amazing how much that part about me being nosy sounded like Darryl. All Carlos needed was a shiny knife and a Lakeport drawl.

"Fine," I said. "I'll be sure to hire an armed guard the next time I want to go out to a fish camp. Which incidentally, I've visited many of in the past. I'll bring backup the next time I want to talk to some mean redneck. Which incidentally, I've probably dated worse guys than Darryl and lived to tell about it."

I jammed a lemon cookie in my mouth so I wouldn't say something I'd really regret. He waited for another outburst. I didn't speak, just took another cookie from the pack and started on that. This time, I took off the top part and slowly licked all the cream filling from inside.

When I caught him staring at my mouth, both of us quickly looked away. He made me so angry. So why did I feel a sudden warmth spreading somewhere south of my belt?

Carlos cleared his throat. Stood up. It gave me a little thrill to see him try to subtly adjust the front pleats on his dark blue dress slacks.

"I've got a lot of work to get back to," he said. "Please don't take this to mean I approve of what you did, Mace, but I'll definitely check out what you found out about the knife-wielding Mr. Dietz."

That was as close as he'd come to a thank-you.

"What about C'ndee and Ronnie? What do you think that connection means?"

Crossing his arms, he stared at me, cop-like: "The case is still under investigation."

"So I spill all the information I have, and you offer me nothing in return?"

He gave me a know-it-all smile, which really chapped my butt. "Sure, Mace, I'll tell you everything I know and have it all over the Himmarshee Hotline before dinner."

I felt a pout forming on my mouth, which I know doesn't look as charming on me as it does on Mama. "I'm not a gossip, Carlos."

"No, but your mother is. And you're only one degree of separation from her."

"Okay, just tell me if there's anything I should know to keep Mama safe."

He gazed into the trees, thinking. Maybe he remembered some of her prior scrapes, because he relented a little. "I will tell you Ronnie Hodges wasn't exactly what he seemed."

SIXTEEN

I RACED THROUGH A yellow-turning-red traffic light on Main Street. A pothole loomed. I swerved to miss it. The Jeep zoomed past the Dairy Queen on the left; Pete's Pawn Shop on the right. An *eeeeek* sounded from the passenger seat.

"My stars and garters, Mace! Would you please slow down? You know you're not Dale Earnhardt, may he rest in peace."

I eased off the gas. Mama had a point. I do love to go fast.

"Thank you." She unclenched her hands from the dashboard and settled back into her seat. "Now, what do you think we should do about Alice?"

Mama had asked me to pick her up after work at Hair Today, Dyed Tomorrow, and then go with her to look in on Ronnie's widow.

"I'm not sure there's anything we can do, Mama. Her husband's just been murdered. She's going to need time to deal with that. The best we can offer is to let her know we care."

Mama angled the rearview mirror toward her, so she could repair her wind-blown hair. As she fluffed and straightened, I said, "Trying to drive with no mirror is a lot more dangerous than going a few miles over the speed limit."

"Try thirty miles. You were doing at least fifty-five when you blew through that red light, Mace."

"Yellow light." I turned the rearview back. "Why can't you just use the mirror on your visor?"

She reached into her purse for her compact. "That stingy, cloudy thing? It won't give me the full effect."

I looked at her platinum-hued 'do. It was smashed on one side, swirled into some kind of circle on the other, and standing up in spikes on the top of her head. It looked like she'd come under attack by a badger bearing styling mousse and a teasing comb.

"Sometimes you don't want the full effect," I said.

Even though I slowed down, we still made it to Mama's in no time. Downtown Himmarshee, such as it is, is only three miles from her house on Strawberry Lane. Pulling into the driveway, I could see the porch light on next door at Alice's. It was just five-thirty p.m., and still sunny. The light had probably been burning since the police processed her porch last night.

The drapes were drawn in the front windows. The day had been hot, and Alice's flowers wilted in their gaily colored pots. Mama's gaze followed mine to her neighbor's home.

"Looks sad, doesn't it?" she said. "What is it about a house after someone dies? You can almost imagine that somehow it feels the loss, too."

I wasn't sure about that. But the house definitely looked empty. Alice's car was likely still at the VFW. I hadn't thought yesterday to look behind the hall to see if Ronnie's truck was parked in the back near the kitchen. I'd have to ask C'ndee if she saw it when she rushed in late to meet us. Come to think of it, there were quite a few questions I wanted to ask C'ndee.

Mama's compact clicked shut, bringing my mind back to the present.

"You ready, Mama?"

When we got to Alice's front door, I knocked softly at first. We could hear the TV blaring, even though the windows were closed and the air conditioning unit hummed next to the porch. When there was no answer, I knocked a little harder.

"Nobody home," a woman's voice called from inside. "Go 'way."

Mama and I looked at each other.

"Alice, honey, is that you?" Leaning forward, Mama yelled into the crack at the edge of the door. "I'm here with my middle daughter, Mace."

A couple of moments passed. Then the TV volume went down. "S'open. C'mon in, Ros'lee."

As soon as we stepped into the house's dark maw, the smell of hard liquor hit me like a fist to the face. A half-empty bottle of bourbon sat on a high counter in a dim shaft of kitchen light. Alice slouched in a recliner in the living room, illuminated by the blue glow of an ancient rerun of *Law & Order*. The guy who played Mr. Big in *Sex and the City* was still a cocky young Detective Logan with the NYPD.

Alice let out a snuffling sob.

"Oh, honey!" Mama hurried to her side.

"I'm all right, Ros'lee."

Mama hesitated just a second before she laid a hand on Alice's shoulder. I had to credit her for not letting her face show the shock she surely felt at her neighbor's appearance. Bits of brown-looking food and what smelled like bourbon made a trail of stains on Alice's ratty pink robe. Her hair was limp and greasy. The bathrobe gaped open, revealing Alice wasn't wearing anything but Alice underneath.

"Mace, honey, why don't you go see if you can rustle us up some coffee?"

With Alice now staring blankly at the TV screen, Mama jerked her head twice toward the kitchen. I got the message.

I might have been resentful that she sent me on an errand while she got down to the business of comforting Alice. But the truth is I'm awful at emotion. Mama and Marty are the ones with the gift. Maddie usually manages to give offense when she thinks she's offering comfort. And I just clam up, as tongue-tied as a fifth-grade boy trying to talk to his first crush.

Alice could definitely use some coffee, and I was happy to have something useful to do. Her coffeemaker was on the counter, and the paper filters in the cupboard overhead. As I hunted around the kitchen for cups and spoons, I heard Mama murmuring in the next room, urging Alice out of the chair.

"Honey, you'll feel so much better once we get you into a shower."

Soon, the coffee was brewing. Steps sounded from the living room. One set was light; the other heavy. I knew Mama was helping her into the bedroom, because I'd hear the two of them stumble slightly every so often. I probably should have assisted, but my face burned at the memory of that gaping robe. Seeing Alice emotionally naked was somehow even worse.

Her bathroom must have been right behind the kitchen. I was relieved when I heard the water running through the wall.

While I waited, I straightened up, trying to make myself useful. I washed a few dishes; tossed away a paper plate half-filled with brown, crusted-over franks and beans. Opening blinds and turning on lights, I headed back to the dining room where I'd seen the bottle of booze.

Alice was devout, and we'd always believed she didn't approve of drinking. If she'd slipped, the fact that someone had butchered her husband was a pretty good excuse. I figured I'd put the bourbon away anyway, take away temptation. If she wasn't accustomed to liquor, drinking the remaining half might kill her.

As I stepped up to the counter, my boot hit something solid. Three cardboard boxes were shoved underneath, lined up against the wall. I glanced toward the closed bedroom door.

Darryl Dietz's voice replayed in my head, accusing me of being a nosy bitch. While I resented the second part of that description, I had to admit he had a point with the first. I opened the flaps on the closest box.

A brown-checkered sport coat lay atop a jumble of men's clothing. I remembered Ronnie wearing that jacket last summer to a prayer breakfast at the VFW. The next box contained big, heavy men's shoes.

I peeked over my shoulder. The door was still closed.

I opened the last box, crammed full of framed photos. Right on top was a picture of Ronnie and Alice, young and smiling. Their hands were clasped together on a gleaming silver knife, poised to carve the first slice from their wedding cake.

I laid the picture on the carpet. Quietly, I extracted another: Ronnie, fishing in Taylor Creek. The next one showed him at the counter of the Home on the Range Feed Store and Clothing Emporium, before his injury. He'd worked there until a pallet of feed bags toppled onto him. Beneath that picture was a cap-and-gowned Ronnie, shaking hands at a podium and holding a high school diploma.

Except for that one wedding photo with Alice, all the shots were of Ronnie. Cross-legged on the floor with framed pictures all around, I was pondering how one box can sum a man's life. But what of the moments a camera didn't capture? A box of those memories might reveal a different life.

"Finding what you need, Mace?"

Mama's sharp voice made me jump. I tried to keep the guilty look off my face.

"What are you doing messing around in there?" Alice looked less drunk now than angry.

"I … Uhmmm." There really was no excuse. "I just wondered what was in the boxes." Alice stalked to the counter, and bent to close the flaps on the first two cartons. She held out her hands. "I'll take those."

"Sorry." I gathered up the pictures and handed them over.

Mama shot me a dirty look. Alice slammed framed photos back in the box. I hoped the glass wouldn't shatter with the force, just because she was mad that I was a nosy bitch.

———

"My, that coffee smells good!"

Mama's cheery words dropped like stones into the strained silence. We'd left the scene of my crime to sit at Alice's kitchen table. I traced a border of morning glories on a blue plastic placemat. Alice stared at the refrigerator. Following her gaze, I saw she'd forgotten to pluck one last picture of Ronnie from underneath a magnet on the door.

"I'm..."

"Thank..."

Alice and I started to speak at the same time. Our eyes met, and both of us looked away.

"Honey, we're guests in your home. Why don't you go first?" Mama patted Alice's hands, which were folded in the prayer position on her placemat.

"I was going to say thank you, Mace, for making the coffee."

"And I was going to say I'm sorry for looking through your personal things. I don't know what got into me."

"I didn't raise her that way," Mama sniffed.

Alice sipped from the cup I poured, gave a little shrug.

The television still droned in the next room. But in the kitchen, it was so quiet I could hear a clock shaped like a blue teapot ticking on the wall. Air whooshed from a ceiling AC vent, rustling blue-checked curtains above the sink. Mama's spoon clinked against her cup as she stirred her coffee. Finally, Alice gave a long sigh.

"I suppose y'all are wondering why Ronnie's things are packed up."

Mama's eyes met mine over our coffee cups. "Well, now that you mention it, honey."

Alice raised her hands in a gesture of helplessness. "I know it's strange, but then everything has seemed strange since Ronnie died. This morning, when I came home from your place, Rosalee, I saw him everywhere I looked in here. The more I saw, the more I remembered how he died."

She rubbed her eyes. "I got those boxes from the shed, and started throwing in anything of his I could find. The more I drank, the better an idea it seemed."

"What idea was that?" I asked.

"That if I could only get rid of all those reminders, maybe Ronnie wasn't really dead. Maybe his murder was just a dream."

She lifted her face to us, eyes brimming with tears. "It didn't work, you know?" Her voice was as small as a child's. "I filled three boxes and Ronnie's still dead."

SEVENTEEN

ALICE'S TEARS SPLATTERED ONTO her placemat, watering the morning glory border. I felt like a heel. Not only had I invaded the poor woman's privacy with those boxes of clothes and pictures, I'd brought on another round of crying.

"I thought maybe you were mad at Ronnie. I remember after I caught my old boyfriend Jeb with another girl, I packed up all the souvenirs I'd saved of him riding rodeo and tossed them in the trash."

"That's hardly the same thing, Mace." Mama sneered at me. "You're comparing a lying boyfriend to a murdered husband. Did you misplace your manners somewhere in that crazy drive over here?"

I hadn't told Mama yet about Darryl, or his stepson's claim that C'ndee jilted him for a caterer in Himmarshee. I was trying to find a roundabout way to discover if Ronnie had been cheating on Alice. Even I knew asking a new widow such a bald question was out of bounds.

To my surprise, Alice's face softened into a smile. "It's all right, Rosalee. I can tell you both that Ronnie wasn't perfect. He slept on the couch a time or two over the years. Then again, I'm no angel, either. Aside from a few spats, though, I'd say we had a pretty good union."

Mama patted Alice's hand. "Honey, every marriage has its ups and downs."

"She should know," I said to Alice. "Sal will be Mama's No. 5."

"Ronnie was my one-and-only. We were just kids when we got married."

I flashed on that picture of them cutting their wedding cake, eyes shining with youth and happiness. What an awful end to what began with such promise for Alice and Ronnie.

The dreamy smile still lit Alice's face. But between the *café con leche grande* from work, and now this cup at Alice's, I needed to use the facilities. Urgently.

"Could I please use your bathroom?" With stellar timing, I barged into what might have been Alice's only happy thought of the day.

Mama glared at me as Alice's smile slipped away. "Help yourself."

I didn't want her to think I was snooping again, so I avoided her bedroom and master bath. Plus, I didn't relish the thought of them sitting and sipping coffee as I was answering nature's call on the other side of the kitchen wall. I found a dark hallway to the guest bath.

When I finished up and opened the door, bright light spilled into the hall. Some pictures were grouped on the wall, with lots of faded spots where Ronnie's photos must have hung. I wasn't being nosy. I was just passing by.

Alice posed for one photo in front of a flat, rural landscape with a silo on the horizon. No puffy clouds or sabal palms. It didn't appear to be Florida. There was another of her with an elderly couple dressed in worn work clothes. The man looked stern, and the woman, tired. Her parents? The picture next to that was of Alice on her wedding day. She's a plain woman, but she was radiant that day, like all brides. I leaned in to see if I could spot any tulle on her dress, now that I know what it is.

That's when I noticed the frame was too big for the picture. Alice stood in a side view, smiling and extending her arms. But a jagged rip down the center of the picture cut off her hands at the wrists. Mama had made me stare at enough wedding photos in magazines that I recognized that side-angle shot. The right half of the photo was gone, the position that always belongs to the groom.

For the moment, I decided to just tuck the sight of that mutilated photo away in my mind. I returned to the kitchen just in time to hear the end of a question from Mama.

"... do about Ronnie's business?"

I hoped she wasn't asking Alice if she'd be up to feeding one-hundred-fifty guests by Saturday.

When Alice didn't answer, Mama quickly said, "Of course, you don't need to decide anything yet, honey."

Alice stared into her coffee. "I never wanted Ronnie to start Pig-Out Barbecue and Catering. Just because you love to eat doesn't mean you should open a restaurant, I told him."

I slid into my chair. "Ronnie surely did love food," I said. "I remember him at that prayer breakfast last summer. Before we discovered Mama was in trouble, he was eyeing that buffet like a beggar at a banquet."

Alice's dreamy smile resurfaced, which made me feel good. "Remember how big he got after he got hurt at the feed store?"

" 'Fatter than a fixed dog,' I think is how Ronnie put it," I said.

"And then he managed to take off all that extra weight," Mama said. "Maybe Maddie should try whatever diet Ronnie went on."

Alice shook her head. "Maddie wouldn't want to do that. Ronnie's weight dropped from sheer worry over that catering business. I tried to tell him we could get along fine with him collecting disability, but he wouldn't listen. He thought all that new money moving into Himmarshee Links was going to make him a millionaire."

"So that's why he started the business?" I asked.

Lining up her spoon in the center of a napkin, she nodded. "And proceeded to pour nearly everything we had into it."

"So Pig-Out wasn't a success?" Mama asked.

Alice's laugh was short, mirthless. "Hardly. Ronnie was at his wit's end. Pig-Out was running through money like green grass through a goose."

I thought back to what Carlos had said about Ronnie not being what he seemed. Could the failing business be what he meant? I knew Mama thought Ronnie was a success: She'd told me often enough she and Sal were paying a premium price for the best. And, according to Darryl's stepson, C'ndee had also believed Ronnie to be a prosperous businessman.

Who else had been misled about Pig-Out? And how had they taken to being lied to?

———

The crickets tuned up for their evening concert. The sun sank low on the horizon, painting the dusk with fingers of purple and rose. It had rained while we were inside at Alice's, and the grass and the leaves on the oak trees glistened.

I took a deep breath of the fresh-scrubbed air. It felt good to be out of that house, with its dark rooms and reminders of death. It felt good to be alive. Why is it in the sympathy we feel when someone dies that there's also a tiny voice inside that says "Thank God it's not me?"

"Mace, you're ringing!"

"What?"

Mama pointed to my purse. "And try not to be rude. You're already on a losing streak."

I fumbled, found the cell, and answered just as I imagined voice mail would be picking up.

"Yeah?" I said, unsure if there was even a caller there.

"Telephone manners!" Mama hissed.

"Is this Mace Bauer?" The voice on the phone was pure Ivy League.

"It is. Who's calling…" And then, for Mama's benefit I added "…please?"

"Anthony Ciancio."

I'd thought as much, but I liked to hear him talk. He was the culture to his Aunt C'ndee's clash.

"Tony!" Eyes on Mama, I put a big smile in my voice. "How nice to hear from you. Everything okay with the Ciancio clan?"

Mama lifted an eyebrow. I listened, and then repeated what he said to get her goat.

"So you think Mama and your aunt have gotten off on the wrong foot. They're so alike, you say, that they're really two peas in the same pod?"

Mama's face darkened.

"You want to take all of us out to dinner? Well, isn't that nice."

Mama's head ricocheted from side to side. She mouthed an emphatic *No!*

"Oh, yes. I agree. Dinner *is* the perfect way to get C'ndee and Mama back on the right track."

Now Mama was grasping for the phone. I ducked and wove, keeping just out of her reach.

"You're absolutely right, Tony. We're all going to be family; and there's nothing more important than family. In fact, my mother's here with me right now."

Mama put a pretend gun to her head, dramatically pulling the pretend trigger.

"Oh, no, we're just shooting the breeze. You're not interrupting." I listened. "Well, if you don't mind me suggesting," I said sweetly, "then the Speckled Perch probably serves the best dinner in town."

My mouth watered at the thought of fried fish with grits, hot dinner rolls, and collard greens. Mama mimed tying a noose around her neck.

"Well, she's a little tied up right now. But I'll tell her you extended a personal invite. Oh, yes, we'll be ready. You'll pick us up at Mama's house. In an hour? Great!"

Mama made like she was tightening the rope, rolled her eyes back in her head, and stuck her tongue out of the corner of her mouth.

"Oh, yes," I told Tony. "Mama is definitely looking forward to it. In fact, she's grinning from ear to ear right now."

EIGHTEEN

THE NOISE IN THE dining room at the Speckled Perch was approaching full din. Bus boys scrambled about, clearing dishes. A couple of high-chaired babies screeched. A waitress rushed out from the kitchen, left arm laden with plates, and shouted to the hostess: "Eighty-six the cobbler."

Dang. That peach cobbler was a specialty. I planned to reserve my second dessert choice, a slice of key lime pie, as soon as we sat down.

"It'll be just a minute, Ms. Rosalee." The young hostess smiled at Mama. "We're getting you a booth cleaned up right now."

Too vain to wear her glasses, Mama squinted at the girl's name tag. *Tracy*. The hostess had probably been one of her Sunday school students, like half of Himmarshee.

"Take your time, honey."

Tony had insisted on dropping us at the front entrance before he parked the luxury car he'd rented to drive south. He'd noticed the unpaved lot was filled with puddles, which I thought was considerate of him. Of course, a little rainwater wouldn't faze me in my work boots. But I could see where Mama, sporting bright orange sling-back heels, might mind the mud.

As they prepared our table, I replayed getting ready in my mind.

"Don't you have anything else to wear, Mace?" Mama had asked, as we waited for Tony to pick us up at her house.

"Let me go take a look in the Jeep, Mama. Maybe I'll find a little black dress and Jimmy Choo heels in the back, right next to the paste bait for my raccoon traps."

"No need to get snippy." She tied a jaunty bow beneath her chin. The scarf was the same shade as her shoes and pantsuit.

"I thought you were never wearing orange again after that jumpsuit they made you wear in jail."

She waved her hand, as if a little stint in the slammer in connection to a murder was of no consequence.

"It's not orange. It's tangerine, and I look good in this shade, Mace." Admiring herself in her full-length mirror, she clipped on matching earrings. "Besides, all that was so long ago."

"It was only last summer," I'd said, more sharply than I meant to.

Why was I so cranky? All I know is that each time Mama added another one of her *tangerine*-colored doo-dads, it left me feeling more plain in my olive drab work clothes and boots. It didn't help when Tony arrived, and let out an admiring whistle when she finally paraded into her living room. All I'd gotten when I answered the door was a flash of those beautiful white teeth and a somewhat formal "Good evening."

I mean, not like I cared. I'd never be interested in a guy who spent more time on his hair than I spent on mine.

As if on cue, Tony and his perfect hair pushed open the door of the Perch. My mind returned to the present. An older couple was leaving at the same time, and the woman dropped her cane. Tony picked it up and handed it back, then held the door open for them to pass through.

"Thank you," said the woman, who looked eightyish.

Tony gave a little bow. "It's a pleasure to assist such a lovely lady."

I swear she blushed.

The young hostess' jaw dropped when Tony walked up to join us. The restaurant's usual male clientele included ranchers, bass fishermen, and the occasional rodeo bull rider with the facial scars and busted-up body to prove it. We don't get too many guys who look like male models in Himmarshee.

"Can I have you?" Tracy immediately clapped a hand over her mouth. "*Help* you," she said between her fingers. "Can I *help* you?"

The dimple in his cheek winked at her. I'm sure Tracy thought it was adorable. "I have everything I need with my two dates." Tony pointed at us.

"I'm starving," I announced.

"Mace is always hungry," Mama stage-whispered. "She burns a lot of calories driving her poor mother crazy."

Ring, ring. Kettle to pot.

Tracy fell all over herself, showing us to our booth and making sure Tony was comfortable. How would it feel to cause a stir everywhere you went, just because the random placement of your facial features happened to be what people find attractive? With Tony—Mama, too—it was more than that, though. There was a certain attitude, an expectation of attention. Not conceit, exactly, but self-confidence by the truckload.

Suddenly a yeasty smell wafted out of the kitchen, focusing my brain on food. "Tracy, would you mind asking the busboy to bring us some rolls as soon as he can? My stomach's growling like a pit bull."

Reaching for her glass of water, Mama's mouth was an inch from my ear: "Could you at least *try* to be lady-like, Mace?"

I leaned in to pluck a napkin from the table's center and whispered back: "I'll remind you of that advice after you've scarfed down two of those doughy nuggets before he even gets a chance to put the basket on the table."

My mood improved once I got a beer and the bread. I offered the basket to Tony, but he passed. Probably worried about those rippling abs under that fitted shirt.

"So, where's C'ndee?" Mama looked at him innocently over her tumbler of sweet tea. "Is she running late again, bless her heart?"

Her voice was cane-syrup sweet, so Tony couldn't be expected to know she was taking a Southern-style shot. He glanced at his watch, which was gold and wafer thin. "Looks that way. Sorry. I know you ladies are hungry."

I swallowed the last bite of my fourth roll. "No problem."

Tony dialed C'ndee's cell, and got voicemail. If his aunt didn't show for dinner, I'd happily take the opportunity to grill him about her love life. Mama didn't seem disappointed by her absence, either. She always did like being the prettiest girl in the room.

"We sure appreciate you taking us to dinner, Tony." Mama dabbed a slab of butter on her second roll. "I thought you'd be tired after that long drive from New Jersey."

He waved a hand. "I like to drive. And I don't sleep well. So if I'm going to be up all night, I might as well be doing something."

"I know how that is. I'm a very light sleeper myself..."

The woman slept like a ton of stone. As I sipped my beer, I tuned out the two of them and surveyed the restaurant. There wasn't much competition for Mama on the female front. A few retiree couples from the RV park finished their early bird specials, the wives showing fleshy, sunburned arms in sleeveless floral blouses. A girl from Marty's high-school class opened baby shower gifts at a table for eight. I wasn't sure whether it was her fourth or fifth, but I did notice she'd gotten bigger with each baby. The fact that about half of her guests were also pregnant didn't keep them from stealing glances at Tony. Studying the menu, he seemed not to notice the attention.

That scarlet-haired senior from the drive-thru was at the bar, wearing a skirt no bigger than a dish towel.

Elbowing Mama, I whispered. "Hey, do you know that old gal flirting with the bartender?"

Mama looked, and then snapped her head around quick. "Dab Holt. She must have moved back. Remind me to tell you her story. It's a doozy. Please say she didn't spot me."

"Nope. You're safe."

I continued my scan. Only one woman in the place might have given Mama a run for her money. She sat alone at the last stool at the bar. She'd spun around, back to the bar, so she could face the dining room. Even at this distance and in low lighting, I could tell two things: She wasn't from Himmarshee, and she was the type to turn heads. She wore sunglasses, even in the dim bar, and tight black leather from tip to toe. Motorcycle boots and a halo of blond curls completed the look. I saw the sunglasses shift just barely toward our booth. So even this goddess was not immune to Tony's chick-magnet looks. I nearly laughed at the thought she might think we were a couple.

"Why are you smiling, Mace?" Mama said. "You said you're sick of Teensy stories."

"Sorry, what?"

"His little top hat for the wedding."

I tuned back into the table talk, rolling my eyes at Tony. "That's not the worst of it. Has she told you that the dog is the ring bearer?"

He burst out laughing. "No way!" He had a really nice laugh.

"Yes, way." I chuckled, and Mama laughed, too.

"What's so funny?"

The voice at my shoulder was cold enough to re-frost my beer mug.

"Well, hey, Carlos. Mace, honey, look who's here!" Kicking me under the table, Mama signaled me to brush the bangs out of my eyes.

I could feel my face turning red. Carlos was the one with the rude tone of voice, so I don't know why *I* felt guilty. It's not like Tony and I had been making out in the booth. I grabbed the bread basket and held it up.

"Dinner roll?" I said.

"I'm not hungry." He scowled.

Before I could ask why he was in a dining establishment if he didn't intend to dine, Carlos said, "I'm meeting someone."

Mama kicked me again. When I didn't open my mouth, she said, "Well, Carlos, why don't the two of you join us for a drink? Is it a friend from the Himmarshee police?"

Carlos peered into the bar, and my gaze followed his. Ms. Sunglasses was watching our every move.

"Not exactly," he spoke to Mama, but now his eyes were on Tony.

"Oh, sorry. Where are my manners?" I said, and performed introductions. "You've met C'ndee, Carlos. Tony is her nephew," I added.

The two men nodded. Tony raised his hand for Carlos to shake, but he didn't get up from his chair. And he made no attempt at the kind of friendly small talk he'd made when he met my cousin, Henry. He and Carlos faced off like two bull gators in the same small lake. There was a chill at the table, and it wasn't the air conditioning.

"I better get going." Carlos clipped off the sentence like it was costing him money. "Enjoy dinner."

Mama barely got out, "Are you sure you won't..." before he'd stalked away.

Several of the women from the baby shower followed Carlos' progress as he made his way to the men's room. Tony might have had the advantage when it came to classic good looks, but add in Carlos' dark, brooding countenance and those bottomless-pool eyes, and the total package is hard to resist. At least that's the way it seemed from the head nods and elbowing coming from the ladies at the table for eight.

It was a big night for beefcake at the Speckled Perch.

I guess my eyes were following Carlos, too, because Tony said, "Why don't you go after him?"

"Me?" I snapped my head toward Tony.

"No, your mother." The dimple winked.

"Believe me, darlin', you do not want to go there with Mace. If I didn't know how old she was, I'd swear by the way she acts she was in junior high. One day she likes Carlos; the next day she doesn't."

She stuck her spoon into my ice water and stole half my cubes for her sweet tea. I glared at her.

"And how does Carlos feel about all of that?" Tony asked.

I traced a finger through the water Mama had sloshed on the tabletop. I wasn't about to answer. Mama, of course, pounced like a left tackle onto Tony's question.

"Well, it never does a man any harm to wonder a little bit about his gal," she said. "Keep 'em guessing, I always told my girls. But Mace has taken that advice to the extreme. Any day now, I expect Carlos will decide he's had just about enough."

Normally, I would have made some smart-aleck remark, but my heart had jumped into my throat, and I couldn't strangle out a single word. While Mama and Tony were dissecting my love life, Carlos had come out of the bathroom and beelined to the bar. Ms. Sunglasses signaled to the bartender, who brought two beers. She got off her stool, greeting Carlos with a big smile.

My plans to grill Tony about his aunt flew from my head.

Sunglasses offered Carlos her hand, and he enfolded it in both of his. And that handshake was a hundred degrees warmer than the one he'd shared with Tony.

NINETEEN

I CRANKED THE JEEP'S ignition in front of Mama's house for a third time. It answered in universal car language: *You're screwed.*

No engine meant no AC, and the June night felt like August. A drop of sweat rolled off my nose onto the steering wheel. I slapped at a mosquito siphoning blood from my neck.

Tony leaned his head into the driver's window. "Sounds like the battery's dead."

Mama had caught a ride home from the Perch, while Tony and I stayed behind to linger over coffee and key lime pie, which I couldn't even enjoy. Trying to act like I wasn't interested in what was going on in the bar between Carlos and Ms. Sunglasses kept my stomach in knots.

All they'd done was talk, but that in itself was saying something. Carlos normally doled out his words like a miser with nickel tips. Yet he and Sunglasses were still there, deep in conversation, when Tony and I left the restaurant.

Now, it was late, and Mama was already asleep. Teensy was likely snuggled deep into his doggy pillow at the head of her bed.

"I'd be glad to give you a jump off my rental car. Have you got any cables?" Tony said.

I shook my head. I'd loaned my set to Rhonda at work. Her battery had been acting iffy, and I didn't want her to get caught out somewhere.

"What about..." Tony started to say.

"Mama's ancient turquoise convertible is in the shop, as usual," I finished.

He slipped his hands into the front pockets of his jeans. "Want to pop the hood and let me take a look?"

And ruin that manicure? "No, thanks," I said. "I'm sure it's the battery. I can't even remember the last time I replaced it."

I turned on the Jeep's headlights and asked Tony to tell me if they lit.

"Sorry. Not even a flicker."

Almost all the houses around Mama's were dark. Folks in a country town like Himmarshee hit the sack early. Only Alice's window showed a blue glow, leaking around the edges of her drawn drapes. She'd probably left the TV on in the living room for company.

Mama did the same thing after Daddy died. For months, she drifted off each night on the couch before she could finally return again to the double bed she'd shared with our father.

"Can I give you a ride home?" Tony asked.

My cell phone lay on the passenger seat. I hated to call Maddie so late. But I also hated to ask a guy I barely knew to do me the favor of driving me twenty miles outside of town to my little cottage in the woods. I told Tony he could drop me somewhere close and dialed my sister's number.

"Hmmpf?" Maddie answered.

"It's Mace."

"Everything okay?" She was instantly awake, a note of fear in her voice.

Having a teenaged daughter and a mama with a penchant for trouble made Maddie aware of what a phone call at eleven-thirty p.m. might mean.

"Everybody's fine," I reassured her. "My battery's dead, and I wondered if I could borrow Pam's car."

Maddie took a deep breath, preparation for a rant. "I sincerely hope you're not going to ask me to get out of bed and come get you somewhere, Mace. What have I told you about keeping a regular maintenance schedule on that vehicle? This would never have happened if you were more ..."

"Yeah, I know, Maddie. More like you."

"Responsible, I was going to say."

I cut her off, or it'd be sunrise by the time she was through cataloguing my character flaws. "Save your breath, Sister. I've got a ride."

"Really?" she said, brightening. "Carlos?"

"Uhmmm ... no."

"Who, then?"

I waited a beat. I knew if I didn't tell Maddie, she'd only march out to meet us at the curb. Frayed blue robe. Sleep mask pushed onto her forehead. Hair in curlers. I figured I'd save us both from that disturbing sight.

"Tony Ciancio," I said. "C'ndee's nephew."

Silence seeped toward me over the phone. "You still there, Maddie?"

Tony asked, "What's going on?"

"My sister's giving me the silent treatment."

"Why?"

"It's a long story, Tony. Thirty-two years long, to be exact."

Finally, Maddie spoke. "I certainly hope you know what you're doing, Mace."

"I've got a dead battery. I need a ride to your house. Tony has a car. It's not that complicated, Maddie."

"It's *always* that complicated, Sister."

The phone emitted the *beep* of an ended call. Maddie had hung up on me.

"So, it's okay?" Tony said. "You can use the car?"

"Yeah," I answered. "For free. But you can bet my sister will find a way to make me pay."

———

The three-mile stretch between Mama's house and Maddie's was deserted. Tony was skilled behind the wheel. Relaxing the vigilant posture I usually assume whenever anyone but me is driving, I gave him quick directions and leaned back into soft leather. The Lexus had a much higher comfort level than my beat-up Jeep.

"Listen," I said, "I wanted to ask you something about your aunt."

Distracted by trying to pretend I didn't care about Carlos and Ms. Sunglasses in the bar, I hadn't gotten to my questions. Tony tilted his head slightly, eyes not leaving the road.

"Do you know anything about who she's dating?"

He laughed. "Now, that's always an interesting topic. Aunt C'ndee has more dates than a calendar. She's a heartbreaker."

Which didn't answer my question.

"Did she say anything about staying out at Darryl's Fish Camp?"

"Just that she couldn't wait to get out of there. There was some kind of bass-fishing tournament in town when she first got to Himmarshee. That was the only place with a vacancy."

"Did she mention she was dating Darryl?"

"No." He shook his head. "I didn't even know there *was* a Darryl. But it's not unusual she wouldn't tell me. C'ndee was married to my dad's brother. After Uncle Frank died, she made some bad choices, went pretty wild. A lot of people in the family thought it was a sign of disrespect. I didn't; but I did learn that where C'ndee's love life is concerned, it's better not to ask questions."

The honey-colored glow from the dials on the dashboard lit Tony' chiseled features. His face looked honest enough to replace Lincoln's on the penny.

"So, you didn't know anything about her running around with Ronnie Hodges, either?"

Surprise flickered on his face. "What?"

"Ronnie," I said. "The murder victim."

"Good god, no! Where'd you hear that?"

I didn't want to tell Tony the information came from Rabe. For some reason, I felt protective of Darryl's stepson. Not that he wasn't big enough to take care of himself.

"Just around," I said. "It's probably a rumor."

Resting my head against the seat, I closed my eyes. It'd been a long day, and I was tired.

Tony tapped the button to turn on the radio. It was the country station, playing "Is Anybody Loving You These Days?" He sang along.

My head must have had a quizzical tilt, because he stopped singing and asked, "What? A Yankee from New Jersey can't appreciate a little Dierks Bentley?"

Good thing my side of the car was fairly dark or he'd have seen me blush. That was *exactly* what I'd been thinking.

"I'm trying to absorb as much local culture as I can. I like to know a place if I'm going to live there."

That sat me up straight. "You're going to live here? In Himmarshee?"

Somehow I couldn't picture Tony eating lunch for the next twenty years at Gladys' Diner. Taking his fancy car for service to Juan's Auto Repair and Taqueria. Choosing his wardrobe from the Home on the Range Feed Supply and Clothing Emporium. There wasn't a pink- or teal-hued polo shirt in the place.

"Is that so hard to believe?" he asked.

"Actually, yes." I aimed the AC vent toward the window. The frigid air was freezing my former sweat drops to ice cubes. "Turn left up there where the lights are shining on that white pillar. You know, your aunt never said anything about starting a business here. How long have you two had those plans?"

Tony didn't answer. Was he stalling, or just concentrating on the upcoming turn into Maddie's neighborhood? Slowing, he eased the car left. "Which way now?"

"Left at the third street." I pointed toward the darkness. "So? How long?"

"At least a year," he said. "We targeted this part of Florida because the coasts are already overdeveloped. There's more potential for growth here. With the new golf course and all, the south end of the county is booming with affluent transplants."

That would make Maddie happy. If the owner of a full-service, event-planning business was projecting enough of a population spike that would want big weddings, birthday parties, and bar mitzvahs, then an honest-to-God shopping mall couldn't be far behind. Unfortunately.

"Maddie's place is on the right. The one with the porch light."

He eased into the driveway, thoughtfully killing his headlights before they could shine into the house. I had to meet this guy's mama.

Engine off, he leapt out of his seat and hurried around the car to open my door. He insisted on walking me to the house. Normally I'm all about equality. But I had to admit, being pampered felt kind of nice.

When we got to Maddie's door, I said, "Thanks a lot for dinner, and the ride. I really appreciate it."

I stuck out my hand, but Tony leaned in close and brushed his lips against my cheek. I'm sure the surprise registered on my face, because he took a step back and cocked his head.

"Hope you don't mind."

"No-o-o-o," I stuttered, still smelling his scent, like tall pines on a wind-swept beach.

"I'm Italian." He shrugged an apology. "We're pretty affectionate."

"It's fine, really."

"Sometimes we even give a kiss on both cheeks."

"Not at once, I hope?"

He laughed. I could get used to the sound of that.

"No. We do it like this." He kissed the same cheek again, lingering a bit this time, and then passed *this close* to my lips on his way to the other cheek.

"Hmm," I said. "The timing must take years of training."

"Not so long, really. I could give you a few lessons if you like."

I put a hand to my cheek. It was so hot, I was surprised there wasn't a blister.

I was just about to say, *Yes, I like*, when I noticed the blind in Maddie's front window shift back and forth. At least she hadn't flicked the porch light or turned a hose on the two of us.

"It … it's getting late," I stammered. "I've got to be up in a few hours."

A smile formed on his lips. I had an inappropriate urge to trace it with my tongue.

"Okay, good night." He stepped off the porch. "But think about those kissing lessons, would you?"

When I opened the front door and stepped inside, I was thinking about just that.

"Look at you: smiling like a billy goat in the briar patch." Maddie's arms were crossed over her blue robe; she had the high beams on her principal's glare.

"I'm tired, Maddie. Can you just give me the keys and save the lecture?"

She pulled them out of the robe's pocket and handed them over.

"What exactly are you playin' at, Sister? You've got a good man, and you're ready to toss him out with the trash."

I shrugged, like a seventh-grader caught without a hall pass. Maybe Mama was right about me.

The door to the kitchen swung open just then. Maddie's husband Kenny came out with a piece of banana cream pie and two forks.

"Evenin' Mace," he said.

I waved. As I turned to leave, I noticed Maddie looking at her husband with pure love in her eyes. It might have been the pie, but I didn't think so. She put a hand on my arm before I stepped out the door.

"You better straighten up, Mace. Maybe your relationship with Carlos isn't perfect. No relationship is. But if a man makes you happy and treats you right, that's as close to true love as you're likely to get. Don't screw it up."

TWENTY

As I ROLLED DOWN the unpaved drive to my little cottage, an owl hooted from a fencepost as if to welcome me home. A thousand stars lit the midnight sky. The beams from the headlights on Pam's ancient VW bounced across the yard, catching a couple of raccoons loping away into the woods.

"Thieves!" I yelled after them.

My nemeses had returned, foiling an elaborate brick-and-bungee-cord garbage protection system. Cantaloupe rinds and chicken bones littered the grass; an empty potato chip bag tumbled across the driveway as the car passed by. I imagined constructing a raccoon-proof concrete garbage vault, complete with a steel top too heavy for them to lift. If I ever figured out how to foil the masked bandits, I could get a job as a government consultant on how to safeguard our borders from evil-doers.

Garbage cleanup could wait until the morning. I parked the car, threw a tarp over its broken convertible top, and made my way to the front door.

Once inside, I saw the red light blinking on the answering machine. I tossed the keys to the VW along with my own set into the gaping jaws of a preserved gator head I keep on my coffee table.

"Did you miss me, Al?" I said to the taxidermist's specimen.

The gator and I had been on close terms once, since I helped wrestle him out of the pool of a newcomer who hadn't pictured a ten-foot reptile with seventy-five razor-sharp teeth as a guest at his swimming parties.

Wila stalked out of my bedroom, making Siamese noises, which meant she sounded like a whole alley full of cats.

"Hush, Wila." I scratched under her neck and on her back near her tail the way she likes. "I know I've been away all day. I know I'm a bad mama. And you're right, a human child probably would have walked out on me by now."

Meowr.

"It could be worse. If you were a little bit bigger, I'd set you on those damned raccoons outside."

Meowr.

"Nah, I'm just kidding, baby. I didn't save you just to see you come to harm."

I shot a guilty look at Al, who had the bad luck of being classified as a nuisance gator after he got a little too used to being around people. That meant he could be trapped and killed, his hide and meat sold for profit.

"Sorry about that, buddy. There are just too many of you in places that used to be wild, aren't there?"

Al didn't answer. But I felt that beady glass eye of his judging me.

I added a little canned cat food to the dry stuff that Wila won't eat unless she's starving. *It's about time*, her body language said.

Pressing the play button on the answering machine, I turned on the AC, shrugged out of my T-shirt and paced off the dozen or so steps from my living room to the bedroom of the tiny cottage. The first message sounded just as I tossed the dirty shirt into the clothes basket in the corner. The voice was pure Ivy League.

"I had a great time tonight," Tony said. "I hope you did, too."

Yeah, except for seeing my alleged boyfriend having a rendezvous with some gorgeous mystery woman, it was a lot of fun.

"I read in the *Himmarshee Times* about a rodeo next month at the Agri-Civic center. I'd really like to go, and I could use a local guide. Would you like to come with me?"

Hmmmmm. Maybe I would.

He went on about how he'd always wanted to see a real rodeo, how he couldn't even believe they had rodeos in Florida, and how I'd have to tell him what was appropriate to wear. That was easy: Wrangler blue jeans, no matter how hot the temperature is. Nothing pegs an outsider faster than wearing Bermuda shorts and man sandals to the Himmarshee rodeo.

I had to give Tony credit. He seemed to really be trying to learn the way of life down here. Not like a lot of newcomers, who move South only to complain about how everything is different than it was up North.

Isn't that the point?

The next message was one I'd saved earlier, when I called from my office to check the machine. There weren't enough hours in my workday to listen to the whole thing.

"Mace, honey, this is Rosalee. Your mama."

Mama always became oddly formal when she talked to the answering machine. I think she pictured it as a secretary, painstakingly writing down each message that came in.

"I was just thinking about our fitting tomorrow morning. Could you please not wear your boots? Obviously, those are fine for tromping through the swamp the way you do. But they'll just ruin the drape of your bridesmaid gown."

I doubted that lime-sherbet nightmare could get any worse, boots or not.

I slipped out of my jeans, brushed my teeth, and washed my morning coffee cup. Mama prattled on past the machine's thirty-second warning, discussing the wedding favors again, telling me about a distant cousin who'd called and shamelessly invited herself to the wedding, asking whether I thought Alice would still want to come to the shower, considering what happened.

"I want to do the right thing, Mace. But, honestly, do you think a woman who just lost her husband to a crazed killer with a knife would want to sit there playing shower games?"

I wondered whether Mama was protecting Alice's feelings or the party atmosphere. She finally began to wrap it up,

"Anyhoo ... oh, yeah, there was something I wanted to tell you about C'ndee ..."

Just as Mama was about to impart some news that might have been of actual interest, the machine cut her off. She probably had blabbed, unaware she'd exceeded the time limit until she heard the dead line. I had half a mind to call her back and wake her up to finish the message.

But it was beyond late now. I wouldn't call her back tonight, or Tony either. In fact I might not return his call at all. I remembered what Maddie had said in the foyer at her house. What *was* I playing at?

I didn't want to dwell too long on that question, as I had no answer. Instead, I took a shower so I wouldn't have to bathe in the morning. I was surprised when I got out and saw the light blinking again. I hit the button to play the new message.

"It's Sal. Sorry to call so late, but I need to talk to you. Call me tonight, no matter what time you get in."

I immediately dialed the number he'd left. "Is everything all right?"

"Fine. But your mudder told me you two went out tonight with Tony Ciancio."

"So?"

"You need to be careful with that guy, Mace."

"Why?"

"I don't want to go into a lot of details."

"Well, he's C'ndee's nephew," I said. "She's close to him and you're close to her. I figured Tony was okay."

"You're right. I do like C'ndee. She was my late wife's cousin. But she don't have good sense sometimes. She married young, and got herself involved with the wrong family."

"Tony's family?"

There was a long pause on the phone. "Just watch yourself," Sal finally said. "Tony Ciancio could charm the underpants off a Puritan."

After Sal's call, I felt tired but not sleepy. I was curious about Tony, even if I decided not to pursue things with him. And that decision wasn't a done deal, despite Sal's warning. I turned on my computer and checked my email. Mostly spam, as usual. I mean, my email address is country*gal*. Don't those marketers know I'm not interested in making my manhood bigger? I deleted a bunch of crap, and then navigated to Google.

I just entered Anthony Ciancio and New Jersey, since I wasn't sure what part of the state he was from. Maybe the last name Ciancio was as common up there as Martinez was in Miami, because there were sure a lot of hits.

Scrolling quickly, I saw some newspaper headlines popping up with the name Ciancio and the kind of words you don't want to see when investigating a potential date.

"Extortion"…"crime family"…"suspicious restaurant fire."

TWENTY-ONE

"Fran, honey, I think you can take it in a smidge more, right here." Mama tugged at a tiny gap on the bodice of my lime-colored abomination. "The Lord saw fit to bless Mace more with broad shoulders than a generous bustline."

I slapped her wrist. "Hands off, Mama!"

The proprietress of Fran's Formal Duds and Frocks leaned back and narrowed her eyes at my gown. "Nope. It's a perfect fit, Rosalee. And Mace has a beautiful build. She's not scarce at all in the bust department. If I made it any tighter, the guests would be staring at the bridesmaid and not the bride."

Mama pursed her lips at the possibility. "Well, if you say so, honey," she finally said. "You're the expert."

Maddie and Marty were still in the back of the shop, struggling into their gowns. There were stays and straps and petticoats, along with highly engineered parts I couldn't even name. Fran had lopped about a foot off the bottom of Marty's dress. She added a V-shaped panel of extra fabric under each of Maddie's arms.

How she managed to nip and tuck and fit three such different shapes was a mystery to me. Then again, I can botch sewing on a button. I pictured her using seamstress magic, like that scene from Cinderella when adorable mice and birds pitch in to sew the ballgown. Of course, if our Fairy Godmother ever saw us in these sherbet-colored getups, she'd wave a wand and make at least five pounds of ruffles disappear.

Standing on a platform upholstered in rose-colored carpeting, I gazed at myself in Fran's full-length mirror. I looked like Scarlett O'Hara meets Ballroom Barbie by way of Kermit the Frog.

A giggle came from the dressing area, followed by Maddie's sternest voice. "I don't find this remotely amusing, Marty. I'm a virtual mountain of those pink melty mints Aunt Ida used to give us every Christmas."

Mama shouted, "Hush, Maddie. You girls are going to be absolutely stunning in those dresses. I've got a surprise for you, too. Remember C'ndee found your bridesmaid's gifts? Well, it's the perfect thing: press-on fingernails to match the colors of your dresses. Isn't that incredible?"

"Incredibly tacky," I said under my breath.

"I heard that! Now, you other girls c'mon out here so Fran can get a look-see," Mama called.

My sisters filed into the fitting room, full skirts gathered up like color-blind debutantes picking their way through mud. Three pairs of eyes rolled in sisterly commiseration. Mama clapped her hands together and held them to her heart.

"Can't you just see them at the ceremony, Fran? My three darlin' girls, as pretty as pictures."

The photo from Alice's wedding popped into my head. That was followed immediately by the memory of Ronnie, stabbed in the VFW kitchen. And that made me think of what I'd discovered on the Internet about Tony's restaurant-owning family. I'd been so focused on figuring out which of my parts went where in my stupid dress that I'd neglected to fill in Mama and my sisters with my news.

"Mama, did C'ndee ever tell you the Ciancio family's restaurant business had some serious trouble with the law back in New Jersey?"

Marty's eyes widened. A straight pin fell from Fran's mouth. Maddie spun to stare at me, her cotton-candy-pink dress rustling like sabal fronds in a stiff wind.

Mama's hand clutched at her throat. "Please don't tell me they poisoned somebody with tainted food."

I shook my head. "No, no food poisoning. More along the lines of extortion and questionable competitive practices."

"Like what?" Maddie asked.

"Like some rival owners beaten bloody and having their restaurants set on fire."

Marty's blue eyes were huge orbs. "Was Tony involved?" she whispered.

"He wasn't mentioned by name in the stories I read on the computer. Neither was C'ndee. But it's got to be the same family, right?" I looked from one of them to the other. "How many restaurant businesses owned by Ciancios can there be in Hackensack, New Jersey?"

Marty shrugged, long hair brushing the orange-sherbet ruffles of her off-the-shoulder sleeves. Mama had no comment, for a change. Maddie, a thoughtful look on her face, picked an invisible speck of lint off her billowing skirt.

"We need to find out more about the Ciancios, Mace." She raised serious eyes to mine. "Tony might be dangerous in a way that I *hadn't* considered."

Before Mama or Marty had the chance to process what Maddie might mean by that, I said, "Sal doesn't seem to like him much, but he won't say why. I'm going to add that to a list of questions I have for C'ndee."

Marty said, "But nobody's seen her, right?"

Mama nodded.

"Maybe we should ask Sal where she went," Maddie said.

"I don't know, girls," Mama said. "They're family. They're thicker than ticks on a fat dog."

"Meaning Sal might not want to tell us what he knows about her," Maddie said.

I thought about our first acquaintance with Mama's fiancé. "Remember how secretive Sal was, and how we were convinced he was Tony Soprano?" I said, as my sisters laughed.

"Who?" asked Fran, who was in her seventies and probably thought HBO was a kind of body odor.

"Like Don Corleone from the *Godfather* movies," Maddie interpreted.

"Not the Mafia again, Maddie." Mama sighed. "Just remember: you girls found out Sal's one of the good guys, despite appearances. Maybe it'll be the same for Tony. Not every man of mystery has a notorious past."

Marty patted Mama's arm in agreement. "When we met Sal, he just wanted to keep his business private. There's nothing wrong with that."

"Humph," Maddie said.

"Yeah, Sal's a private guy, all right." I shot Mama a look. "Now just imagine the poor man marrying the Mouth of the South."

That started a round of bickering about which of us was the biggest gossip.

"Well, maybe I am *interested* in people, girls," Mama concluded. "But I'm never mean, like some I could mention." She glared at Maddie, who acted like she didn't notice.

"I was always taught, and I tried to teach you girls, that if you can't say something nice you shouldn't say anything at all."

"Now, Rosalee, where's the fun in that?" Fran's smile was devilish, even bisected by several straight pins. "And what did y'all mean before about the Mafia?"

Marty whispered, "The day Ronnie Hodges was killed, somebody chopped off the head of a wild pig and left it on Alice's front porch."

Fran gasped.

"I said then that it looked like the kind of calling card the Mafia would leave," Maddie said.

"Which Maddie knows because she watches the movies."

We ignored Mama's smart-aleck tone. "It was like a warning," I told Fran.

Lowering herself onto a stool next to the rose-colored platform, she spit the straight pins into her palm. "That's just awful."

"Ronnie's company was called Pig-Out BBQ and Catering, " I explained. "Maybe somebody doesn't want Alice to continue the business."

Mama said, "*Alice* doesn't even want to continue it. She told us it was bleeding money."

Marty winced at the word choice. "Maybe somebody was trying to send a message to other restaurant owners to get out of the business or what happened to Ronnie..."

"... and that poor hog," Fran interrupted.

"... will happen to them," Maddie finished Marty's thought.

"Maybe we should warn the Pork Pit and the Georgia Pig," I said.

"Don't forget that guy along State Road 70 with the trash can smoker who calls himself Pig Pickin's," Mama said. "He could be a target too, if somebody has a thing against barbecue."

We all thought about that for a moment. Finally, Maddie shook her head firmly.

"Impossible," said my sister, who never met a pulled pork platter she didn't love. "It has to be about something else."

TWENTY-TWO

I GAZED INTO THE woods of Himmarshee Park, all cool and green. The late-afternoon sun slanted through the branches of a cypress tree, washing me in slivers of golden light. This wooden park bench beat any pew beneath stained glass in a grand cathedral. In a way, the park *was* my cathedral.

"All set, Mace?"

Rhonda's voice startled me out of my meditation on the glories of the outdoors.

"You bet, Boss. Heading home?"

She lifted an arm to show me her purse. Her car keys were in her hand. "You should have a dozen or so people show up for your nature walk. Some of the old folks from Leisure Lake trailer park are coming over in a van."

"Sounds good."

I actually preferred the senior citizens to students from Maddie's middle school. Kids that age are tough to impress. The boys always try to act tough, and the girls squeal like idiots if they so much as see a spider.

"By the way, Mace..."

I cocked my head at her.

"Please show some patience if people ask stupid questions. Not everyone knows as much about the outdoors as you do."

"I'll be an ambassador of good will, Rhonda."

She looked skeptical. But she waved anyway, gliding across the wooden deck outside our office. Her keys jingled like a soundtrack at a high-fashion runway show.

I glanced at my watch. It was almost six, which meant Rhonda was well past her quitting hour. I felt grateful, and not for the first time, that no one had ever seen fit to make me a manager.

The sunset walkers would arrive within forty minutes or so. And that would give me just enough time to feed the handful of injured or unwanted critters currently living in the park's makeshift zoo. I hurried to the animal enclosure, where I was welcomed as usual by the white-striped presence of Pepe No Pew.

The de-scented skunk had been a pet, until his owner cruelly released him into the wild. As I pulled dinner together, he padded to the front of his pen. On the menu for Pepe: A chicken neck, a selection of chopped fruit and vegetables, and a couple of crickets and worms tossed into his pen so he could find them later.

Our residents generally included a few of the "nuisance" animals I trapped in my part-time job. The park had a wildlife license as part of our educational mission. I tried to expose visitors to some Florida critters; tried to convince them co-existence was possible. If only people could see how beautiful the corn snake was, for example, and how it wouldn't hurt them if left alone, they'd be less likely to want it dead.

Or, that was my hope anyway.

"Hey, buddy. You get your mouse tomorrow," I called out to the snake.

The creature lay coiled in the corner next to an elevated den I'd made of rocks, straw, and branches. A screen over the top of the pen kept him from slithering out.

"Not a bad crib, huh? You'll be going back to the woods soon. Just think of this as an all-expenses-paid snake-cation."

Carrying a large tray with the animals' food, I made my way around the enclosure: The possum got a little moistened cat chow, bite-size chopped fruit, a raw egg, a splash of yogurt and, for the fish course, a couple of thawed silversides.

The raccoon got wet dog food, supplemented with a bit of fruit, fish, an egg, and a thawed baby chick.

My last stop was Pepe's pad. Without his scent, the skunk was defenseless in the wild. So, he was stuck with us for life. Dropping food into his shallow bowl, I leaned in for a chat.

"You're getting as fat as a fixed dog, you know that, *Monsieur*? Maybe we need to get you a little skunk-sized treadmill. Would you like that?"

Pepe raised his head. He seemed a tad dubious about that treadmill.

"Yeah, I know. I could stand to lose a couple of pounds myself. You should have seen me holding my breath to zip up this brides-maid's monstrosity that Mama's making me wear on Saturday. Believe me, Pepe, that dress is awful enough without a big rip down the back to show off my lily-white butt."

Pepe returned to his bowl as a low chuckle came from the entryway. I whirled, and felt my face catch fire.

"Tony! I didn't hear you come in."

He flashed a bright smile in the dim light of the enclosure. "I didn't want to interrupt your Dr. Doolittle moment."

"Yeah, Maddie gets after me for talking to the animals, too. It's not like I think they're going to open their mouths and talk back."

"Of course not."

His tone was amused. I couldn't tell if he believed me. Better to change the subject. "What brings you to Himmarshee Park?"

"I saw a little blurb in today's newspaper about the nature program. I thought I might be late. I stopped on the way to rescue a turtle trying to make it across the highway."

Coming a bit closer, he peered into the snake's section. He pulled back with a grimace, side-stepping away. So Tony was okay with turtles; snakes, not so much.

"The paper said this is the last walk until the fall brings cooler weather. I hoped you'd be leading it."

I sensed another blush coming on. I was acting as silly as Maddie's squealing schoolgirls. I had serious business to discuss. I couldn't afford to be distracted by Tony's charm, or those mesmerizing white teeth.

"Listen," I said, draining all the levity from my voice, "I need to ask you some questions."

"Should I have a lawyer present?" He smiled again, but a chill edged his voice. "Maybe your cousin Henry would agree to take me on as a client."

"You don't need a lawyer, Tony. And I apologize ahead of time if I'm out of line."

I took a deep breath. "I was curious about you, so I went on the Internet and searched with your name."

"And?" The cool edge had hardened to ice.

"And I found a lot of stuff about the Ciancio family being involved in restaurant-related crimes."

He advanced a couple of steps toward me, then crossed his arms over his chest. His green eyes, smiley and warm before, were Arctic pools now.

"And?" he said, with a hint of menace.

I stepped to my right, positioning the snake's pen between us. Tony moved no closer. I took the plunge.

"And I just wondered if any of the bad things that happened to your family's restaurant rivals in New Jersey had anything to do with what happened to Ronnie Hodges down here."

My question hung in the air. Tony lowered his chin and stared at the ground for the longest moment.

I could hear Pepe's nose hitting the rim of his bowl. The raccoon splashed water as he washed his food. An ibis' throaty call reverberated from deep in the swamp.

I was beginning to consider the sanity of raising this topic with a bunch of animals as my only witnesses when I heard a door slam in the distant parking lot. Faraway voices sounded. Human voices. Potential witnesses' voices.

Tony's face came up, his head tilted toward the lot. His gaze returned to meet mine.

"I wondered how long it would take for my family history to follow me here." He seemed more resigned than angry. "It sounds like the other nature walkers are on their way. I don't want to get into this now, Mace. I will tell you I had nothing to do with what you read about. My whole life, I've been trying to live down who my father is. What my family is."

A flicker of pain lit in his eyes. I felt bad about putting it there. I resisted the urge to smooth out the wrinkle now marring his model-worthy brow.

The clamor of voices grew as my visitors made their way along the path. I also heard the rumble of a powerful motorcycle traversing the wooden bridge at the park's entrance. The sound seemed out of place, since the bikers I've met generally prefer chicks and bars to birds and trees.

"I'd better get back to the office to meet them." I nodded to the door. "I'll understand if you don't want to come along."

His smile had been stripped of several thousand watts. But he managed a weak grin. "No, I really do want to see the park. And it's not like you're the first person who ever asked about my family. I'd like to talk later, though. Explain where I'm coming from."

"Sure," I said.

Collecting the food tray, I started for the exit. Before I could juggle the unwieldy tray to reach for the door handle, Tony jumped to open it for me. Apparently having a Mafia don for a daddy doesn't rule out having nice manners.

As he stepped aside to let me pass, Tony bumped against the snake's pen. A low hiss sounded as warning.

TWENTY-THREE

As TONY AND I approached the wooden walkway outside the park's office, I could barely believe who was among the nature walkers milling about.

The usual retirees were there, sporting bright clothes and sunburns. There was a serious-looking, thirtyish couple; binoculars around his neck, *Birds of Florida* in her hand. And there was the mystery woman from the bar at the Speckled Perch, outfitted again in dark glasses and black leather.

I greeted everyone, exchanged introductions, and outlined where the wooden boardwalk would take us. Then I addressed Ms. Sunglasses.

"I'm sorry, I didn't catch your name."

"Jane Smith."

Yeah, right, I thought. "Would you like to leave that in the office?" I gestured to the motorcycle helmet she carried.

Clasping it tightly to her side, she shook her head. "S'fine."

"Everybody ready to spot some wildlife then?"

My answer was a chorus of yeses and smiles from the seniors and Tony, and nods from the birdwatchers. The sunglasses seemed to aim past me into the distance. No acknowledgment, not even a head nod. Not exactly Ms. Congeniality. She'd certainly seemed friendly enough last night, chatting up Carlos in the bar.

Maybe she was hung over because they'd stayed up all night, drinking and yakking. My stomach clenched like a fist. It surprised me how much it hurt to think that maybe talking wasn't all the two of them had done.

We started out on the walk. It had to be one of the strangest I'd ever given. I always tried to draw out the visitors, asking folks where they came from originally. Few locals from this part of Florida would voluntarily walk through the woods in June at sunset unless there was the promise of shooting something, too.

On this walk, I got back a Pennsylvania, a few Ohios, and a Michigan. Tony piped up with New Jersey from the back.

We all turned to Ms. Sunglasses, waiting for her answer. Her lips opened just wide enough to mutter two words, "All over," before she pressed them shut again.

She made Darryl from the fish camp look like a motor mouth.

Stone-faced and silent, she hung back from the rest of the group. Which would have been fine, if she'd shown the slightest interest in taking in the view from the boardwalk. But she seemed more intent on watching us than observing nature. I couldn't say for sure, though. Despite the darkening sky, she never removed the sunglasses. And she didn't participate, not even when I called the walkers to a railing to see a huge gator lolling in the swamp below the boardwalk.

"How big is he?" one of the Ohioans asked. Flashes went off on digital cameras.

"A ten-footer, at least," I said. "A good way to tell, if all you spot is his head above water, is to estimate the number of inches from his eyes to the tip of his snout. His body will be about the same number in feet. Course, if we weren't on this boardwalk, and he was close enough for you to count inches, you might never get the chance to tell anyone else how big he was."

Everyone laughed but Ms. Sunglasses. She leaned against a far railing, regarding me with a frown.

A little farther on, we came to a hardwood hammock. I pointed out a cardinal flitting by, and a delicate air plant nestled high in a crook of an oak tree. "A lot of people think air plants are parasites, but they're not. They don't get nutrition from the tree; they only use it for support, like a trellis."

"Do the alligators eat the air plants?"

The birdwatchers snickered at the question. Remembering Rhonda's warning, I looked down at the water, and then way up high to the tree. I forced a smile for the gent from Ohio.

"No, sir. Gators definitely prefer the meat course to the salad bar."

"Aren't orchids air plants, too?" asked one of the retiree wives, from Pennsylvania.

I glanced across the boardwalk. Ms. Sunglasses stood rigidly, dark lenses pointing my way.

I answered, "Yep, orchids and Spanish moss, too. Air plants are also called epi…epi…epiphytes."

As I stumbled over a word I'd used dozens of times before, I knew the mystery woman was making me nervous. And I wasn't alone. The seniors watched her furtively, taking in her biker regalia. Tony kept looking over his shoulder, as nervous as a seventeen-year-old trying to buy beer. Only the birders seemed unconcerned by her lurking about like a nature-walk spy. They were too busy sharing binoculars and jotting field notes to notice her odd behavior.

I was relieved when the hour was finally up, and I could bid the whole group goodbye. Tony thanked me, and then hurried off with the rest of the group toward the parking lot. The biker woman hung back, aiming her sunglasses at the upcoming programs on the bulletin board.

Was she reading them? I couldn't be sure. I prayed she wouldn't return for any of the events I led. She gave me the creeps.

"I'm about to close up the park," I finally said to her. "Can I help you with anything?"

"Jane Smith" shook her head without turning, and took her time finishing up at the board. Then, suddenly, she spun around and left without a word. She moved across the deck like a Florida panther, surprisingly quick and silent for a woman in big black motorcycle boots.

Fishing for my keys in the pocket of my work pants, I watched as she followed a curve in the path. She disappeared into the shadowy woods. I wanted to be sure she was gone before I turned my back to unlock the door. Staring hard into the woods, I listened for what seemed like a long time. The voices of the walkers grew faint as they reached the parking lot. The doors on the retirees' van slid open and closed. Two car doors slammed; the birdwatchers, no doubt.

I waited, straining to catch any other sounds.

Just then, my cell phone rang on my belt, startling me. I answered, and it took me a couple of moments of spotty reception to realize it was a phone solicitation. Cursing, I cut off the call.

Seconds later, a motorcycle engine roared to life. Ms. Sunglasses, I presumed. She revved it and took off, shifting gears on her way out of the park. I heard the bike slow, then pull onto the highway, and accelerate again.

Feeling silly, I let out the breath I'd been holding.

As I listened to the motor's rumble, growing distant, I realized I never heard the slam of a single door on the last car in the lot. What had happened to Tony?

———

The sun's final rays were sinking behind the trees. Darkness was approaching fast.

I'd done one last check on the animals, and set the answering machine to take incoming calls. As I prepared to leave, I slipped bug spray into one pocket, and a flashlight into the other. Then I grabbed a heavy club we keep by the door, just in case we run across a wild hog defending its territory or offspring.

As soon as I walked outside, mosquitoes circled and whined, hungry for blood. I sprayed the repellent into my hands, and rubbed them across my face. All I needed was some honking big mosquito bite on my bridesmaid's nose to ruin Mama's Special Day.

We never held the sunset walks during summer, because it gets too wet and too buggy. Couldn't find enough masochists to show up. I enjoyed a silent chuckle, envisioning tender-skinned visitors slapping and dancing on the boardwalk in August, and started onto the path to the parking lot.

I was well into the woods when I heard a rustle in the brush.

Of course, it was just an animal of some sort. This time of day, they're either settling down somewhere safe for the night, or starting out to look for smaller prey. An image flashed through my mind of the mystery woman, and that big motorcycle helmet. That could surely do some damage if she decided to go on a hunt for prey.

The park was alive with familiar sounds: the breeze sighed in the trees; a gator grunted from Himmarshee Creek; small things scurried through palmetto scrub and dead leaves. As I wended my way toward the distant lot, I thought I heard a less familiar sound. Almost like a ragged breath. I shined my flashlight into the deeper woods. All I saw were trees.

And then I heard it again, distinctly. Rapid breathing, like after physical exertion. In and out; in and out.

"Who's there?" The breathing halted. No animal knew enough to do that. "Tony?"

No answer. I tightened my grip on the club, and began to walk a little faster.

TWENTY-FOUR

"Mama? It's Mace."

"Honey, where *are* you?" Her pout was audible over the cell line. "I thought we could go over the order of the toasts for the reception one more time."

Please, God. No.

"I don't think so, Mama. I'm on the highway on my way home from work. I'm running late, and I'm beat."

I'd made it to the parking lot without incident. Tony's car was gone. Maybe the breathing I thought I heard in the woods was just a trick of the wind through the trees.

When Mama didn't respond, I said into the phone, "Remember that strange woman Carlos was talking to last night at the Perch? In the bar?"

"Of course I do, Mace. She'd be kind of hard to forget, what with all that black leather. Now, not every woman could carry off that much black. But with her blond hair and that gorgeous shape, I have to admit it looked terrific on her."

Thanks, Mama, I thought. Just what I needed to hear.

"Anyway," I said, "that same woman showed up at the park this afternoon for the sunset walk."

"Was she wearing black again? You know, if she'd just add a colorful scarf in an accent color, she would really have a great look. Maybe turquoise, or aqua, even pink, with that mass of blond curls. Was she wearing..."

I cut Mama off. "Yes, she was in black. No, there was no scarf. Now, if we can move on from the fashion segment, I'd like to give you the rest of my news."

"I'm all ears, Mace. Though I must say it wouldn't kill you to pay just the smallest bit of attention to fashion. If you'd just put on a little lipstick now and then..."

My knuckles were showing white on the steering wheel. "Mama!"

"Oh, all right." The pout was back. "What's your news?"

I was going to tell her all about Tony showing up, and me raising the topic of his family. But at just that moment, I saw an oncoming car fast approaching the little bridge over Taylor Slough. State Road 98 narrowed at the bridge, and the highway demanded my full attention.

"Hang on, Mama. I'm driving over Buzzard Bridge."

The spot earned its name because so many wrecks had occurred that the buzzards hung out, waiting for carnage.

"Mace, be careful!"

I edged to the right and slowed a bit, as the other car blew past me with just a foot or so to spare. There was still enough twilight, and we were close enough, that I could see the driver's eyes. They were wide with fear under the brim of his Walt Disney World cap.

Maybe he'd ratchet down the gas pedal on that rental car when he came to the next narrow crossing.

"Okay," I began, before I was immediately distracted again.

This time, it was a scene in a thicket of trees alongside the road. A tall blonde stood beside a Harley-Davidson motorcycle. Black, of course. A big, fancy car was parked right next to the bike. The car gleamed, golden, under my headlights. A heavy-set man with a cigar in his mouth leaned casually against the driver's side door. The car was a very distinctive Cadillac.

"Well, *that* was weird," I muttered as I sped past.

"What's weird, Mace? Would you please speak up? It's really hard to hear you on that cello-phone."

"I just saw Sal, pulled way off on the shoulder along 98. He was talking to that same blond woman from the bar."

Mama gasped. Apparently she had no trouble hearing me now.

"Well, you have to turn around and go back there! Find out what Sal's doing out in the woods with some gorgeous young gal."

I looked in the rearview mirror. There was nothing but dark road behind me. "They're not exactly in the woods, Mama."

"Woods, highway, whatever. Turn around right now, Mace."

I hesitated. Mama already had talked me into a god-awful, ruffled mess for Saturday, wearing a most likely horrifying hairdo, and carrying the most ridiculous parasol known to womankind. It'd cost me, but I decided this request was going to be my line in the sand.

"No, Mama. I will not turn around. It's been a long day. I'm tired, and I'm hungry. You can ask Sal yourself why he was out here along the road with her."

I didn't add that the thought of any kind of confrontation with Ms. Sunglasses made me nervous. She was strange; she was just as big as me; and that helmet looked plenty heavy.

"Well!" Mama's exhale was full of indignation. "I'd certainly do it for you, Mace."

Did I dare go there? Ah, what the hell.

"I know, Mama. And that's the difference between us."

"Excuse me?"

"I'd never *want* you to do it for me. You're acting like you're in junior high, sending another girl over to the lunch table to find out if some boy still likes you. For God's sake, you're a grown woman! You're going to marry the man on Saturday."

There was a long pause on the phone. "This connection must be real bad. I thought I just heard you disrespecting your mama."

"No disrespect intended. I'm just saying you should talk to Sal. I'm not going to be your go-between."

"Fine!"

"Good."

I was gaining on a slow-moving truck, hauling a noisy cargo. An awful smell wafted toward me on the night air.

"Whew! I'm coming up on a truck full of hogs and a double center line, Mama. I need to get off the phone and pay attention so I can pass this old boy who's driving as soon as I get the chance."

There was silence on the other end.

"Mama? Did you hear me?"

"What if Sal is like No. 2, Mace? What if he's like him?" Her voice had turned small, shaky.

I felt a rush of sympathy. Number 2 was by far the worst of Mama's ex-husbands. He'd started cheating within days of their marriage, taking up with a cocktail waitress from the casino hotel where they honeymooned in Las Vegas. After that, there'd been a long and humiliating procession of Other Women.

I eased off the gas a bit, letting the smelly truck gain some distance. "Mama, Sal is a good man."

"Maybe too good to be true."

"Now, you know that's not right. Sal is nothing like No. 2. Just talk to him. I'm sure there's a reasonable explanation."

She sighed, a sound heavy with remembered pain. "I could never go through it again, Mace."

"I know, Mama. You're just having pre-wedding jitters, that's all. Everything is going to be all right, I know it. You and Sal are going to be as happy as Rhett Butler and Scarlett O'Hara."

There was a long pause from Mama's end.

"You didn't watch that movie I loaned you, did you, honey?"

"No. Why?"

"Because Rhett walks out on Scarlett in the end."

TWENTY-FIVE

A CLAW-LIKE HAND LANDED on my right shoulder. Maddie shrieked from the backseat of Pam's VW. "Watch where you're going, Mace! You nearly knocked over my manatee mailbox."

"Sorry," I muttered.

Mama had sounded so upset, I decided to round up my sisters and pay a visit for moral support. We'd just picked up Maddie, and we were enroute to Mama's now. Marty was in the front, like always, because she's prone to carsickness. Maddie was in the back seat because, well, who ever heard of a front-seat driver?

Grinning at me, Marty leaned over to extract Maddie's fingernails from my shoulder.

"You know, Mace..." My big sister settled back into the seat, but her tone said she wasn't ready to let an opportunity for further criticism pass her by. "God gave us rearview mirrors for a reason."

I glanced at Marty and rolled my eyes. She giggled.

"Actually, Maddie, some racecar driver in 1911 at the first Indianapolis 500 gave us rearview mirrors," I said.

Maddie harrumphed. "Nobody likes a know-it-all, Mace. And God surely put the idea into that driver's head."

"You're probably right, Maddie. But just so you know, I missed that ugly mailbox of yours by a mile."

Maddie was about to start another round when Marty said, "Sisters, enough! Now that we're all here, Mace, what were you going to tell us about Sal?"

I filled them in on seeing him with Ms. Sunglasses, and how Mama had some kind of flashback to the bad old days with Husband No. 2. We were used to the Mama Drama, but we also knew the awful toll that second marriage had taken on her.

"It's post-traumatic stress," Maddie said with certainty.

"Thank you, Dr. Laura," I said.

"I mean it, Mace. She's facing the same set of circumstances—getting married. Now, she's reliving the anguish of getting hitched to the wrong man, and wondering if she's making the same mistake again."

"So why didn't she go through that with Nos. 3 and 4?" Marty asked.

"The same stimuli never presented themselves," Maddie said. "It's as simple as that."

Along with her college French, Maddie also took a few psychology courses. Who's the know-it-all now?

"Sounds like a bunch of hooey to me, Maddie," I said. "Mama's probably just over-reacting, as usual."

Marty twisted a long strand of hair around her finger. "How bad did she sound?"

"Hard to tell on the cell, Marty. That's why I wanted us to go see her. Y'all know how rash Mama can be. I just don't want her to do something crazy."

"Wouldn't be the first time," Maddie said.

"Remember when she got into a fistfight at a party with that one woman No. 2 was running around with?" I asked my sisters.

"Those were some good deviled eggs that gal brought, though," Maddie said.

I nodded. "Yeah, it was a shame the whole platter ended up on the floor, with Mama and the hussy rolling around in them like wrestlers on TV."

Marty sighed. "She was cleaning stains off that sherbet-colored pantsuit for days."

I turned on the radio, classic country. Tammy Wynette was singing "Stand by Your Man," a real oldie. We made it onto Main Street, and almost to the song's chorus before another shriek rattled the windows from the back.

"Great Uncle Elmer gone to heaven, Mace! Didn't you see that woman stepping out of her car at that parking spot? You came so close you about took her door off."

The more Maddie picked, the heavier my foot felt on the accelerator. Childish, I know. But I hated having my driving criticized. Especially when everybody in Himmarshee County knew to clear out of the way when Maddie Wilson got behind the wheel. I gunned the VW, which whined in protest.

"Speed limit's thirty-five, Mace."

Marty's quiet, reasonable voice made me realize what a baby I was being. Lifting my foot off the gas, I looked in the rearview at Maddie. "Sorry."

"Humph!" Maddie crossed her arms over her chest.

None of us spoke for the next few minutes. Soon, I turned onto Strawberry Lane. As we passed by Alice's house, I saw the drapes at her front windows were still drawn. The porch light shone on her flower pots, filled with sad, wilting plants. If Mama weren't so pre-occupied with The Wedding of the Century, she'd surely have been next door to her neighbor's, seeing to poor Alice and her dying geraniums.

I eased the VW into Mama's drive. "Well, sisters, we'll know soon enough if this is Mama as Usual or Red Alert," I said.

As we piled out of the car, Teensy's high-pitched barking sounded through the open windows. You'd think that crazy dog would recognize the three of us by now. I swear he barked like that just to annoy me.

"Teensy!" Mama shouted. "Shut the hell up!"

The three of us nearly dropped in our tracks between the pit-tosporum hedges on Mama's front path. The S-word *and* cursing?

"Uh-oh," Marty breathed.

"Uh-oh is right," Maddie echoed.

The front door flung open. Mama stood on the other side, the squirming dog in her arms. Her eyes were red and puffy; her plati-num-hued 'do a collapsed soufflé. She was missing one of her raspberry-sherbet colored shoes, and her big toe stuck out of a huge run in the foot of her knee-high stocking.

She burst into tears.

"Girls, the wedding is off!"

TWENTY-SIX

MARTY COULDN'T HELP IT. She giggled. She does that sometimes when she's nervous. Looking horrified, she clamped a hand over her mouth. But the more she tried to hold back, the harder her shoulders shook with suppressed laughter.

"Sorry, Mama," she managed to squeak out.

The look Maddie aimed at our little sister could have formed icebergs on Lake Okeechobee. "I don't see what's so funny, Marty."

Marty couldn't speak. Her knees had gone weak. She propped herself against the frame of the front door and simply pointed into the foyer at Mama and Teensy. The harder Mama cried, the louder the little dog yowled. The two of them sounded like the most talentless duo ever kicked off *America's Got Talent*.

"S-s-so glad I could a-a-amuse you, Marty." Mama hiccupped accusingly. "Maybe when the remainder of my life falls apart, you can get your sisters in on the joke, too."

Mama plastered a haughty look on her face and pulled herself up to her full height, four-foot-eleven inches. But it's kind of hard to project dignity when you're absent one shoe, your mascara has melted into raccoon eyes, and a Pomeranian is trying to wriggle out from the armpit of your raspberry-hued jacket. I felt a chuckle coming on, too.

"Oh, for God's sake!" Maddie pushed past us through Mama's front door. "The both of you are completely useless."

"Are not!" Marty and I said at the same time, which kicked my chuckle into all-out laughter.

Maddie wrapped a protective arm around Mama's slender shoulders, and then glared at us over the top of our mother's smooshed 'do. Marty and I only laughed harder.

The next thing we knew, Mama and Maddie had turned their backs on us. The foot with the raspberry shoe kicked out to the door, slamming it in our faces. I heard the deadbolt lock rotate with force.

"You can join us when you learn some manners," Maddie called out through the open window.

I raised my eyes to Marty's. The guilty look on her face probably mirrored my own. Our ill-timed guffaws had run their course. Like school kids sensing real trouble on the bench outside the office, we took a few moments to compose ourselves. Then I knocked at the door.

"May we come in now?" I tried to make my voice sound serious. Mature.

Marty leaned to the window and added, "We promise to be good."

Heavy steps vibrated on the other side of the door. Maddie. I didn't hear the dog's paws scrabbling over the floor, though. Teensy was probably with Mama in the kitchen, sulking.

"Beautiful timing, sisters," Maddie hissed as she opened the door. "Now Mama is sad *and* mad. She's furious at you two."

Mad was good, I thought. I'd rather see her angry than moping and beaten down like she became in that last year of her marriage to No. 2. Marty and I arranged our faces into appropriately chastened expressions. We slunk in behind Maddie as she led the way into Mama's kitchen.

"Good evening, girls." Mama's tone was frosty.

"Evening, Mama." We tried to sound contrite.

Marty and I silently took our seats. A box of pink wine sat on the kitchen table. The glass in front of Mama was half full. Maddie was busy, putting out gingham-checked placemats, and pulling more glasses from the cabinets. I waited as she poured our wine, and drew a tumbler of tap water for herself. Mama kept her eyes on the table, fiddling with a ceramic salt shaker shaped like a duck. Still sniffling a bit, she traced the line of the duck's yellow-gingham collar.

I caught Maddie's eye and gave a slight nod toward Mama's wine glass. Maddie slid it under the box's pour spout and filled it to the brim. When the rest of us had taken our first sips, I broke the silence.

"Mama, you can't possibly mean you're backing out of the wedding. Surely this is something we can work out?"

Silently, she lifted the tail end of a raspberry-sherbet scarf she wore around her neck and dabbed at her mascara-muddied eyes. I hoped the scarf wasn't Dry Clean Only.

Marty tore off a piece of paper towel from the roll on the table. Maddie fished a compact out of her purse and handed it to Mama.

Never one to ignore the presence of a mirror, she popped it open to take a peek.

"Jesus H. Christ on a crutch." Mama snapped the compact shut like it caught fire. "I look a fright."

"It's not that bad," I said loyally.

"It's mainly the mascara," Marty added.

"That and your hair," Maddie pointed out helpfully.

Mama opened the mirror again. "I always said I'd never cry over another man, girls. And here I am." Examining the damage, she fluffed her hair's flattest side and picked off mascara clumps with the paper towel. She extracted her Apricot Ice lipstick from her pantsuit pocket, and swiped it twice across her lips.

Then she handed the compact back to Maddie, took a big swallow of wine, and squared her shoulders. "Enough is enough," she said.

I didn't like the final sound of that.

"What happened, Mama?" I glanced at the swiveling hips on her Elvis wall clock. "It's barely been an hour-and-a-half since we talked. How could Sal go from the love of your life to the scum of the earth in such a short time?"

She took another big swig of wine, not even bothering to blot the lipstick stain off the glass. "Plain and simple, girls," Mama said. "He's a liar."

My sisters and I looked at each other. When Mama gets that made-up-her-mind tone, it's easier to push a Brahma bull up a steep hill than it is to get her to see any alternatives.

Marty shook her head. "I've never known Sal to lie."

"Well, then, you don't know him very well, Marty, because he flat-out lied to me about that woman Mace saw him parking with."

"They were just standing there. They weren't 'parking,' Mama."

An imaginary picture immediately popped into my head of Sal and Ms. Sunglasses wrestling like horny teenagers on the roomy seat of his Cadillac. Now I'd have to recite the first several stanzas of "'Twas the Night Before Christmas" to banish the image from my mind.

"Well, whatever they were doing, he denied even being out there at all. And he kept trying to get me off the phone, like I was annoying him for even asking."

She swallowed more wine, and stared out the window into the night. When Mama spoke again, her voice was soft and distant. "I'm telling you, girls, Sal sounded just like Husband No. 2. I remember it so well, this one time when I called to check on him when he was home sick from work. That lying S.O.B. couldn't get me off the phone fast enough. I found out later he wasn't sick at all that day. Number 2 had some hoochie-mama from an Orlando strip club in my bed at the exact moment I called."

My heart went out to her. We'd all known No. 2 was a rat. But we were still young when they were married. She'd never shared those kinds of carnal details.

"That's awful." Marty put a hand over Mama's on the table.

Mama shrugged. "That wasn't the first time. Wouldn't be the last."

Maddie topped off her glass of wine.

"Maybe it wasn't Sal out on the road," Marty said, but even she sounded doubtful. "Are you certain you saw them, Mace?"

Maddie snorted. "Mace can pick out a hawk on a pine branch at fifty yards and tell you if it's a red-tailed or a red-shouldered. And Sal is a lot bigger than a hawk."

"Yeah, he's more like a buzzard," Mama said.

Now she was name-calling. I just wished I'd turned around on that highway and checked on Sal and Sunglasses, like Mama asked me to. We'd have the real story, and her imagination wouldn't have had a chance to spin out of control.

We all fell silent, each with our thoughts. Then, Maddie got up to rummage around in the refrigerator. She returned with three-fourths of a butterscotch pie in one hand and two take-out containers from the Pork Pit in the other. I rose to get out some plates and silverware, while Marty slipped the take-out into the microwave.

"I couldn't eat a thing," Mama said. "I'm too upset."

Maddie cut her a small slice of the pie anyway. Mama pushed the plate way off to the side of her placemat, even though butterscotch was her favorite.

Once my sisters and I had filled our plates, Maddie announced: "Well, I like Sal. I'm not going to believe the worst about him until I hear what he has to say."

Last summer, Maddie's attitude toward Sal had been the last to change. But once he won her over, she was in his corner for life. Even if he was a New Yorker.

Marty defended him, too. "Can't you give Sal the benefit of the doubt, Mama? Remember there were a lot of things he wouldn't—couldn't—tell us last summer. But everything turned out all right in the end, didn't it?"

Mama didn't answer. Marty's question hung in the air, which was rich with the tangy smell of barbecue sauce, the aroma of macaroni and cheese, and the sweet scent of that pie, topped with a mountain of whipped cream.

Mama's fork darted over her placemat for a tiny bite of her pie.

Encouraged, I said, "Your wedding shower's tomorrow night at Betty's, isn't it, Mama? Be a shame to let all Betty's preparations and those nice gifts go to waste."

She regarded her left hand under the kitchen light. "I suppose I'd have to give Sal back his ring, too."

Maddie added, "Not to mention, the deposits you'll lose, canceling at this point."

I heard Marty's sigh of relief when Mama slipped the plate to the center of her placemat and really started in on the pie. She had it about half-gone when Teensy gave a yelp and skittered out from under the kitchen table toward the front door.

"Is that barbecue I smell?" a man's deep voice boomed over Teensy's barking. "Y'all better have saved me a plate."

Our cousin Henry made his way into the kitchen, Mama's Pomeranian yapping at his heels. Teensy did a few revolutions around Henry's ankles, the pitch of his barking climbing higher each time he went airborne.

"Aunt Rosalee, I love you to death, but if you don't silence that little varmint, I'm going to marinate him in sauce and stick him on a barbecue spit."

Mama gasped, snatching Teensy off the floor and clutching him to her chest.

"You wouldn't!" she said.

"Oh, I would," Henry answered, but his grin belied the threat.

As Henry took a seat, I put a quarter-rack of ribs on a plate, and then doused the meat in warmed barbecue sauce. When I handed it to him, he licked his lips. "You got any cornbread? And how 'bout some baked beans?"

Maddie harrumphed. "You'd think an uninvited guest would be grateful for what he's served."

"Hush, Maddie." Mama slapped her on the wrist. "You know Henry's never a guest in this home. Henry's family."

As Mama got up to fetch his favorite sweet tea from the refrigerator, Henry leaned around her back and stuck out his tongue at Maddie. She balled up a paper towel and tossed it at him. It bounced off Henry's forehead and hit Teensy, asleep on the floor.

"I saw that!" Mama's tone was serious, but I noticed the trace of a smile on her lips.

Say what you will about Henry, and we three sisters have said plenty. We always could count on him, though, to make Mama smile. And that was just what we needed tonight.

Henry tore through his food, as focused as if he were presenting a case to keep a client off Death Row. Mama helped herself to another little sliver of butterscotch pie. Marty made coffee, and Maddie and I cleared the table.

When Henry stopped for a breath before his dessert course, he slapped himself on the forehead. "I almost forget to tell you my news!"

"Yes, even you might have trouble talking while you're choking down half a pig." Maddie handed him a length of paper towel.

"I noticed you weren't exactly dainty either, Maddie, shoveling in that pie." Henry mopped the lower half of his face.

"Your news?" I prodded.

He took his time wiping barbecue sauce off each finger, extending the dramatic moment like the grandstanding attorney he is: "Word is down at the courthouse that C'ndee Ciancio is being sought for questioning in the investigation into Ronnie's murder."

Marty's hand flew to her throat, just like Mama's. And it must have been a comfort to Henry to see my older sister's mouth drop open in surprise. "You're not serious?"

"Maddie, I'm as serious as the bride's daddy at a shotgun wedding," Henry answered. He looked at me, waiting for my reaction.

All the little questions I'd been juggling about C'ndee ran through my mind. Her links to Tony's family, with their shady restaurant dealings up North. The fact she ran around with Darryl Dietz, and then, apparently, with Ronnie, too. Her odd behavior the day I discovered Ronnie's body; and how she'd made herself mighty scarce ever since.

I knew it would disappoint Henry, but I wasn't surprised.

"C'ndee's the perfect suspect," I said.

"Well, this is just horrible, Henry." A frown wrinkled Mama's brow. "If C'ndee gets tossed into the slammer, what am I supposed to do about food? We can't order supper in a sack from the Burger King for a hundred-and-fifty wedding guests."

"Good Lord, no!" Henry said.

"By the way, Henry, that's the same wedding Mama was all set to cancel a half-hour before you got here," I said.

He raised his brows. "You were calling off the wedding?"

Mama waved her hand dismissively. "Not really."

Maddie snorted. Marty's eyes went wide. I shrugged at my sisters.

"Well, I was upset. But I've given it a little thought." She held out her hand, examining her engagement rock. "I'm not getting any younger, girls. This may be my last chance for happiness."

We waited.

"Now," Mama continued, "all we have to do is make sure my fiancé's not a cheater and my caterer's not a killer."

TWENTY-SEVEN

A COFFEE VENDING MACHINE in the breezeway gulped my quarters. Choosing the buttons for cream and sugar, I waited impatiently for my order to be processed.

I'd just returned from a quick circuit of the park and a morning check on the animals. I was desperate for caffeine, and our office coffeemaker was still on the fritz.

Maybe I'd go small appliance shopping on Saturday now that the wedding was off. No, wait. It was on again. I wondered how many times that would change in the two days remaining before Mama's Special Day.

Whir. Clunk. No cup; no coffee; no coins returned.

Despite a bad feeling about my odds, I fed more money into the slot. *Beep. Whir. Splash.* The machine spit out a soupy brown liquid, minus the cup. There went my second seventy-five cents, dribbling down a silver drain that seemed to grin at me.

Before I returned to the office, I aimed my work boot and added a kick to the smack I'd just given the coffee machine. It resisted my persuasive efforts.

"We've got to call for service on that stupid machine again …" I had a foot through the door when a tantalizing aroma stopped me where I stood.

Rhonda saluted me with a take-out cup. "Look what Carlos brought!" Her eyes rolled up in ecstasy as she sipped.

My hand flew to smooth my hair. I always claim I didn't inherit an ounce of Mama's vanity, but that's not strictly true.

Rhonda swallowed and whispered, "You look fine. Pinch your cheeks for some color. And straighten your shirt."

Tucking in my T-shirt, I whispered back, "Where is he?"

"Men's room. *Café con leche* is on your desk."

I nearly spilled the coffee with milk when I spotted what was sitting right next to the cup. A perfect red rose in a glass vase. I raised my eyebrows at Rhonda.

"He didn't say. I didn't ask."

Carlos had never struck me as the red rose type. My mind returned to last summer when Jeb Ennis had carried daisies to me here at the park. I hoped this day ended better than that one had.

I was staring at the rose, lost in my memories, when I heard Carlos' voice beside me. "Do you like it?"

I jumped, snatched back to the present. To Carlos. I leaned to sniff the flower. "I love it. It's beautiful."

From her desk across the room, Rhonda nodded happily.

"What's your angle?" I asked him, and watched as my boss's encouraging smile turned into a frown.

Carlos's face darkened, too. "I don't have an *angle*, Mace. I just thought it might cheer the place up."

My gaze followed his around our workspace, with its walls painted institutional tan. A mountain of files towered in a corner. A jumble of feathers, bones, and animal skulls I was cataloguing for a wildlife exhibit covered the top of a long folding table. An oversized events calendar hung crookedly from the back wall. Large windows were a sole saving grace, allowing us to see out to the trees and sky beyond.

I gave him a smile: "I apologize. The rose is exactly the thing for this mess. Thanks."

No words slipped from the locked vault behind his lips.

I saluted him with the cup. "This couldn't have come at a better time, either. *Gracias.*"

His stiff posture relaxed, just a bit. He waved his hand. "*De nada.*"

Behind his back, Rhonda mimed wiping sweat off her brow.

"Do you think we could take a few minutes outside?" he asked.

Rhonda waggled her eyebrows suggestively. I turned my head so I wouldn't laugh. I was already treading on slippery ground with Carlos.

"Sure," I said, and led the way to the door.

"Don't forget to feed Ollie 'til he's stuffed. I don't want another near miss with a furry creature when the kids come to visit today," Rhonda called after us.

"Ollie's never full, Rhonda. He's an opportunistic eater, like my sister, Maddie."

Rhonda said, "You should stick around to watch Mace feed the alligator, Carlos. He chomps whole raw chickens like canapés. He has one forbidding set of jaws."

"So the bite on Mace's gator is pretty nasty, huh?" Carlos smirked.

"Fearsome." She returned his grin.

"Kind of like someone else at the park, someone with a big mouth and a mean bite?"

I resented his implication. My bite wasn't *that* mean.

"Absolutely!" Rhonda said. "Just remember, when that other someone snaps at you, she doesn't mean you any harm. Unlike Ollie, she won't kill you if you get too close."

"I'll keep that in mind."

As the two of them high-fived, I held the door. "After you, Mr. Comedy Central."

He bowed and stepped through. I shot Rhonda an "I'll deal with you later" look over my shoulder. She shook a long, elegant finger at me.

As we settled ourselves onto the wooden bench in the breeze-way, my mind returned again to the day that Jeb had brought me the daisies. We'd sat together right here. I could almost feel the hot patch of skin where our thighs had touched. At least they'd touched until Carlos arrived, and I jumped away from Jeb like I'd gotten an electrical shock.

Was I playing the same game again? Carrying on and flirting, this time with Tony Ciancio, to avoid taking the relationship with Carlos to the next level? I stared into the trees, as if I could find my answer written on the branches and leaves.

"*Peso* for your thoughts, Mace."

Carlos was staring at me. My face burned. Could he tell how confused I was? When I didn't answer, he asked, "How's the wedding planning coming? Everybody's dresses fit?"

I looked at him sideways. The last time he referred to the wedding, he'd called it stupid. And now he wanted dress details? That plus the rose added up to strange.

"What?" he asked.

"You know Mama would love to have you at the wedding. But you've shown zero interest before now. Even Sal runs the other way when wedding talk comes up, and he's the groom."

He looked into my eyes. "I'm coming to the wedding. I care about you, Mace. So of course I care about your mother, too."

Uh-oh. I hoped we weren't going to talk about "us." I wasn't sure what "we" were.

He put a finger under my chin to lift my face to his. "You know that's true, right?"

I pulled away, ducking my chin into a nod. I traced the outside seam on my workpants.

"Your enthusiasm is inspiring," Carlos said dryly.

"I'm sorry." I raised my eyes to his. "I feel like my emotions are on hold. I'm distracted, and nervous about Saturday. I've been trying to imagine who might have murdered Ronnie, and why. And I'm worried the killer's next move might end up derailing Mama's wedding, or worse."

Saying my fears aloud made me think about what Henry had reported. "We heard C'ndee is a suspect."

His brows shot up. "Who told you that?"

"Himmarshee is a small town, Carlos. People gossip."

"What else are people saying?"

"Well," I ran a thumb along the slat of the bench, thinking. "They're saying she was running around with Ronnie. And that her boyfriend before Ronnie has a violent temper. And that she's made herself mighty scarce in these last couple of days."

"I see you've been busy."

"Is she a suspect, or not?"

His features hardened into his cop look. "You know I can't talk about that. This is an active investigation."

"I'm not the enemy, Carlos."

He was quiet for a moment. He finally said, "Then what are you, Mace? I thought we were the opposite of enemies, but now I just don't know. What are we to one another?"

I stared out into the park again. A blue jay scolded me from a cypress branch. I could feel Carlos' gaze on me, waiting. But I didn't know what to tell him.

"Okay, I guess that's my answer."

He rose from the bench. I put a hand on his arm. He shook it off.

"Just give me some time," I said.

"You've already had time." His face was a wall. "But as long as I'm here, there is something else I need to ask you."

I hoped at least I'd get an easier question this time. "Go ahead." I was eager to change the subject.

"I went out to that fish camp you told me about. No sign of Darryl, and nobody knew anything about him, or at least that's what they told me." He crossed his arms over his chest, like an interrogator. "You said you talked to the son, right?"

"Stepson. Name's Rabe."

"Well, Rabe is supposed to be there this afternoon. I told the rest of them I'd be coming back. I think I'd have more luck talking to people out there if you were along. Would you mind?"

I thought of Darryl with his knife at that fish-cleaning station. He'd be singing a different tune with The Law standing beside me. And I couldn't wait to see that redneck bastard squirm.

"Of course I'll come," I said. "And Carlos?"

He cocked his head.

"I knew you had an angle."

TWENTY-EIGHT

It was a long ride to Darryl's Fish Camp. Tension hung in the front seat like a heavy curtain between Carlos and me.

My Jeep was back in service with a new battery, thanks to Sal. Carlos and I decided to take it, since his unmarked car, a white Ford Crown Victoria, screamed plainclothes cop. I drove. Carlos rode shotgun.

He'd spent most of our forty-minute trip to the south end of Lake O ignoring me, making calls on his cell phone in rapid-fire Spanish. It was rude on several levels, but I cut him a break. I hadn't exactly been Emily Post when he came to visit at Himmarshee Park.

I'm sure he thought I was jerking him around. He was entitled to cop an attitude.

The way he was machine-gunning Spanish words into the phone, I didn't have a prayer of understanding him. I can puzzle out simple words and a few sentences, as long as the verbs are present tense, the speaker goes really S—L—O—W—L—Y, and there are hand gestures and facial expressions to help me along.

Carlos, however, seemed in no mood to help me along.

I did catch a tender tone to his voice in the first call, and the word *abuela*, which I remembered meant grandmother. My mind went back to the first time he told me about his granny, and the way she spent hours in the kitchen cooking his favorite Cuban dishes, even though she was well into her eighties. That was when we were getting to know each other. What had happened to the bond between us? Sometimes I wanted to make it stronger; other times it seemed I was taking it apart, piece by painful piece.

His present conversation sounded like business, though I couldn't be sure. For all I knew, he might be placing an order for tomorrow from the new Cuban lunch counter outside of town. If so, I wondered if he remembered how much I liked those sweet fried bananas. I thought of the first time he made Cuban food for me. His face had been joyful as he fed me a forkful of delicious *plátanos*. We'd gone directly from the kitchen to his bedroom. No one can tell me food isn't an aphrodisiac.

Now, I stole a glance at him in profile. His jaw was set in a hard line; his face closed and cold. No joy. He stared impassively at the scenery—sugarcane fields that seemed to stretch forever; a flat road shimmering in the June sun; the occasional agricultural truck lumbering by on the opposite side of US Highway 441.

"So you talked to your grandmother?" I finally asked, when he made no move to speak.

"About her." His brow furrowed. "She's sick."

"I'm sorry." I remembered how I felt when Maw-Maw started failing. I resisted the urge to reach over and stroke his cheek. "I hope it's not serious."

"She's eighty-six, Mace. At that age, anything is serious."

"I'll ask Mama to add her name to the prayer list down at Abundant Forgiveness, Love and Charity Chapel."

"Thanks. Can't hurt. I know a lot of the old ladies at Saint John Bosco in Little Havana have been lighting candles, too."

He shifted on the passenger seat. Tapped his fingers on one knee. "How much farther?"

"We're almost there. But if you need to take a whiz, I can pull over into the weeds."

His lip curled. "As inviting as that sounds, I don't have to go. I'm just trying to remember where the fish camp is. There aren't many landmarks out here. Everything looks the same."

"Unlike Miami, where all the strip malls and condos display such unique and interesting differences."

Now, why did I say that? Did I want to start a fight?

"I think we've already established that Miami is evil and ugly—though millions of tourists a year might dispute that—and that Himmarshee is paradise. If you don't mind snakes, bugs, and accents so thick no one can understand a word people up here are saying."

"Accents?" I raised an eyebrow. "At least *we* speak English!"

"Marginally."

I thought of Carlos, with his precise diction and careful grooming, meeting up with Darryl, with his muddy bare feet and redneck growl. I couldn't help it, I started to laugh.

"Son, jest wait 'til we git to that camp," I drawled. "You ain't seen nuthin' yet."

Before long, the Jeep was rattling over the ruts in the dirt driveway. This time, I noticed that somebody had used the fish camp's metal sign for target practice. Whoever had done it was a pretty good shot, too. Blue sky showed through a hole where the eyeball of a largemouth bass used to be.

"Where's the lake?" Carlos asked.

"Can't see it from here. The shoreline's behind a dike, at least thirty feet tall. Two hurricanes in the 1920s killed a couple of thousand people out here, which made the government sit up and pay attention to flood control."

I dipped my chin toward the boat dock as we passed by. "You get into the lake by taking one of those boats and traveling the rim canal."

He frowned. "They don't look very seaworthy."

"Well, nobody plans to take them to sea. This isn't exactly ocean-fishing out here, Carlos. Most everybody at a camp like this one would just load in a cooler of beer and some bait and shove off."

As he cast another glance over his shoulder at the boats, I scanned the dock and the fish cleaning table. No sign of Darryl.

As we approached the cabins, I felt a vibration through my left boot in the floor board of the Jeep. Rolling down my window, I got a blast of Rabe's oldies rock. If the boy was going to indulge his inner head banger, he really should learn to balance the treble and the bass.

Carlos grimaced and stuck a finger in his left ear. "¡Ay, Dios! What is that?"

"Megadeth," I answered. "Countdown to Extinction."

He shot me a skeptical look.

"What can I say?" I shrugged. "I went through a brief arena rock phase in college."

Slash, the dog, barked from the porch. I could barely hear him over the music. Rabe stepped out of the door to Cabin No. 7, wiping his hands on a red mechanic's rag. He leaned to turn down the boom box, which sat on the warped wooden floor of the cabin's porch.

I tooted my horn twice, and waved out the window. Rabe walked down the steps into the bright sun, squinting at us from under his worn straw cowboy hat. He gave a slight nod, and commanded the hound to stay.

As Carlos and I got out of the Jeep, Rabe glanced over each shoulder. Then he plodded toward us across the weed-filled yard.

I made quick introductions. As they shook hands, Carlos' eyes narrowed, taking measure of the younger man. Rabe towered over him, but he had none of the chest-puffing posture of some big men. His face was blank; neither friendly nor hostile. If anything, he seemed a bit nervous, eyes darting from the camp's entrance, to the cabins, to the boat dock.

I wondered if that was leftover from childhood, when Rabe must always have worried about what corner Darryl would come around next.

"I told Detective Martinez how you and I talked," I said. "He's very interested in finding your stepfather."

His gaze lit on Carlos' eyes. "Yeah, that's what I figured when I heard you were out here yesterday askin' questions. I told Darryl you'd want to talk to him, and all. 'Bout an hour ago, though, he said he planned to go fishin' off Osprey Bay Island. Said if you wanted to see him, you could take a boat and come on out there."

"Can we get there by car?"

Rabe looked at me, local to local.

"No," he said slowly. "It's an island. In the lake. You get there by boat."

I saw a flicker in Carlos' eyes. Annoyance at being talked down to? Something else?

"We'll wait for him here," he announced.

Rabe shrugged. "Suit yourself. Be a long wait. Darryl usually don't come in until close to sunset."

My watch said it was twenty-two minutes past noon.

"I can't stay here all day, Carlos. I've got work to do at the park. Plus, Mama will truss me up and shove me in the oven like a Thanksgiving turkey if I'm late for her bridal shower."

I thought about our agenda of shower games. Maybe sticking my head in the oven wasn't a bad alternative.

Carlos surveyed the boats next to the dock. "Are there life jackets?"

Rabe and I exchanged a glance.

"Yeah, we keep 'em under the seat up front. But the boats at that dock belong to guests. You'd be taking the camp's boat. It's pulled up over yonder next to the chickee hut, at the dock by the beach."

"A beach?" I said.

"Yep. Unusual for these parts." His voice swelled with pride. "We hauled in a bunch of sand and made a fake shoreline on the canal for when we have cookouts and such."

"Was that Darryl's idea?" I asked.

Rabe spit on the ground. "No way. My mom and I have been pretty much running this place. All Darryl does is drink, brawl, and fish."

Carlos pressed his lips together. Swallowed again. "Will the camp's boat be any newer than those at the dock?"

"Do you have a problem with boats?" I asked.

"I don't have a *problem*. I'm just not crazy about being on the water."

"You're Cuban. You lived in Miami. And you don't like the water?"

"Not every Cuban comes to the United States on a raft, Mace. My family is from the interior, the island's agricultural region. We were always cattle people, not coastal people."

Rabe dug into his pocket, and extracted a green tin of chewing tobacco. He offered some to Carlos, who declined the hospitable gesture.

"Listen," Rabe said, as he tucked a pinch beneath his bottom lip. "The boat'll be fine. It gets a lot of use. Nobody's gotten hurt yet."

"Always a first time," Carlos grumbled.

"For real, man." Rabe's grin revealed the dark tobacco staining his bottom teeth. "You'll be fine."

Finally, Carlos nodded his assent.

"Good, then." Darryl's stepson stuck his hands in his overall pockets and turned toward the beach. "Y'all can follow me."

TWENTY-NINE

Navigating slowly through a lock leading to Lake Okeechobee, I broke into the *Gilligan's Island* theme song from behind the boat's wheel: "Well, sit right down and hear a tale..."

By the time I reached the verse about the ill-fated three-hour cruise, storm clouds had gathered on Carlos' face.

"Sorry," I said. "Couldn't resist."

As we hit open water, several moments passed in silence as I opened the throttle, familiarized myself with the give in the steering, and settled as comfortably as possible in the elevated captain's chair behind the wheel. There was a big rip on the seat's plastic upholstery, and I felt a damp spot from the soaked stuffing spreading across the butt of my work pants.

The fish camp's boat was a 16-foot fiberglass skiff, and only half as crappy as some of the vessels we'd seen at the dock. Carlos sat in the front, on the flat surface of the bow, facing me. I spotted a fish hawk pass overhead, fat prey squirming in its talons.

"Better watch out." I pointed skyward. "If that osprey drops his dinner, it might knock you out. Talk about your unidentified flying objects."

Carlos barely raised his eyes. Not even a chuckle. He sat stiffly, his fingertips touching a life vest next to him. There'd only been one vest in the hold. It was mildewed, ratty-looking, and faded by the sun from orange almost to white. Darryl apparently wasn't big on strict compliance with Coast Guard safety standards. I'd handed the sole life jacket to Carlos.

Frowning, he pinched it between two fingers and held it out for inspection. Even from the back of the boat, near the stern, I could smell the fish stink on it.

"Just keep it within reach," I'd told him. "I don't think we'll be hitting any icebergs."

Now, we were heading into a notoriously shallow area of the lake. I tilted the motor up, bringing the propeller closer to the surface and away from the sharp rocks and thick grasses that lurked below. The boat's flat bottom was a blessing. When the lake was low, I'd seen many vessels with V-shaped hulls run aground in these waters.

As soon as we were through the shallows, I lowered the prop and throttled up again. Carlos scanned the vast surface. "All I see is lake. Where's this Ostrich Island?"

"Osprey." I bit back a smile. Outsiders! "It's not much farther."

The motor purred. The boat might not look like much, but Rabe knew his way around an engine. Though ancient, the Evinrude seemed to be in tip-top shape. The breeze was picking up. Puffy white clouds skidded across a brilliant sky. The wind gave the lake a bit of a chop. The boat thudded over the waves, making for a bumpy ride.

"If—you'd—slow—down—it might—be—a—little—smoother." Carlos' words stuttered out in time to the boat's bounces.

"If I slow down, we might not catch up to Darryl."

The boat pounded the water. I glanced at him. His face was white.

"You don't get sick, do you? This chop's not much, but I know Marty gets seasick staring at a glass of water."

"I'm not sick." He clamped his lips shut.

"If you say so. But you might want to sit back here, where you can look forward. And if you do feel queasy at all, it helps to stare at a fixed point on the horizon." I gestured to the far distance, where blue sky met the dark waters of the lake.

"How—*thud*—do you find a fixed point—*thud*—when you feel like you're strapped to a basketball—*thud*—in full dribble?"

I looked at my watch. "We're maybe fifteen to twenty minutes away."

"You didn't tell me we'd be navigating the entire lake."

"Not even close. Lake Okeechobee is thirty miles from east to west; about the same from north to south. After Lake Michigan, it's the second-biggest freshwater lake that lies entirely within the continental United States."

"Very impressive, professor, even though I've heard the stats before." He turned his head right and then left. "It's still too much water for me."

With an almost imperceptible shudder, he cast his eyes down to the deck.

We were silent for a bit; me watching the compass on the console and the shapes of the clouds crowding the sky; Carlos apparently memorizing the squiggly lines running through the boat's fiberglass finish.

When the engine sputtered, his head jerked up. "What's that?"

It sputtered again and then coughed.

"Crap," I said. "It sounds like we're out of gas."

He grabbed for the life vest.

"No worries. I checked the second tank before we left. It's full." I shut off the motor. "It'll just take a couple of minutes for me to change the fuel line to the full tank."

I was busy, tending to the tanks, pumping the gas, starting the engine to get us underway again.

"Mace?" Carlos said.

"Hmm?"

"Is there supposed to be water back there, inside the boat?"

"Well, a little water is normal. It might be rainwater from that storm a couple days ago. Or maybe some spray from the wake."

"I'm not talking about a little water. I'm talking about a lot."

I felt a tiny stab of fear. "C'mon over here and take the wheel. And don't worry, Carlos. Everything's fine."

A moment later, I'd revised that assessment. "Shit."

"What's wrong?"

I stooped at the transom, where earlier I'd seen the boat plug securely stuck into the drain hole when we set off from Darryl's camp. Now, the plug was missing. When I stopped the boat to change the tanks, water had flooded in. It swirled now around my boots, soaking the toes.

"We've taken on some water." I tried to squeeze out all inflection, making it a simple declaration of fact. Neither good nor bad.

"What?!" His voice rose. The boat lurched right as he jumped up from the seat, his shoes hitting a flooded deck. He stared for a long moment at the water eddying around his feet.

"We'll probably be all right as long as we keep moving," I said. "The water should drain out."

I don't think he even heard me. His breath was coming in ragged gasps.

"This cannot be happening again." Staring at the flooded deck, his eyes were huge; the color gone from his face.

He stepped away from the wheel. I grabbed it. He moved to the bow, struggling to don the stinking life vest. The frayed strap with a clasp at the end fell apart in his hand. The fear in his eyes scared me. I'd never seen this man when he wasn't in control of his emotions.

"Hang on, Carlos. We need to keep moving."

I put a hand on his arm. He shook it off. And then he gave a short nod, almost to himself. He leaned down, removed a revolver from an ankle holster, and laid it carefully on the console.

"You don't understand. I cannot stay on this boat."

I had one hand on the wheel, my other arm reaching out to him as he stepped toward the bow. "Wait, Carlos ... I ..."

I'd barely gotten out those words before he climbed up, shut his eyes, and crossed himself. Then he stepped over the side, dropping feet first into the dark waters of Lake Okeechobee.

THIRTY

CARLOS' ARMS FLAILED. THE unclasped life vest floated up, tight against his neck. Water splashed wildly. I cut the engine and stretched out on the bow, reaching a hand toward him.

"Look at me!" I yelled. "Right here! Look at me."

Panicked, he paid no attention, just kept fighting the lake. The thrashing motion of his arms whipped up the water around him, like a hurricane's surge. His head went under.

I stood on the bow, wiggled out of my T-shirt and boots, and went in after him. It took just a moment or two to reach the spot where he'd gone down. I grabbed his shirt collar and pulled him back up, still fighting.

"Carlos!"

As he turned his head to the sound of my shout, his chin barely grazed the surface of the lake.

"Stop struggling! You're okay. Just stand up."

His brows drew together in a question. The windmill of his arms slowed. Realization slowly dawned.

"The lake is shallow," I said. "You're less likely to drown out here than to get attacked by a gator. And with the way you're splashing around, one of these big boys is going to mistake you for a distressed animal. He'll make you his dinner."

Standing now, he untangled the vest from around his neck. A sheepish look crept across his face.

"Walk around to the back of the boat with me. I'll show you where to climb in."

"But the boat's sinking."

"Not yet. But the longer we stay stopped in the water, the more likely that is. Even if it does sink, we'll scuttle the piece of crap. We can probably wade all the way to shore."

I scanned the lake, saw no other boat traffic on this weekday. Where were the weekend anglers, the "bassholes," when we needed them?

"Good thing you didn't jump in with your gun," I said. "We can use it to scare away the gators."

Casting an uneasy glance over each shoulder, he hurried after me to the stern.

"I guess I looked pretty stupid, jumping over."

I'd seen real terror in his eyes. Nothing stupid about that. "Not at all," I said.

Where had that fear of boats and his blinding panic come from? I wasn't going to ask him. He'd tell me when he was ready.

Once we were onboard, I quickly searched through a bin below the console. A bottle opener. Bug spray. An extra set of keys. A screwdriver. And then, success.

"This is what we need." I held up a spare plug. "As we get underway, bail as quickly as you can with that bait bucket. If we can get moving, the boat will angle up on plane, and the water should drain."

I started the engine as Carlos set to work. His confidence seemed to grow with each bucketful of water he tossed overboard. The lighter we got, the faster we went, until water streamed out through the open hole.

"Can you navigate again, while I see if I can get the plug in?" I asked. "We're headed back to the camp, so just keep the compass pointing east."

Grabbing the wheel with new assurance, he turned his face toward the sun. It seemed like he'd faced some awful fear, and was grateful to have survived to see daylight again.

I leaned over the transom, felt for the drain hole, and worked the plug in with the heel of my hand. "I got it!" I finally yelled. "Hallelujah."

I saw Carlos' shoulders relax. I was still soaked, and the rush of the wind felt cold. I stripped off my wet bra and was about to shrug back into my dry T-shirt, when he turned his head to say something. I couldn't help but notice how his eyes flickered across my breasts. I quickly pulled my shirt over my body.

He'd seen me naked before, of course. But for some reason I felt embarrassed. I found a nylon jacket under the bench seat, and tossed it to him.

"You might want to take off that wet shirt. The sun feels warm now, but you'll get cold at this speed in the wind."

He caught the jacket. I stood next to the captain's chair, steering as he changed into the dry jacket. When he was done, he took back the wheel, and I moved to the side to lean against the gunnel.

"Thanks, Mace. And thanks for saving us."

I waved a hand, like it was nothing. "Guess we won't end up in watery graves at the bottom of the lake after all."

A look of pain raced across his face. I immediately regretted my lame attempt at levity.

"Sorry."

He shrugged. "I should be used to it. It's been many years."

"But you're not."

"No."

Neither of us spoke for a time. The engine whined. The throttle was fully open. We still headed east, back to the camp. A shift in the wind had smoothed the lake's surface.

"Do you want to reverse course, go find Darryl, now that we're not taking on water?"

"No. I need to regroup."

"Regroup how?"

He lifted his wet pant leg and showed me his ankle, trailing lake vegetation. "Well, dry clothes, and minus this green stuff in my holster, for example."

"It's called water lettuce."

Ignoring my botany lesson, he said, "I want the upper hand when I meet up with our friend Darryl. Do you think he sabotaged the boat?"

As soon as Carlos mentioned sabotage, a news story from a few years back popped into my head. The focus was on dirty tricks in a bass fishing tournament. And then I got a quick image of a spool of fishing line I'd seen on a table under the thatched-roof of the chickee hut.

"Oh, man." I slapped my forehead.

"What?"

"Fifty-pound test line. When I saw it today at the camp, I wondered why anybody would have such strong line for lake fishing. It wasn't for fishing. You tie a length of it to a boat plug, add a big hook at the end, and where the water's shallow, the hook snags something on the bottom. Pop. There goes your plug."

Carlos cocked his head toward the transom. "Would Darryl know that trick?"

"I'm sure he has knowledge of anything that's illegal, unethical, or just plain mean. But would he take a chance like that with a cop, given what surely must be a prior record?"

Carlos nodded. "Good point, which raises the next question: Who all had access to this boat before we set out on the lake?"

I thought about Rabe, lurking by the dock the day I talked to Darryl. I hoped Carlos' answer implicated Darryl instead of his stepson.

"My money's on Darryl," I said, remembering how his black eyes had glittered with cruelty. "And speaking of predators..."

I pointed to the lake. A big gator glided by, head atop the water, powerful tail moving to and fro under the surface. The distance from eyes to snout tip was at least a foot.

"¡Dios mío! That's a monster."

"Twelve feet, at least," I agreed.

Carlos swallowed hard. "What if he'd been swimming by a few minutes earlier?"

"Well, he wasn't," I said. "We were lucky."

His eyes got a faraway look. "Just like I was lucky before."

I didn't want to push him. But my curiosity was growing. And he *had* brought it up.

"What do you mean, 'before'?" I asked.

He took so long to answer, I thought maybe the wind had swallowed my question.

"*Mi hermano.*" His voice was so soft, I had to lean in to hear him. "My brother."

Goosebumps rose on my arms, and not just because I was still half-soaked.

"He drowned," Carlos said.

"When?"

"A long time ago. He was seven. I was four. We'd gone to the coast."

His knuckles whitened on the steering wheel. He stared at the horizon.

"My brother didn't want to take our uncle's little boat into the ocean. But I begged to get closer to the dolphins we'd seen swimming offshore."

Carlos' gaze moved across the lake. Was he seeing those long-ago dolphins frolicking? What else did he see in that endless water?

"My brother wasn't like other older brothers. He never picked on me, or bossed. He was happiest when he could make me happy. I remember him frowning up at these big, dark clouds forming in the sky. But I wanted to catch up to those dolphins so badly, I cried…"

His voice faded. He shook his head.

"The weather changed?"

He nodded. "The rain fell so hard, it felt like needles piercing the skin on my bare arms. And it was cold. Which is strange, because Cuba was always warm. My teeth chattered. Waves kept sloshing into the boat; my feet were soaked. I complained I was freezing. My brother stood up to look for a towel, or anything dry."

Lifting a hand over his face, he pinched the bridge of his nose. It was as if he wanted to force the memories far back into his mind again.

"I'm so sorry, Carlos."

When he spoke again, he sounded emotionless, like an expert testifying in court. "A big wave hit, and knocked Raul off balance. Before I could make a move, he'd fallen over the side. He must have banged his head as he went over. It seemed like it happened so fast. Raul could swim, but I couldn't. I was afraid to jump in. But I kept watching, calling his name. He never surfaced. And the waves kept sloshing over the sides of the boat."

I pictured Carlos as a four-year-old: Drenched. Frightened. Watching the water rise in the boat. My heart nearly burst.

"I kept praying for the dolphins to rescue him, to swim him to safety."

His voice was barely a whisper. I took a step closer. "How'd you get to shore?"

"Some fishermen were coming in, running from the storm. They saw me alone in this nearly sunken boat, out there in the ocean. I told them Raul had fallen in. They looked for him, but I'd already drifted from where he went under. His body was never found."

He stared into the sky, watching a big cloud. Then he spoke again. "I'm not even sure why I jumped over today. I was afraid of the water, but I was even more scared the boat would sink. It doesn't make any sense."

Pure panic never does. I wasn't sure how to comfort him. What would Marty say? I moved closer and put a hand to his cheek. He leaned his face into my hand, resting it there for a moment. When he pulled away to look at me, his eyes shone darkly with guilt and pain and unshed tears.

I brought my mouth to his ear and whispered, "It wasn't your fault. You were just kids."

"That's what everyone told me. But I heard the talk. I noticed how people stared. I watched my mother turn away. Her grief over Raul was so strong, she could barely stand to look at me."

I thought of the close relationship between Carlos and his grandmother, and the fact he rarely spoke of his mother. And once, when I'd asked, he said he had no siblings. My mama might drive me crazy, but I couldn't imagine my life without her, or my sisters.

"Was it just the two of you?"

A short nod. "I must have wished a million times to take back those five minutes on the shore, when I begged him to go. I've hated boats ever since."

I felt my face burn over my stupid jibes. Had I really sung the *Gilligan's Island* song?

The rise of the dike was clear in the distance.

"We're getting close to Darryl's camp," I said.

He cleared his throat. "Thanks for listening, Mace. You've always been easy to talk to."

"I just wish I could wave a wand to give you a do-over of that day."

"Me, too." His smile was tinged with sadness. "You would have liked Raul. He was kind and gentle. Much nicer than me."

I smiled at him. "Oh, I don't know, Carlos. I happen to think you're pretty nice."

He lifted an eyebrow. "Really? As nice as Tony Ciancio with his Rolex watch and sailboat tan?"

"Nicer, in fact." I touched his cheek. "And you've got a pretty good tan yourself."

Now that the color had returned to his face, his skin looked yummy, like butterscotch toffee. I had the urge to lean over and taste it.

He laid his palm over mine, pressing my hand against his face. Then he turned his head ever so slightly, just enough for his lips to meet my open palm. When they did, what felt like an electrical current jolted me clear down to my bare feet.

"Hmmm," I said. "That's nice."

"It's been a while for us, hasn't it?"

"Too long."

"How much time before we get back to the camp?"

"Too much," I murmured.

Our eyes met. My heart pattered. What had I been doing, playing around? *This* was the man I wanted. And I wanted him right now.

He gestured to his soaking-wet slacks, which showed each muscle and bulge quite clearly. "Do you think they'll let us use a cabin when we get back to the camp? Maybe clean up and dry off?"

I concocted a fantasy of Carlos and me in the shower, working one another into a lather. As a lascivious grin spread across my face, I wondered: Did I look as predatory as that big gator?

THIRTY-ONE

I WAS STUDYING THE shade of purple on Betty Taylor's front door, trying to determine if it occurred anywhere in nature, when Maddie answered the bell.

"Why are you so late? Mama is madder than a box of frogs!" She wrinkled her nose. "And what is that stench? You smell like something they left behind in the cast net."

Maddie's eyes moved from my head to my feet.

"Those boots are soaking wet, Mace! Betty'll throw a fit. She just had her lavender carpet cleaned for Mama's bridal shower. You better strip off those stinking things before you come inside."

At the word "strip," I felt my face get hot. My eyes darted away from Maddie. Memories of what Carlos and I had done all afternoon in an empty cabin at the fish camp filled my head. Skilled at reading the body language of guilty middle-schoolers, Maddie gave me an assessing look.

"Well, at least you have some color in your cheeks. We'll tell Mama you're trying out a new blush for the wedding."

"I…"

She raised a crossing-guard's hand. "Stop right there. I don't want to hear it. I just hope you're using protection."

If my face was red before, it was burning now. "Maddie, please! I'm not one of your students."

"No, you're just acting like one. Do I know the lucky man?"

I pressed my lips together.

"Was it Tony?"

I shook my head.

"Is it that rodeo devil, Jeb Ennis, back in the saddle again?"

Another head shake.

"Oh, no you didn't! Are you playing around with poor Carlos again?"

I folded my arms across my chest. "He wasn't exactly complaining."

"Give him time. I have no doubt you'll be back to making him miserable once the afterglow's gone." She *tsked*. "Now, get out of those nasty boots and slap a smile on your face. We've just started a game of Pin the Tail on the Groom."

I raised my eyebrows. "Sal's here?"

"Yes, everything's patched up; Mama's over the Mystery Woman. But now, Sal's the life of the party, and he's stealing her spotlight. She might just give him the hook."

As I stood on the mat to remove my boots, Maddie muttered as she moved down the hallway: " 'All the modern showers have the bride and groom together, Maddie.' That's when I *should* have said, 'Since when is Himmarshee modern, Mama?' "

I heard a loud whoop of female laughter from the next room. And then Sal's Bronx honk boomed, "Careful there, Dab! Another

205

inch closer and I couldn't perform my husbandly duties on the honeymoon."

Ohmigod! It was the hussy from the drive-thru!

I came into the living room, barefoot, just in time to see a blindfolded senior citizen in a silver lamé mini-dress, holding a fabric donkey tail in her hand. The sticky swatch at the end was aimed perilously near Sal's private parts. As Dab gave a sultry laugh, Mama did a slow burn on the couch.

As I sat, she hissed, "I never should have invited that shameless woman. She's flirting with Sal, right in front of me, and I'm the bride!"

"Shhh," Marty whispered from the floor. "Dab looks like she's been rode hard and put up wet. You've got nothing to worry about."

"And she's ancient," Maddie said. "I doubt she's flirting."

"Well, I'm sixty years old …" Mama started.

"You're almost sixty-three," Maddie corrected.

"Thank you, Maddie. I didn't know you were running the Florida Department of Vital Statistics in addition to the middle school." She smoothed her hair and lowered her voice. "As I was saying, Dab's only got about ten years on me. A woman, and especially that one, doesn't forget how to flirt just because she gets older."

Mama seemed to notice me on the couch for the first time. "If it's a woman who ever knew how to flirt, that is."

I let the shot roll off my back. I was just grateful she was focused on Dab instead of on my late arrival. Or my bare feet. Or the color in my cheeks from incredible sex.

"Didn't you say she had a doozy of a story, Mama?" I asked.

"Only if you think dancing naked on stage in a cage in Las Vegas is a story." Mama raised a hand, ticking off items on her fingers. "Or, it's a story being married more times than me, even though she claims we're equal because she actually married the same man twice. Or, doing time in prison..."

"Uhmmm, Mama?" Marty said. "You've done time, too."

She waved her hand. "That was just jail, honey. And it was all a mistake. Dab Holt got sent up for murder, I heard. They say she shot a man in Reno, just to watch him die."

Marty snorted a swallow of pink wine out her nose. Maddie said, "For heaven's sake, Mama! You're quoting a lyric from a Johnny Cash song."

"Well, I can't help that, Maddie. Maybe he wrote the song about Dab."

"How come we've never met her? She sounds fascinating," I said.

Dab was snake-dancing around Sal, using the donkey tail like a stripper's scarf.

"My goodness, Mace! I tried to give you girls a good example growing up. I wouldn't have exposed you to a woman as bad as Dab."

Maddie said, "Dab beat out Mama for Miss Swamp Cabbage in 1965. They never spoke again, until Mama decided to make amends by inviting her to the shower."

"The vote was rigged." Mama fluffed her hair. "I suspect she did a special favor for one of the judges. Plus, she was too old, according to the rules. She lied about her age!"

"Imagine that," Maddie said.

"How'd she come by that unusual name?" Marty asked.

"Her daddy called her that because she was so tiny; just a little dab," Mama said.

I looked at Mama's frenemy, doing a shimmy now, the shiny fabric of her dress stretched tight across her breasts. They perched unnaturally high and round on her skinny frame, like two honey-dew melons on a grocer's shelf.

"I guess she got her nickname before she got the implants," I said.

Betty came over just then with a cup of punch and a plate: A deviled egg, a pig-in-the-blanket, some spicy bean dip with a few tortilla chips, and three ham-and-cheese roll-ups.

"Bless you, Betty. I'm starving."

"Well I could tell you didn't stop home to eat, Mace, 'cause I know you would have done something with that hair."

My hand went to my mass of snarls. I couldn't remember if I even washed it after my dip in the lake. There hadn't been much time for hair care once Carlos joined me in the shower.

"Is that a new shade of blush, Mace?" Betty asked. "It's very be-coming. But, honey, you have got to come in to Hair Today, Dyed Tomorrow and let us fix that mess on your head. You can't walk down the aisle in that beautiful dress with hair that looks styled by a weed whacker."

"Amen!" Mama said, though her eyes were still fastened on Sal and Dab.

Now, Dab was affixing the tail to Sal's upper arm. She gave his bicep an appreciative squeeze. Mama sat on the edge of the couch, as if she was about to launch herself like a missile at Dab.

"My Lord!" Dab's voice sounded like sex and cigarettes. "You must really work out. And I *do* hope that's your arm."

Marty giggled. I leaned behind Mama and raised my eyebrows at Maddie. She grinned.

"Looks like you *are* never too old," she said.

Mama rocketed off the couch, shouting, "Next!"

She grabbed the blindfold off Dab. I thought she'd yank out a handful of her scarlet bouffant, too. But she just gave Dab a tight smile.

"Maybe you'd better sit down and rest a bit, honey." She patted Dab's arm. "Those varicose veins must act up something awful at your age."

"I guess at your age your eyesight's not what it used to be, Rosalee." Hiking a high-heeled foot onto Betty's coffee table, Dab displayed a surprisingly shapely leg. "I don't have any varicose veins."

Pushing past Dab to claim her rightful place on stage, Mama tied the blindfold gingerly, so as not to muss her helmet of hair. Since I was woefully familiar with the Mama Show, I turned my attention to my food and punch while I checked out Betty's home.

And I'd thought Hair Today was a purple palace. Her home made the salon seem sedate. The living room drapes were mulberry velvet, with low-hanging swags in the same shade. The over-stuffed couch was plush, and as purple as an eggplant. The carpet was a thick pile, closer to lilac than lavender. About the only thing that wasn't purple was the TV, and it wore an orchid-hued doily like a lacy hat.

In her sherbet-colored pantsuit, Mama looked like a tangerine in a bowl of plums.

Among a dozen or so guests, I recognized some of Mama's bingo buddies and several of her fellow church-goers. D'Vora, from the salon, chatted with Charlene, the waitress from Gladys' Diner. Alice Hodges sat by herself, an untouched plate of food on her lap. Her clothes were clean and pressed, and she wore a hint of lipstick. She'd tried to fix herself up. But her eyes were still blank; her complexion sallow. It seemed as if no one wanted to breach the force field of mourning that surrounded her.

Just as I was about to stand up to go check on Alice, the doorbell rang. Glancing at her watch, Betty frowned. She'd probably been hoping to have us all gone in time to sit down with her feet up, a plate of leftovers on her lap, and *American Idol* on the tube.

"Rosalee, were you expecting another guest?" Betty asked.

Slipping off the blindfold, Mama did a quick survey of the room. "I invited my nephew Henry so Sal wouldn't be the only man. He said he couldn't make it until later, though."

Sal cleared his throat. "It … it … might be C'ndee."

Mama's brows shot up.

"She called this morning to say she'd taken a little trip to the coast. She said she was really sorry she missed dinner with you and her nephew at the Speckled Perch. I told her to stop by tonight so she could tell you in person."

"Well, isn't that nice." Mama gave Sal one of her looks. Translation: She'd like to hand him that blindfold and stand him up at the wall of a firing range.

He tugged at his collar. "Sorry I forgot to mention it."

"I'm sure you are."

The bell ding-donged again, an impatient sound. As Betty hurried to get the door, every other pair of eyes in the room watched Mama and Sal to see what would happen next. Even Alice seemed to shake off her sleepwalking state to attend to the pre-wedding drama.

Maddie started humming the theme from *Jaws*.

THIRTY-TWO

"Oh, my Gawd! That cake is absolutely GORGEOUS!" C'ndee's big voice blasted from the dining room. "I have to visit the little girl's room, but be sure to save me a slice."

"Cake," Maddie and I chorused.

"That's a wonderful idea," Marty called out, in a voice brimming with artificial cheer. "Mama, why don't we go into the other room and cut the cake?"

A murmur of assent went around the room. Mama cast one more withering glance at Sal, who seemed to shrink a little under the glare.

"Poor guy," I whispered to Maddie. "He better man up if he wants to go *mano a mano* with Mama."

"You know it. She likes a challenge. If she can walk all over him, he won't last long enough to board the *Maid of the Mist* on their honeymoon."

"They're not going to Vegas?"

"Nope, Niagara," Maddie said. "She has bad associations to Vegas, what with Husband No. 2. Then again she's been to Niagara Falls, too. Was that with No. 3 or 4?"

Marty hissed under her breath, "Hush, the both of you! You'll jinx the wedding."

The party relocated to the dining room, where all of us attempted to stay on our best behavior. Mama's snit was quickly forgotten, and she was already laughing and kidding again with Sal. She dabbed her finger in a bit of stray icing, and got on her tiptoes to put a dollop on his lips. Then she kissed it off.

Sal beamed as the two of them shared the process of cutting, plating, and passing pieces of cake. The thick white frosting was decorated with dark purple roses, no surprise. *Best Wishes, Sal and Rosalee*, was written in cursive, in a lighter shade of purple.

I was working on an exit strategy that would allow me to eat cake, and still get out the door before that shower game where guests squeeze a nickel between their knees and try to walk. Whoever drops her nickel first is definitely not a virgin. Considering the afternoon I'd spent, I doubted if I could squeeze my legs around a basketball, let alone a nickel.

Our plates full, my sisters and I returned to our positions in the living room. As Maddie savored a jumbo-sized icing rose, Marty said, "Are you going to talk to C'ndee, Mace?"

"You bet I am. If she ever makes it out of the 'little girls' room.' What in the world is taking her so long in there, I wonder?"

Maddie shuddered. "Maybe she got some bad seafood over there on the coast."

My older sister had once eaten some bad raw clams in Vero Beach. She'd been convinced ever since that the only good seafood was frozen, deep-fried, and served with a side of hush puppies.

Knowing Maddie's taste for retelling the Revenge of the Clam story, in detail, Marty changed the subject. "I called the park today, Mace. Rhonda said you'd left with Carlos." Her eyes sparkled with curiosity.

I ignored Maddie's tongue clucking. "He asked me to go with him to question that lowlife, Darryl. We took a boat from the fish camp, but we never made it to Osprey Bay Island."

"That's because they took a little detour." Maddie was wearing her know-it-all look.

"Well, we started taking on water. Carlos went overboard, and nearly drowned. And we barely escaped being eaten by a giant gator. So, I guess you could say we were detoured."

"What!??" My sisters gasped.

Mama walked up with Sal, hands entwined like teenagers. "Did I miss something?" she asked.

As they sat, I launched into the tale of the Missing Drain Plug and How I Saved the Day. I was savoring the contrite look on Maddie's face, when a hubbub arose and interrupted me.

"Get your hands off me, you hick!" The voice was loud, angry, and pure Joisey.

"Don't call me a hick, you hussy!" That one was rural and shrill. Alice.

The voices were coming from the hallway, near the powder room. We all looked at one another. Then we leaped off the purple couch, plates of cake forgotten. We heard a loud *thump*, like a body getting shoved into the wall. Then *slap*, the sound of an open hand hitting skin. Just as we rounded the corner into the dining room, Alice and C'ndee came staggering out of the hallway. Each had a handful of the other's hair.

"Let go!" Alice screeched.

"You first!" C'ndee countered.

Betty started clearing her souvenir shot glasses and Princess Diana plates off an accent table. Sal roared, "C'ndee! Stop it right now." The two women circled, round and round.

"She started it." C'ndee landed a kick with her red stiletto on Alice's shin. "Bitch!"

Alice hopped on one foot. "Whore!" she yelled, connecting with a solid punch to C'ndee's left breast.

"Ouch!" C'ndee cried, as everyone but Sal cringed.

He bulled his way through the moving mass of shower guests turned fight fans. He almost made it to the battering duo, even had one beefy arm stretched out to separate them, when C'ndee gave Alice a mighty shove. Alice grabbed at her opponent's left shoulder and held on as she fell backward.

The two of them toppled together onto the dining room table. The punch bowl tipped, spilling a juice mixture of cranberry and pineapple, with lemon-lime soda. A fruity smell rose in the room. Globs of lime sherbet dotted Betty's carpet, like green islands in a lilac sea. Then the cake slid from the table, splat onto the wet carpet. The two women went next, coming off the table only to lose their footing in frosting, sherbet, and bridal shower punch.

Mama clutched her hand to her throat. "Make them stop, Sal!" she wailed. "They're ruining my shower."

As I watched Alice and C'ndee tumbling across the floor in white frosting and pink punch, I had to disagree with Mama. This was the best bridal fete ever.

THIRTY-THREE

MAMA AIMED A DISPOSABLE camera at me and clicked. Little red dots from the flash danced in front of my eyes.

"My stars and garters, Mace. You look like the governor just signed your death warrant. Would it kill you to crack a smile? You're supposed to be playing a beaming bride."

I hadn't been able to escape the shower games. I slapped down my "bouquet," a paper plate adorned with ribbons from the shower gifts, on Betty's coffee table.

"I'm wearing a veil made out of toilet paper, and y'all have me wrapped like a mummy with at least three rolls. I look more like an explosion in an outhouse than I do a bride, Mama."

The excitement had died down. Betty brought out store-bought cookies to replace the ruined cake. My cousin Henry had arrived. And with Mama and him fixing the votes, guess who got roped into portraying Himmarshee's next bride?

Sal had finally managed to pull apart C'ndee and Alice. D'Vora took the widow Hodges into Betty's bedroom to help her clean up.

C'ndee, cursing, stormed out the front door with Sal right behind her. I started to make my exit right behind them, but Marty and Mama stopped me.

"We've got to stay and help Betty," Marty said.

"My shower is a disaster." Mama's lower lip quivered.

Maddie clapped her hands like the teacher she'd once been. "Why don't all of us pitch in to help Betty pick up, and then we'll all play the wedding gown game?"

"That sounds like a great idea," Marty immediately chimed in.

I wasn't the only one to roll my eyes and start for the door. But Maddie shot the dissenters her principal glare, and we all fell into line.

Now, I was the make-believe bride, and Mama was snapping pictures, probably figuring a TP wedding dress might be the only kind I'd ever get. Meanwhile, Henry was taking advantage of the fact I'd been toilet-papered into paralysis to steal a cookie off my plate.

"I saw that! It's not my problem you got here late and missed both the catfight *and* the cake, Henry."

"Mace, please," Mama said. "A bride is supposed to be gracious and giving, not surly and snide."

"You must not have ever watched that *Bridezilla* show on TV," I told her.

Henry gulped down the stolen cookie and then reached for the last one on my plate. "Aunt Rosalee, you can't expect Mace to play along. She's extremely literal. She was never blessed with a good imagination. Mace sees only toilet tissue where we might see a lovely white gown."

"That must be the problem. It's a *white* gown!" Dab's stage whisper was followed by a burst of laughter.

Henry popped my cookie into his mouth.

"Thanks for the analysis, you overeducated weasel. I forgot about your legendary imagination: Michelangelo, Shakespeare, and Henry Bauer, Himmarshee's Courtroom King of the Slip-and-Fall."

Henry and I might have gone a round if Betty's doorbell hadn't rung just then. Our exhausted hostess yelled from her reclining chair, "It's open."

A few moments later, Sal trudged into the living room. Head hanging, shoulders slumped, C'ndee limped in his wake.

"C'ndee has something she wants to say." He nudged her to center stage.

The room was so quiet, I could hear the remainder of my punch gliding down Henry's gullet.

"Start tawking," Sal said.

"I'm sorry, Rosalee, to have acted the way I did at what should have been a happy day for you." C'ndee looked down as she twisted her hands. "And, Betty, I'll pay for the cake, and whatever we broke. I'll also take care of getting your carpet cleaned."

She lifted her eyes, scanned the crowd, and then stepped backward as if to leave.

"You're not done yet, George Foreman." Sal gripped C'ndee's wrist. "Where's Alice?"

"Let her through," came a muffled voice from the back.

Arm around Alice's shoulders, D'Vora led her into the living room. She wore a loaner running suit from Betty, purple of course.

She'd had a shower, but I noticed punch-colored pink splotches on her white canvas shoes.

C'ndee looked worse than Alice, though. She'd repaired her makeup, but her mass of curls was flat and sticky in the back. A clump of purple-and-white frosting showed clearly. A rip gaped at the left shoulder of her leopard-print blouse, and the spike heel of her right shoe had snapped off. That explained the limp.

Sal elbowed her in the ribs. "Well?" he prodded.

"I'm sorry, Alice."

C'ndee's voice was more like a breath than a whisper. Her dark lashes were wet against her cheeks.

For a long moment, Alice said nothing. Then, letting loose a sigh that shook her whole body, she began to cry.

C'ndee's eyes flickered up for an instant to Alice's contorted face. Looking horrified, she quickly returned her gaze to the floor.

I felt awful. The fight had been entertaining, like a white trash pileup on *Jerry Springer*. But this raw emotion wasn't funny. Marty and Mama moved quickly to comfort Alice. She waved them away.

"I'm okay," she stuttered between sobs. "It's ... it's not C'ndee's ... fault. I hit her first. I'm not crying over the fight."

At that, C'ndee lifted her face. She dug in her pocket, pulled out a pack of tissues, and peeled off a couple for Alice.

"Thanks." Alice blew her nose. "It's Ronnie ... it's everything, you know?" she looked at several of us in turn.

"We know." Mama patted her shoulder.

"Of course," another guest echoed.

"I knew he was cheating." She dabbed her eyes, took a step toward C'ndee.

"You weren't the first," the widow told the mistress. "You wouldn't have been the last."

As a dozen pairs of eyes focused on C'ndee, her face turned as pink as the spilled punch. I was surprised. I wouldn't have imagined she was capable of feeling shame.

"Ronnie told me your marriage was all but over." She raised her face to Alice's. "He said you were getting a divorce. I've been cheated on myself. I know how it feels. I didn't mean to hurt you."

Surprisingly, Alice smiled. "You mean with Ronnie, or with that hard kick you landed on my shin?"

A chorus of giggles rounded the room. Relief flashed across C'ndee's face.

"If it makes you feel any better, these were three-hundred-dollar shoes." C'ndee raised a foot to display the broken designer creation. "And I can't find the heel anywhere. I even searched Betty's front yard on hands and knees."

Alice said, "Yes, I think that does make me feel a little better." She lifted her shoe with its pink stains. "At least these were just from the markdown bin at the Sebring dollar store."

Everybody laughed, including C'ndee. Then the levity quickly left her face. "I mean it, Alice. I really am sorry. About everything."

She reached out a hand. The widow took it. They shook, and kept their fingers entwined.

"Ronnie wasn't completely lying, you know? He and I had stopped living as man and wife. I took my marriage vows seriously, but I was so angry after he strayed."

She looked out Betty's front windows to the dark street outside. I thought of that wedding picture at Alice's house, with the groom razored out.

"But now that he's gone, I realize I still loved him." She gave a sad shrug. "Too late."

Alice's words and a sense of loss hung in the air. Maddie whispered, "It's a good time to question C'ndee, Mace. Everybody's being so honest."

At my other shoulder, Marty warned, "Don't you dare! Mama can't take another title bout."

Heeding Marty's advice, I held my tongue. Maddie plowed into the silence, voice carrying like she was yelling at kids in a cafeteria food fight.

"There's something we've been wondering, C'ndee."

"What's that?"

"Have you heard you're a suspect in Ronnie's murder?"

The color drained from C'ndee's face. Alice dropped her hand like she'd been scorched. Sal, who'd been edging away during the emotional apologies, stopped dead.

"No, Maddie, I hadn't heard that." C'ndee's voice was icy. "Where'd you get your information?"

"Yeah, who told you dat?" Sal's accent got stronger under stress.

Maddie gestured vaguely. "People gossip."

I was grateful she didn't give me up. But when I looked at Sal, his penetrating gaze was burning me two new eyeholes. I immediately felt guilty.

C'ndee recovered her confidence, brushing off Maddie's question. "Gossip? That's all? That's something I'm used to."

She turned and put both her hands on Alice's shoulders. I noticed the two of them were about the same size, but C'ndee had muscles in the places where Alice had flab. She was at least fifteen years younger than the widow, and in much better shape.

"I swear to you, Alice, I had nothing to do with your husband's death."

Alice returned her gaze, seeming to seek—and find—something in C'ndee's eyes. "I know they're going to find the person who really did kill Ronnie," she finally said. "I don't believe it was you."

C'ndee exhaled. "Thank you. And if anybody tries to prove otherwise, I have access to some very sharp lawyers."

It wasn't long after the two women's heart-to-heart that Betty got up from her easy chair and announced she was tuckered out. "Anybody who wants to stay, feel free to lock up."

Seeing the hostess don her bathrobe is a sure-fire party ender.

After Mama made the three of us promise to clean up for Betty, she left with Sal. C'ndee and Alice had caused the entire ruckus, so it seemed fair that they pitch in. But, given Alice's loss, and the fact none of us were crazy about C'ndee, my sisters and I didn't press when they both wanted to leave with the rest of the guests. Henry, of course, couldn't be bothered to help with what he considered women's work.

We were standing at the sink, doing as Mama told us to do.

"Henry never did have to lift a finger!" Marty washed a plate, and then handed it to me to dry.

"Aunt Ida ruined that boy, if you ask me." Maddie took the plate from my hand and stacked it on the clean kitchen table.

"Then again, he did grow up having to eat Ida's cooking." Marty handed me another plate.

"Speaking of Ida, remember when Uncle Teddy got drunk and tossed his wife's brother into that vat of Ida's potato salad at one of Mama's receptions?" I dried, passing off to Maddie.

"How about when Ida took a barbecued rib and smacked that woman Henry was dating?" Marty giggled.

"Yep, that was Wedding No. 2. Beef rib. It was a big one." Maddie squirted more soap into the sink.

"She deserved it," I said. "Ida walked in on her in the bathroom with the groom. He claimed he drank too much. Mama should have known right then that No. 2 was a scoundrel."

We worked in silence for a while: Wash, dry, stack. Wash, dry, stack.

Finally, I said, "Speaking of scoundrels, I never got C'ndee alone to ask her about that snake, Darryl. He wasn't much of a husband to his wife, but if C'ndee was messing around with him, that means she was doing it with two married men. I'm not sure I buy her Little Miss Innocent act from today."

"You're so suspicious! If Alice can find trust in her heart for C'ndee, so should we."

"Mace has a point, Marty. Think about it: Two wives she was doing dirty," Maddie said.

Just then, the doorbell rang.

"Go awaaaaay," Betty groaned from her bedroom.

"We've got it, Betty." I hurried to answer the door.

Dab Holt waved at me through the living room window. When I opened up, she said, "Sorry, hon. I left my wrap behind."

She found it behind the dining room buffet, probably misplaced during the excitement over the fight. I'm surprised no one heard it drop. The shawl was silver, and looked like the heavy chain mail knights used to wear.

"So, you and my mama go way back?"

"Ages, hon. Your mama's a few years older than me, though."

I ducked my chin to hide my smile. I could have beat around the bush some more, made polite conversation. But it was late, and I was nosy. Besides, Dab didn't strike me as being too concerned with niceties.

"Mama said you shot a man in Reno. Is that the truth?"

"It was Carson City, hon." She adjusted the wrap around her shoulders. "And I didn't shoot him; I stabbed the son of a bitch. I'd do it again, too. I'd just make sure my aim was better."

THIRTY-FOUR

As I PASSED THE turnoff to the Pork Pit, my stomach grumbled. Talk about your conditioned response. I was as predictable as Pavlov's dogs. I made a U-turn, and circled back to the side road to the barbecue spot.

The food was tasty at Mama's bridal shower, but those few ham-and-cheese cigars hardly filled me up. After all, I had saved a drowning man and then ravished him all afternoon. How many of my fellow shower-goers had burned *those* kinds of calories before the event?

I pulled into the gravel parking lot, no doubt grinning as a few choice moments with Carlos replayed in my mind. I was probably blushing, too. Out of the corner of my eye, I saw something that immediately snapped me back to the present time and place.

"Meat is Murder!" The shout came from a large pig, enormous costume head bobbing in time to the words.

"Love Animals, Don't Eat Them!" chanted a second, smaller pig.

They looked like characters at Disney, if Disney had a farm animal theme park.

As I parked, I noticed a couple of customers hurrying past the pigs into the Pork Pit. The man held the woman close, as if one of the porcine pair might pounce.

"Murderer!" the first pig yelled at me as I got out of the Jeep. Deep voice. Masculine.

"Boycott Barbecue!" the smaller added. That voice was familiar, and it sounded like she was running out of steam.

I walked closer to the shoulder of the road where they stood, and peered at the little pig. A smooth cheek and a blond dreadlock showed through the face hole.

"Linda-Ann, is that you?"

The big head nodded. "Hey, Mace, how you doin'?"

"Well, I'm fine, but what's all this with the pig suits? How long have you been out here?"

"We're protesting," the big pig said.

"Eight hours today," Linda-Ann added. "And it's our second day. This is the boy I told you about." She pointed a plush pink arm at her companion. "Trevor, this is Mace."

"How do you do?" He extended a soft cloven hoof.

I shook it. With greater maneuverability than I'd have thought, he tightened his grip on my hand.

"Please don't go in there, Mace," he pleaded. "Have you ever seen a video of an animal slaughterhouse? We can show you things you wouldn't believe."

"Uhm, no. But thank you anyway." I tried to extricate my hand. "You know, Trevor, my sister's a vegetarian. I realize there are good arguments against eating meat. But I don't see how dressing up like Halloween and screaming at people gets your point across."

He clutched my hand more tightly. "Exactly! We have to do more to reach people, don't we Linda-Ann? We have to try harder to get our message across."

I thought I detected a lack of enthusiasm in her nod. But it was hard to tell. Maybe the giant head was just getting heavy.

"We're passing out fliers next week at the rodeo," she said.

"Didn't you used to barrel race with that Quarter horse of yours?"

"Trevor says rodeo events are cruel to the animals."

My hand was still in its plush prison. "Well, it was nice to meet you, Trevor." I pulled hard. He pulled back.

"Please, Mace." His voice rose. "You can't go in there to eat. It's immoral."

"You're entitled to your opinion. It's a free country. But we're just going to have to agree to disagree on this issue."

He finally let go, and I immediately stuck my hands in my pockets so he couldn't trap me again. Raising his arms to either side of the giant head, he lifted it off. His dark eyes burned with passion and idealism and maybe some desperation. Had I ever felt that strongly about anything?

"You should love animals, not eat them." His voice quaked with emotion. "When you do, it's like you're the animal's executioner."

Were those tears filling his eyes? It may just have been a reflection from the restaurant's neon pink Pork Pit sign.

I was about to step away, when his words triggered a memory.

"Speaking of executions, did y'all hear about the wild hog's head that was left at Alice Hodges' front door?"

Linda-Ann's head wobbled from side to side. Shock registered on Trevor's face.

"What do you mean?" he asked.

"Alice is the one whose husband got killed at the VFW this week." When Linda-Ann turned her head to explain to Trevor, her voice missed the mouth hole and came out muffled.

"Alice's murdered husband ran a barbecue business," I said. "The day he died, somebody cut off a wild pig's head, and left it on the widow's porch."

"That's so cruel!" the pig's foot flew to cover Trevor's mouth.

"Well, it was already dead," I said.

"But the disrespect that shows!"

"To Alice or the hog?" I asked him.

He considered. "Well, both."

"When you said y'all have to do more to get your message across, I was just wondering how far you'd go to do that?"

Trevor's brows knit together in confusion. For a guy in graduate school, he didn't seem that brainy. Maybe he was too tall for his available blood supply.

"Mace is accusing us of having something to do with that hog's head," Linda-Ann explained.

I put up a hand. "Not accusing. Just wondering."

Revulsion raced across Trevor's face. Then he got angry. "How could you say something like that? I'd sooner cut off my own head than hurt a pig, wild or not. I'd never, ever, *ever* hurt an animal!"

A stray drop of spittle flew my way. I stepped back. "Sorry. I didn't mean to imply anything."

A big-bellied trucker got out of his rig on the road's shoulder and headed for the Pork Pit. Without another word to me, Trevor slipped his pig head on again. "Boycott Barbecue!" he shouted at the trucker. "Meat is Murder!"

The big man didn't even break stride. He just flicked a cigarette butt at Trevor's pig head and kept walking.

"That was rude!" Linda-Ann called after him.

The cigarette bounced off the plastic head and fell to the gravel. Crushing it under my boot, I headed for the door.

Inside, almost every table was taken. The protest didn't seem to be making much of a dent in business. It wasn't until I'd gotten my take-out order of ribs, pulled pork, and all the fixin's, that I thought about what Trevor had said.

I'd never, ever, ever hurt an animal!

If they'd still been outside, I would have asked Trevor how he felt about hurting a human.

THIRTY-FIVE

MATCHED AGAINST THE SWEET, spicy smell of barbecue sauce, my willpower caved on the drive home from the Pork Pit. One hand on the wheel, I gnawed on a second take-out rib as I made the turn onto my property. Moments later, my mouth hung open, the rib swam in a pool of sauce on my lap, and I struggled to figure out how Tony Ciancio's green Lexus came to be parked under an oak tree in my front yard.

I flashed my brights. He flashed back. So at least I knew he wasn't hiding in a closet inside my house with a silencer on his gun, waiting to kill me. I really had to cut back on my diet of Mafia movies.

Tony got out of his car and raised his hand in a wave. In his aquamarine polo shirt and pressed khakis, he didn't look like a hired hitman. I parked, and he walked over to meet me.

"Hey." I opened the door to the Jeep. "How in the world did you manage to find me way out here?"

"GPS," he said. "I called your mother and she gave me your address."

Of course she did. Tony was an eligible male, Mafia ties or not.

"I'll admit I had my doubts on some of these dark, lonely roads. I didn't think the computer knew where the hell it was sending me."

He slapped at a mosquito on his neck.

"C'mon, let's get inside," I said.

"Can I carry anything?"

I handed him the take-out, making note again of his courtesy. Too bad I'd have to rudely inform him I was involved with someone else. After my afternoon interlude, I felt closer than ever to Carlos, especially with the glimpse he'd allowed me into his childhood pain. I was through playing games.

Once we were inside my cottage, I started putting out plates and silverware as he arranged the take-out on the kitchen counter. "You hungry?" I asked.

"Starving. Do you have enough?"

"Plenty." I didn't want to mention I usually buy enough for three people and manage to eat it all myself. "I love barbecue."

"Yeah, I can see that." Smiling, he pointed to the corner of his own mouth and his chin. "You've got a little evidence right there."

I studied my reflection in the glass door of the toaster oven. Tony's description had been kind. I looked like I'd had a ring-side seat at a wrestling match held in a vat of barbecue sauce. And there was that big blotch of orangey red on my lap, too.

Dabbing with a wet paper towel, I said, "Yeah, those little packets of moist napkins they give out are a joke. I need to be run through a car wash after I eat at the Pork Pit."

Tony laughed. "I don't mind seeing a woman enjoy her food. It always kills me when I take a girl on a date, she orders some expensive entrée, and then sits and picks at a salad."

"I hear ya," I said.

"That won't happen with you, right?"

He flashed that dazzling smile, and I saw Carlos' face float in front of his. The feel of Carlos' hands on my body was so recent, I think my skin still sizzled where we'd touched.

"Yeah, about that, Tony. We need to talk."

"Uh-oh. That doesn't sound good."

I dished some mac-and-cheese and coleslaw onto his plate. I held up the carton of collard greens. He sniffed, and made a face, so I finished off his portion with a serving of pork and several ribs.

"Let's eat before we talk, okay?"

"A condemned man's last meal, huh?" His smile was on its lowest setting.

I blurted out, "I'm serious about someone else."

He tilted his head. "That cop in the bar?"

I nodded.

"Well, I could see that. You barely took your eyes off him." Shrugging, he plucked a rib off his plate. "Can't blame a guy for trying."

That was it? I was relieved it wouldn't be a long, drawn-out discussion. But I was a little insulted at being dispensed with so easily. Then again, Tony probably didn't lack for female company. No doubt a honey or two waited for him back in Hackensack.

Being insulted apparently had no effect on my appetite. I slathered butter onto a piece of cornbread and reached for my third rib.

We ate in comfortable silence, punctuated only by an occasional "Pass the salt, please," or, "Can you hand me another paper towel?"

When we finished, Tony helped me tidy up, and we took our beers into the living room.

"Nice alligator." He pointed to the preserved head on my coffee table.

"My key-catcher. He's an old friend."

I figured I'd save the rest of the story for after I changed out of my work clothes. I had so many sauce spots on my shirt, I looked like I'd been performing surgery.

"Make yourself comfortable. I'll be out in a minute."

He waved an arm, already settling onto the couch. "Take your time."

In my bedroom, I traded my dirty T-shirt for a clean one, stripped off my boots and slacks, and retrieved my favorite pair of sweats from a hook on the closet door. Maddie's not the only sister with post-barbecue fat pants.

Stealing a glance in the mirror, I noted my chin was sauce-free, and my teeth harbored no stray collards. The hair was a different story; too far gone after the lake and what came after to repair without a shower and shampoo. But the sex with Carlos had been worth a few snarls.

"You know, that is one beautiful smile, Mace," Tony said as I returned to the living room. "It's a shame you're spoken for."

I'm pretty sure I blushed, either from the compliment, or from fear that Tony guessed exactly what had prompted my smile.

Just then, a Siamese rocket streaked from the bathroom to the bedroom.

"What was that?"

"Wila. My cat. Normally, she greets me at the door. But she's not used to having company."

He wrinkled his nose. "I'm not much of a cat person. I like dogs."

"Yeah, I'm with you on that. But Wila is pretty cool. She's super smart. And once she gets to know you, she'll stand up on her hind legs and wait to be petted just like a dog."

He looked skeptical.

"No, really. I inherited her, kind of against my will. But she's grown on me."

As if the cat could sense we were talking about her, she let out a loud meow from her hiding place under my bed.

"That's right, Wila," I called. "You're Mama's good little gal."

Now I'd revealed myself as one of those women who pad around the house in sweatpants and talk to their cats. It was a good thing I *wasn't* interested in Tony.

When I sat in the chair across from the couch, he leaned over and clinked his beer bottle against mine. "This is nice, Mace. I don't have too many women I can relax with and just be friends."

"To friendship." We toasted again. "And, speaking as a friend..."

"Uh-oh." His eyes became wary. "The interrogation."

"We never got the chance to finish that conversation we started by the animal pens. Then you disappeared so quickly after the nature walk. You seemed nervous around that blonde with the motorcycle helmet."

His eyes flicked upward for just a moment. Was it a sign he was thinking up a story? Or, was he trying to remember the blonde? She seemed pretty hard to forget.

"Everybody seemed nervous around her." Tony took a swallow from his beer. "She was strange."

I'd give him that.

Still …

"Yeah, she was. But you seemed more nervous than the others. It was almost like you knew her."

"Nope." He shook his head. "But I pegged her. Did you ever see the old film *Fatal Attraction*?"

I nodded.

"That woman at the nature park had bunny-boiling stalker written all over her."

She didn't strike me that way, but I decided to defer to Tony's experience as a ladies' man.

We sipped for a while in silence. Finally, I broached the topic of his background.

"About your family …"

"Here it comes."

"Sorry, but people in Himmarshee have some pretty wild imaginations." I wasn't going to get into *which* people. "Those criminal cases involving your family and the restaurants up north definitely have people talking."

"And what are *people* saying?" His voice was level, but his jaw was tight.

"Do you really want to know?"

He nodded.

"Well, that Ronnie was in the catering business and that all of a sudden your aunt shows up, and then you do, with plans to go into the catering business."

"Event planning."

"Which includes catering," I said. "Which makes Ronnie a rival. And then Ronnie 'The Rival' very quickly ends up dead."

All of a sudden, I retrieved a fact that had been floating around in my brain since I trapped that snake for the newcomer. "Not only that, but somebody saw your green Lexus in town the day before you said you arrived. The day Ronnie was murdered."

He let out a long breath. "Wow. You don't pull any punches with your friends, do you?"

I shook my head.

"First of all, who said they saw me? Because I wasn't here until that morning I met you at the diner. And second, I guess I'd rather hear about this crap from you than from that cop, Martinez."

"So?" I said.

"So, what?"

"Did you have anything to do with Ronnie's murder?"

"Jesus, Mace!" The words exploded from his mouth. "You invited me into your house. Your life. We ate; we drank. Are you really telling me you think I'm capable of killing that man?"

I shrugged. His face settled into resignation; more sad than angry.

"It's typical. You know a little bit about my family, and you think the worst of me. Most of the stuff the feds and the newspapers say isn't true, by the way."

"I'm sorry, Tony. I'm just telling you what people are saying."

He twisted the bottle in his hand, staring at the beer as it sloshed against the sides. "I've been to the best schools. I've studied, and worked, and tried as hard as I could not to become my father." His voice was a whisper. "And yet, whenever anyone looks at me, The Family is all they see. I'll never be able to get out from under that."

"Tony, I …"

The ring of the telephone interrupted me. I'd finally broken down and ordered caller ID for moments just like this. I glanced at the readout.

"Sorry, I have to take this."

Head lowered into one hand, he waved me away with the other.

"Hey, Carlos."

I walked with the phone the few steps to my bedroom, closing the door. Privacy would still be minimal. The walls of my little cottage were solid cypress. But the interior doors were cheap, made of hollow wood.

"Hey, yourself." His voice was warm, caressing. Then he switched to his business tone. "I've got some information I'd rather you hear from me than the Himmarshee Hotline."

"Is everything okay?" My heart began to race. "Nothing's happened to Mama or my sisters, has it?"

"No, no," he quickly reassured me. "It's about C'ndee Ciancio."

I instinctively turned my back to the bedroom door. Either I was shielding Tony from bad news, or trying to prevent him from eavesdropping. I wasn't sure.

"I've got her down here at the police department."

"Is she under arrest?"

"No. I just told her we're going to have a little chat, like you say in these parts."

"And she didn't ask for a lawyer?"

"She says she has nothing to hide."

She was either telling the truth, or it was the bravado of a big-city girl in what she thought was a hick town police station. It wouldn't be smart of C'ndee to underestimate Carlos.

"Well, thanks for telling me," I said.

"I need your help to spin this, Mace. Word is naturally going to spread..."

"I'm not a gossip."

"We've been through that before. Let's just say word will spread. I want you to play it just like I've told you: 'C'ndee's in for a little chat. She may be of help to the investigation.' Can you do that for me?"

"Sure."

His voice changed back to a lover's tone. "What are you doing right now?"

I immediately felt a rush of guilt, and tried to make my voice sound normal. Carlos had a lie detector hard-wired into his brain. "Nothing much. Finishing up dinner."

"Well, I'm thinking of you."

"Right back at ya." I imagined Tony listening in. "I know you're busy; I'll let you get back to work."

We said our goodbyes and rang off, and I returned to the living room. Tony sat upright, the defeated posture was gone.

"What was that all about?"

I hesitated for a moment. He'd find out one way or another. "Your aunt," I said. "She's down at the police department."

I repeated what Carlos had told me to say, but Tony seemed to barely hear me. He'd already yanked his cell phone out of his pocket and started punching in numbers. The look on his face was frightening in its intensity.

"Yeah, Arthur. It's me. We've got a little trouble in Himmarshee," he said into the phone. "Who do you know in Florida who can get here quick?"

His speech was rapid-fire, the cultured cadence slipping into New Jerseyese.

"Goddammit, Arthur! That is not what I want to hear. What do you think I pay you for?"

He stood up and walked to my front door. "That's unacceptable, Arthur. We're talking about my family."

He turned his back and walked outside. But not before I'd seen the hard set to his jaw and the ice in his eyes. I felt like I was watching *The Godfather*, at the moment when a young Michael Corleone makes his transition from nice college boy to cold-blooded killer.

THIRTY-SIX

"Mama's social merry-go-round is making me motion sick."

That was the closest Marty would come to a complaint. But as we gathered at the Speckled Perch to decorate for Mama's party, Maddie ranted enough for the three of us.

"The whole thing is unseemly," she huffed. "Drinking in the middle of the day. A bachelorette party, at her age! And this *is* marriage No. 5. Mama's no blushing virgin."

"Maddie!" Marty looked around to see who might have overheard, but the place was dark, quiet, and empty.

We'd arrived early as the appointed decorating committee. The Perch was normally a dinner and night spot, but the owner agreed to open for the lunch gathering as a favor to Mama. The party would begin at noon.

The manager, dark smudges under his eyes, clip-on tie askew, looked like he climbed off a cot in the back to come let us in. He'd disappeared after unlocking the door, but not before I noticed specks of toilet paper on the spots where he'd cut himself shaving. We waited in the dimly lit dining room, but he hadn't returned.

"I don't think that manager's a morning person," I said. "I'm going to find him, and see if I can get him to at least turn on some more lights."

Rising from the table in the dark, I promptly banged my shin on a chair. Just as I let out a curse word, the lights in our half of the dining room came on.

"Timing is everything, Mace," Maddie said.

We quickly got to work, hanging green garland with white paper roses, and a big sign that said *Best Wishes!* The latter was a bit bedraggled, since Maddie had kept it in her garage since Mama's last wedding, four years ago. As we strung and taped and hung, we dissected the latest news about C'ndee.

"Carlos might have had her come down there, but she didn't stay overnight," Marty said.

"Who told you that?" I was a little miffed she had a better pipeline than I did.

"I stopped at Gladys' for coffee, saw Donnie Bailey from the jail," Marty said. "He said Carlos never arrested C'ndee."

Finger poised at my button, Maddie went ahead and pushed. "Looks like that beau of yours is keeping secrets, Mace."

"It's a murder investigation, Maddie. Not pillow talk." I ratcheted back my snippy tone. "Besides, Carlos already told me she came in voluntarily. He asked her in for a chat."

Maddie pursed her lips. "And she ran right in, with no lawyer? That's weird, considering her family's connections."

"*If* you can believe what you read in the papers," Marty said.

I handed her the roll of tape. "Reporters can't just make things up, Marty."

Maddie stood back to scrutinize our handiwork. She unfastened Marty's garland and re-taped it, more to her liking. Marty and I sniggered behind her back.

I thought about filling them in on Tony's reaction. But I didn't want to suffer Maddie's lecture on how he came to be at my house last night when Carlos called with the news.

"Do you think C'ndee will show up to the party?" Marty replaced a bit of the drape Maddie had straightened.

"Of course," Maddie said. "That woman has more brass than a lamp factory."

The restaurant door swung open, sending in a shaft of sunlight and the chatter of women.

"Looks like the guests are starting to arrive. I'm going to duck into the Ladies before the party gets going," I said.

I was inside a stall when I saw two sets of legs make their way to the bathroom mirror.

"I hope they serve those little fried mushrooms from the menu here. They're yummy," the first woman said.

"So is the bartender." I recognized the sex and smokes sound of that second voice.

The first woman tittered. "It sure was nice of them to open up just for Rosalee's party. I heard the owner is a former boyfriend of hers."

"Frankly, who isn't?" Dab Holt asked. "The woman has more exes than KFC has wings."

I bit my lip to keep from laughing. I hid in the stall until I heard them leave, and then rushed back to the table and shared the joke with my sisters.

"At least Mama's never taken a knife to any of her exes," Maddie said.

"Dab told me yesterday the wound wasn't fatal," I said. "She said she did some time, but her conviction got overturned on appeal. Her attorney claimed she was a battered woman."

"Humph," Maddie said. "I can't imagine anyone pushing that gal around."

Marty said, "That's not fair, Maddie. You never know what goes on behind closed doors."

We were gabbing about whose checkered romantic past was worse, Mama's or Dab's, when Mama breezed in, Alice on her heels. Alice turned right, and Mama joined us.

"Well, I'm glad to see you three looking so cheerful. I thought you'd be crabby about having to come to another one of my many, many affairs."

We burst out laughing. Mama raised an eyebrow, leaned toward us, and sniffed. "You girls haven't been getting into the liquor already, have you?"

"No, ma'am," we answered as one.

———

By half past twelve, the party was in full swing. True to his word, Mama's ex had arranged for a fried-food extravaganza. There were mushrooms, onion rings, and jalapeno poppers. Another platter held catfish, shrimp, and hush puppies. Celery was the only green thing not battered and fried on the table, and it was drenched in blue cheese dressing to go with the hot wings.

My stomach would be tied in knots right through the wedding.

All of a sudden, light slanted in from the open door and a hush fell over the crowd. Alan Jackson sang "Who's Cheating Who?" on the jukebox. C'ndee stood for a moment in the sunbeam as if basking under a stage light.

When she made a beeline toward the bathroom, my sisters and I rose from the table and followed. We crowded in behind her as she primped at the mirror, outlining that full mouth in fire-engine red.

"Ladies," she said, with a pop of her lips.

"C'ndee," we chorused. And then Marty retreated to the wall as Maddie and I stepped all over each other to ask our questions.

"What did Carlos question you about?" I began

Maddie elbowed me aside. "Are you going to jail?"

I nudged her back and stepped to the mirror. "Where'd you disappear to?"

Maddie yanked the collar of my shirt and cut in front. "Is your nephew in the Mafia?"

C'ndee backed against the sink, holding up her hands. "Marty, call your sisters off, would'ya? For Gawd's sake, I thought you Southerners were supposed to be so polite!"

Maddie crossed her arms and glared. I mumbled an apology. "We just have so many things we want to ask you."

"I'll take Maddie's last question first." C'ndee held up a finger. "No, Tony is not in the Mafia. And, as a proud Italian-American, I resent your assumption that he is."

"We read about the family's criminal enterprise up north," I said.

She recovered quickly. "Sins of the fathers, ladies. You can't blame Tony for his dad's business dealings. Not that I'm saying any of that crap in the papers is true."

I started to interrupt, but she held up a hand. "I believe I have the floor, Mace. Secondly, I'm not going to jail. Tony was about to call in the legal pit bulls when I phoned him last night to tell him I wasn't being held, or even formally questioned. That cop, Carlos, was nothing but nice."

"Really?" I couldn't help myself.

She nodded. "He was much more interested in Darryl than in me. Now ladies, I don't believe in regrets when it comes to men. But if I did, I'd regret my ... uh, dalliance ... with Darryl. That is one nasty *cafone*."

"Amen." I wasn't sure what a *cafone* was, but I figured it wasn't good. "Does Carlos think Darryl killed Ronnie?"

She shrugged. "Hard to tell." She opened the lipstick again and re-applied.

"As for where I went ..." She blotted her mouth. "I just needed time alone to think. I really did care for Ronnie. More than you might imagine. We planned to go into business, but it was more than that. I thought we'd settle down, maybe even marry, after he and Alice were divorced."

C'ndee's voice shook a bit. I looked at Maddie, whose arms were still tightly folded. Marty's face, though, mirrored the sad expression on C'ndee's. I came down in the middle: not as skeptical as Maddie; not as trusting as Marty.

C'ndee dropped her lipstick into her big purse and snapped the top with finality.

"Now, I'd like to get a drink and offer your mother my best wishes." She glanced at her rhinestone-clotted watch. "I have a little surprise for her, too. Should arrive at any minute."

She pushed through the door and we followed, three little ducklings brought into line.

Spotting Linda-Ann loading up on fried fish, shrimp, and wings at the buffet, I detoured in her direction. My sisters flanked me. After we said our hellos, I pointed to her plate.

"Guess you're not a strict vegetarian."

"Don't tell Trevor." She popped a shrimp into her mouth, not looking terribly guilty.

"Linda-Ann, didn't you hear anything I said about being true to yourself?"

Marty chimed in. "Mace gave you good advice, honey. You should do things because you believe in them, not because somebody else forces you."

"Trevor never forced me."

On the jukebox, Charlie Daniels launched into the loud fiddle solo on "Devil Went Down to Georgia." Maddie leaned right into Linda-Ann's face. "You're telling us you dressed as a pig and scared those poor folks at the Pork Pit because you wanted to? Linda-Ann, I know you were never a top student, but you couldn't be that dumb."

I pinched Maddie's left arm. Marty tugged on her right to drag her from Linda-Ann's personal space.

"Let's find a table," my little sister said.

The lights were only on in half the dining room; the rest of the room was closed. The only empty seats were at Alice Hodges' table. I led the way across the dance floor.

"Okay if we sit down?" I asked.

Alice nodded without looking at us.

"Are you getting enough to eat?" Marty said. "Can we get you anything?"

The food on her plate looked untouched. A glass of wine, on the other hand, was nearly gone. A second, full glass, awaited.

Alice glanced up. "I'm fine." Her gaze rested on Linda-Ann. To the younger woman's credit, she held out her hand.

"I'm Linda-Ann, Mrs. Hodges. I'm real sorry for your loss. I knew Ronnie from when he worked at the feed store. He used to add in a little something extra once in a while for my horse, Lucky. He sure was a nice man."

Tears sprang to Marty's eyes. But Alice kept her composure. "Thank you, dear. That's kind of you to tell me that."

We took our seats. An awkward moment passed, when none of us seemed to know what to say. But Maddie has never seen a silence she can't fill.

"We were just talking to Linda-Ann about how she and her boyfriend dressed up like pigs for a protest."

Alice raised an eyebrow.

"Trevor says we should love animals, not eat them," Linda-Ann recited. "Trevor says meat is murder."

She clapped a hand over her mouth. "Sorry, Mrs. Hodges."

Alice gave her a weak smile.

"Her boyfriend's beliefs are very passionate," I explained.

"I'm a vegetarian now, just like Trevor." Linda-Ann seemed to remember the animal parts crowding her plate. "Well, not a hundred percent."

Maddie harrumphed. "Trevor sounds like a fanatic, Linda-Ann. How much do you really know about him?"

In her kindest tone, Marty said, "Honey, I'm a vegetarian, too. But it should be enough to do what *you* think is right. You don't have to bully everybody else into doing the same."

Linda-Ann tossed another shrimp in her mouth, chewed and swallowed thoughtfully.

"We never do what I want to do. It's always protest, protest, protest. To tell the truth, I do feel kind of stupid yelling at people in that pig suit. And the plastic head smells nasty inside."

She made such a face, my sisters and I laughed. Even Alice smiled. "I can't imagine dressing up in that costume," she said. "I grew up on a hog farm. I've seen pigs enough to last a lifetime."

Just as Garth Brooks started up on the jukebox with "Friends in Low Places," the door flung open. It let in a shaft of light, along with the best-looking cowboy I'd ever seen. Black hat, fitted snap-button shirt with most of the snaps unfastened, and leather chaps that showed off exactly what he was packing in those skin-tight Wranglers.

"Here's our entertainment, girls." C'ndee's shout was part side-show barker, part Jersey turnpike toll-taker. "Now, get those dollar bills ready and crank up the sexy!"

THIRTY-SEVEN

A FUNERAL HOME HUSH fell over the Speckled Perch. Disapproval radiated off most of Mama's guests. The mouths of the rest of them hung open in shock. On the jukebox, Garth Brooks wound up, leaving the place in complete silence. The sexy cowboy pushed his hat back on his head and frowned.

"This is the place, isn't it?" he asked C'ndee.

"Surprise, Rosalee!" Aiming for gaiety, C'ndee struck a desperate note instead. "This gorgeous hunk is named Houston."

Linda-Ann breathed, "Ohmigod! He used to date a girl I went to high school with. He is *so* hot."

Whispers spread through the room like ripples in a pond. Panic flickered in Mama's eyes, but she hadn't lived through three rotten marriages in the gossip capital of Florida for nothing. She clapped her hands together and plastered on a smile. "C'mon, gals. Houston is here all the way from Texas."

"He's from Apopka, Florida," Linda-Ann said in my ear.

"Let's show him a warm Himmarshee welcome," Mama chirped.

"I wouldn't mind giving him a warm something," Linda-Ann whispered.

My sisters and I were probably the only ones to detect the pleading in Mama's voice. Houston leaned down and hit the play button on his boom box. "Boot Scootin' Boogie" issued forth.

"We'll start out with something safe. Who wants a line dance lesson? Don't worry, ladies. I don't bite."

"I'm in!" Linda-Ann leaped from her chair, hand raised high.

"Me, too!" That voice belonged to Dab. She'd piled her hair into a pouf on top, like a scarlet-colored feather duster. Her painted-on eyebrows were black question marks. Gold lamé hot pants shimmered as she strutted onto the dance floor, fairly drooling at the sight of Houston.

Poor guy. His bite wasn't the one he should be worried about. True to his word, Houston kept things G-rated as the women got warmed up, drinking cheap pink wine and dancing the Electric Slide.

But before long, whoops and hollers and bumps and grinds came from the dance floor. As the levity—or maybe the lewdness—intensified, Alice quietly made for the door, leaving by herself. Meanwhile, C'ndee basked in the glow of bringing the perfect gift to the party. I sat on the sidelines, nursing a beer.

"Mace, do you have any singles?"

I nearly toppled off my chair. Maddie's face was flushed; her hair in sweaty wisps.

"Well, we have to support Mama, don't we?" she asked.

Oh, what an opportunity to rag on my normally prudish older sister. But in a show of solidarity, I rummaged through my purse, found six singles, and divided them evenly among Maddie, Marty, and me. As we elbowed our way through the crowd on the dance floor, we saw Houston sitting shirtless on a chair. Mama perched on his lap, wearing his cowboy hat at a rakish angle.

"You go, Rosalee!" someone yelled.

"A dollar for a kiss!" came another voice.

"A kiss?" Dab shouted. "Hell, I'll give ten dollars, but I expect a lot more than a kiss!"

Mama slipped a bill into the waistband of Houston's tight jeans. He'd just leaned in for a smooch when the hollering and whistling suddenly died. A shaft of daylight shone weakly onto the dance floor. The now silent crowd began moving and jostling, this way and that. Oblivious, Mama and Houston locked lips. When they finished, he gave her bottom a little pat.

"Rosalee!" The roar was like a taunted bear at the Bronx Zoo. "I saw that!"

Mama leaped off Houston's lap so fast, the force sent him and his chair over backwards. He unconsciously brushed his jeans, like he was wiping dust after getting thrown in the rodeo ring.

Sal raised his fists. "You better get up, Cowboy, so I can knock you down again." Mama's face was redder than Dab's duster 'do. She rushed to her groom's side. But Sal kept stomping toward Houston, as if Mama wasn't hanging from his arm like a suitcase. Houston got up. He hung his shirt from an elbow, hefted his boom box onto his shoulder, and then headed for the door.

"It's been fun, ladies, but a fight's not part of the show," he said over his shoulder.

"Don't turn your back when I'm talking to you."

Sal's voice was chilling. Mama let loose his arm and retreated into the safety of the crowd. Houston stopped, put the boom box on a table, and spun slowly toward Sal. His hands flexed into fists. I could almost see the testosterone coursing through his veins.

Linda-Ann breathed in my ear: "Your mama's beau better watch out. Word is Houston is a bastard in a bar fight."

I sized up the fighters. Weighing in at well over three hundred pounds and standing six foot four, Sal wore his customary golf duds. Today's knickers were peach-and-aqua plaid, with a pom-pom beret in matching fabric. I had to wonder where he found peach knee socks to go with the golf shirt.

Houston squinted at Sal like a gunfighter in an old Western. Was it for effect, or had the haze of smoke from the kitchen fryers finally gotten to his eyes? He was a half-foot shorter and at least a hundred pounds lighter than Sal. But there were muscles on top of his muscles in his arms and broad shoulders. And, from all those years of hanging on to bucking broncos, he could squeeze Sal's neck like a toothpaste tube if he ever got him in a leg hold.

I was still calculating odds when Sal pounced like a panther, fat but still fast. Before the cowboy knew what hit him, Sal had lifted him off the floor. Then he spun him around like a TV wrestler, and sent him flying into the food table. When Houston rolled off, weaving, hot sauce from the platter of wings coated his bare back like bright orange suntan oil. An onion ring hung from one ear.

He'd just lunged at Sal when the manager, fully awake now, stepped in between the two men with a raised baseball bat.

"You gentlemen are gonna have to take this outside or we call the cops. Ladies, if either of them makes a move toward the other, dial 911."

Suddenly transformed from a hormone-addled audience to a crowd of upstanding citizens, a half-dozen women scrambled through purses and pockets for cell phones. Collecting his hat, the boom box, and some bills scattered on the floor and buffet, Houston made for the door. As light slanted in, and then disappeared with the closing door, Mama rushed to the victor's side.

"Are you hurt, Sally? Is anything broken?"

"You mean besides my heart? I can't believe you'd kiss another man like that, Rosie. We're supposed to walk down the aisle tomorrow."

Mama traced a pine knot on the dance floor with the toe of her boysenberry pump. To my surprise, Maddie stepped forward. "It was all in fun, Sal. We just got a little carried away. Mama only went along because C'ndee arranged for Houston to come perform. She didn't want to hurt your cousin's feelings."

C'ndee piped up, "That's right, Sal. I thought I'd ruined the party until Rosalee got everyone involved. It was innocent fun."

He looked at me. I unrolled the two dollars I'd been clutching in my hand and showed him the crumpled bills. Maddie and Marty did the same. Hitching up his pants, he blew out a mouthful of air.

"Well, I didn't see nobody else kissing the guy. And I didn't see his paw on nobody else's butt."

"Mama's the bride, Sal. She had to go first," Marty said. "We do this at bachelorette parties all the time. It's traditional."

Maybe in New Jersey, I thought.

Marty was lying like a car salesman with a quota. But she sounded so sincere, and those blue eyes looked so innocent, that Sal bought it. When his shoulders rose in a *What-are-ya-gonna-do?* shrug, I heard Mama's relieved sigh all the way across the dance floor.

Since the stripper was gone and the food table was trashed, the party started breaking up. Linda-Ann caught me by the door of the bathroom. "Can I ask you something, Mace?"

I glanced at my watch. One forty-five. I'd promised Rhonda I'd be back to work by two o'clock.

"Sure." I stepped into the bar, where it was dark and quiet. Linda-Ann followed me.

"I was just wondering if you know what time Ronnie got killed on Monday?"

"Not exactly. In the morning, though, sometime before nine o'clock. We were supposed to meet him at the VFW. I went to look for him when he didn't show up."

Linda-Ann tugged at one of her dreadlocks. "I heard you found the body. That must have been weird."

I nodded, not wanting to relive the experience. "Why'd you want to know about the time?"

Her eyes darted around the bar, like she was afraid someone might be lurking in one of the booths. Finally, her gaze settled on a spot on the wall, somewhere north of my right ear. "No reason, really. I was just curious."

"C'mon, Linda-Ann."

She studied the end of her dreadlock. Finally, she raised her eyes to mine. "It's about Trevor."

I waited.

"He's been staying with me, and normally he sleeps really late because he's up half the night researching animal rights stuff on the Internet."

"Um-hmm," I said.

"It's just that he wasn't in bed when I woke up for my shift on Monday."

She had my attention.

"I even went out to the porch to look for him. I thought he might have fallen asleep on the couch, where he has his computer set up. But the computer wasn't on. And when I looked out the window, Trevor's car was gone."

THIRTY-EIGHT

RHONDA CLAMPED A MANICURED hand over her mouth. "No way, Mace!"

I raised my right hand, courtroom style. "Sal helicoptered the half-naked cowboy right into a platter of hot wings. If I'm lyin' I'm dyin', Boss."

"What is it with your family's parties and food fights? Don't y'all know you're supposed to eat food, not roll around the floor in it?"

I shrugged. "Don't blame me. I've always believed I was switched at birth from a much classier family."

The phone rang on Rhonda's desk. She answered, and raised a pink-nailed index finger for me to wait. But the conversation started veering into budgets and volunteer hours and I knew she'd be a while. I curled my hands into paws and put them up next to my face—our shorthand symbol for critters. Rhonda motioned me toward the door, and I went to check on the animals.

The park was deserted, just as I liked it. On a weekday, parents were at work and their kids were in school. By June, most of the tourists and snowbirds had fled back north for the summer. First stop: Ollie's pond. The gator lolled on the sandy bank with a cattle egret perched on his back.

"Hey, bird," I called. "You feeling lucky today?"

Neither member of the unlikely duo paid me any mind.

I continued across the open area between the pond and the animal pens. My eye caught a flurry of movement to the right. A red-tailed hawk flew from a high pine, intent on making something small and furry into supper. I scanned the field, seeing if I could spot what the hawk saw. And there it was: a flash of dark brown against the parched, dun-colored grass. At this distance, I couldn't tell if it was a mouse or a young rabbit. It made no difference to the hawk, who dove just at the edge of the woods.

Had his prey made it safely into the cover of brush?

In another moment, I had my answer. The bird lifted, and soared overhead, a mouse writhing in its grasp. That was nature—prey or predator. At least the hawk only killed for food. I couldn't say the same about man. Or woman, for that matter.

Heading for the woods, I started to think about the list of people who might have had reason to kill Ronnie. But no matter where else I looked, I kept returning to the Ciancios, and the family's ruthlessness with business rivals. I remembered how Tony's charm disappeared when he was on the phone, how those smooth edges sharpened before my eyes.

Prey or predator?

I entered the deep shade, under a thick canopy of oak and hickory and Southern maple. A cardinal flitted among the green, calling out a sharp *Chip. Chip*. I followed its progress to the ground, where it hopped about in search of berries or bugs. Looking down, I saw the nature path was getting bare in spots. I'd have to make a few calls when I returned to the office, see if I could find some free mulch to spread.

As I studied the patchy spots, I noticed something out of the ordinary at the edge of the path. It looked like fabric of some sort, maybe a discarded towel or a large rag. I got closer, and lifted it with my boot. First a sleeve, and then a pant leg dropped out of the bundle. It was a workman's jumpsuit, colored beige. Stooping for a closer look, I turned the garment over and opened it to the front. Rusty, brownish stains stiffened the cloth. Dried blood covered the coveralls.

———

"What did you do then, Mace?"

Marty's eyes were wide. We'd met at Mama's after work. For a change, I had everybody's undivided attention.

"I dropped them where I found them, backed out the way I'd come, and called Carlos. When I left the park, the police were still combing the woods."

"Do you think they found the knife?" Maddie's ice cream had melted, forgotten in a bowl on Mama's kitchen table. "Was there any identification with the clothes?"

"I didn't hear anyone mention anything about a knife before I left. I didn't see any ID. And the coveralls looked pretty standard. Could be they aren't even connected to Ronnie's murder."

Mama sipped a cup of strong coffee, antidote to the sweet pink wine she'd overdone at her bachelorette party. "Why else would someone have left them where you'd find them? It must be a message, Mace. Isn't that right, Sal?"

He nodded, mouth full of a fried baloney sandwich Mama had made him. They were cooing like courting doves again. Mama had managed to convince Sal he was sexier than any dancing cowboy. And Sal had shown her how much he cared by starting a brawl in a bar over her honor. He was beginning to fit in after all in Himmarshee.

"Who do you think left them?" Marty asked.

"The million-dollar question," Maddie said.

"I saw the label before I dropped them. It said Work Tough. And they were a size Large, which doesn't narrow it down much. Almost anybody could fit into a man's large, except maybe Mama and Marty, and you, Sal."

Mama got up for more coffee. "Anyone else want a cup?"

She held up the pot. Sal, starting in now on a slice of butterscotch pie with whipped cream, raised his hand. It had been a while since Sal wore any size without a couple of XXs.

"Think about it," I said. "Darryl's tall. So is Tony."

Sal wiped his mouth with a napkin. "I don't trust that guy. The only reason he hasn't been arrested yet is that he's smarter than his father. I wish C'ndee had never married into that family."

"Speaking of C'ndee," Maddie said, "there's a woman with some meat on her bones. She'd wear a man's large, for sure."

"You girls have the wrong idea about C'ndee. You'll see," Sal said.

At that moment, an image of Ms. Sunglasses popped into my mind. She was also a big gal, and looked as strong as many men. But what was her connection to Ronnie, or to anyone else in Himmarshee? I wanted Sal to give me the scoop on Sunglasses, but I wasn't about to bring her up in front of Mama.

For the time being, at least, she'd have to remain a mystery.

I said, "Don't forget Trevor. He's scrawny, but he's an inch or two over six feet." I brought them up-to-date on Linda-Ann's revelation that he'd been MIA on Monday. "True believers can always find a way to justify violence."

Marty tucked her hair behind her ears. "I don't think it was him, Mace. Maybe he carries the animal rights issue too far, but to commit murder?"

Sal snorted. "Some of those nuts have bombed the homes of medical researchers who use animals. Murder's only a step away."

We were silent for a moment. Maddie lifted the spoon from her ice cream, and watched the soupy liquid dribble into the bowl. "How come nobody's mentioned Alice?" she asked. "She's certainly big enough, both for the coveralls, and to have gone up against her late husband."

Marty said, "I *was* surprised by that flash of rage when she went after C'ndee at Mama's shower."

Mama added more sugar to her coffee. "I don't buy it. The poor woman is simply under a lot of stress. I've known Ronnie and Alice for ten years. Well, just Alice now. She's in the choir at Abundant Forgiveness."

Sal dug at an errant piece of pie crust with a toothpick. "Even churchgoers and do-gooders go bad, Rosie. Alice wouldn't be the first woman, or the last, to carve up a cheating husband with a knife."

———

The honeyed scent of Confederate jasmine wafted from a planter on my porch, a gift from Marty. So far, I hadn't managed to kill it. Wila hadn't knocked it out of its pot. And some rare bug that only eats jasmine in June hadn't devoured it. I breathed deeply, enjoying the aroma and the delusion that I was a gardener.

The drive home from Mama's had passed by rote, I'd been so preoccupied. Now, all I wanted was a beer and my bed. A cousin coming in for the wedding was supposed to bunk with me. But she was delayed, and I was relieved. I did not want to play hostess tonight.

Unlocking the front door, I stepped inside, grateful for the peace and quiet. It took only a moment to register the fact that the house was too quiet. Where was the cat? Where was that reproaching meow as she demanded to be fed?

"Wila?"

A second or two of silence followed my call. And then I heard the distinct sound of someone breathing.

I didn't switch on the light. I knew my cottage better than anyone. The darkness might give me an advantage. I felt for Maw-Maw's heavy cane, and then pulled it from the stand at the front door.

A match scratched and lit. The flame revealed the face of "Jane Smith," cigarette in her mouth, sitting comfortably in my grand-dad's old chair. Before she exhaled to blow out the match, I saw a teardrop tattoo high on her cheek, where her sunglasses normally sat.

"You won't need a weapon, Mace." The voice was flat and emotionless. No accent. "The two of us are just going to have a little talk."

I tightened my grip on the cane. "How'd you get in here?"

She turned on a lamp on the table beside Paw-Paw's chair; held up my key. "You had this hidden on top of the door jamb. Very original."

I'd left it there for my absent cousin. Stupid.

I stared at the teardrop, trying to remember its significance. Something about prison. Oh, yeah. Convicts add a tattooed drop for each murder they've committed. My mouth went dry.

"What do you want?"

"Like I said…" she took a drag from her cigarette, blew the smoke my way, "… a little talk."

The menace in her voice sent my heart charging into my throat, where it pinned my tongue to the mat. I stood rooted, trying to weigh my options. I could run, but I feared turning my back on her. I could make a move for Paw-Paw's shotgun in the bedroom closet, but I'd have to get past her to do it. I could jump her, and hope that black motorcycle helmet at her feet wasn't as lethal as it looked.

She stared at me, as if she were reading my thoughts. Her eyes were bottomless, as dark and unfeeling as the black leather she wore. Her hand moved across her chest and toward the inside of her jacket. Certain it would emerge gripping a gun, I closed my eyes and began to pray.

THIRTY-NINE

I HEARD THE HUM of my refrigerator. A short mew from Wila in the bedroom. And the even breathing of Ms. Sunglasses.

What I didn't hear was the crack of a gunshot. Slowly, I opened my eyes. "Jane Smith" assessed me from across the room. An amused smile curved up one corner of her mouth.

"Are you going to whack me?" I asked her.

Her laughter softened the hard planes of her face. Holding up a hand with a pack of matches in the palm, she made a show of slipping them back into her inside jacket pocket.

"What makes you think I'd whack you?"

I spun a convoluted story about how we'd had some strangers and a series of unusual crimes in our little town over the last couple of years, and how everyone was waiting for the next awful thing to occur. Finally, I told her she reminded me of Angelina Jolie in *Mr. and Mrs. Smith.*

"Angelina played an assassin," I said.

"Thanks for the compliment."

Her finger traced her teardrop tattoo. My heart made a reappearance in my throat. When she rose from the chair, I backed up against my front door. But all she did was pick up a book from my coffee table and open it to the first chapter. It was Patrick Smith's *A Land Remembered*.

"Any good?"

"Yeah. It's all about Florida history."

Tucking the book under her arm, she made a circle around my living room. She leaned close to the wall to look at a picture of my sisters and me with Mama, when we rode the Florida Cracker Trail. She paused at another photo, this one of my grandparents squinting in the sun in an orange grove. Putting the book down, she pulled out the top drawer on my TV cabinet. She lifted and inspected a couple of DVDs, and then a spare remote, and then a lopsided vase Maddie did in ceramics class. The vase only comes out when I know my big sister is going to visit.

When Ms. Sunglasses stooped to slide out a box of CDs from under my stereo, annoyance outweighed my fear. "Can I help you with something?"

"I wouldn't turn down one of those Heinekens you have in your refrigerator. I think we both could use a beer."

"You snooped around in my kitchen?"

She shrugged.

Would this turn out like that scene in every crime movie, where the killer allows the victim a final drink before blowing him or her away? I went after the beers anyway because she was right. I *could* use a little something to take off the edge.

As I grabbed the bottles and a couple of napkins, I kept my ears fine-tuned. Would I hear her unholster a gun? Take off her jacket so she could move more freely with that garrote she surely had to strangle me? Walk into my bedroom and leave a bomb under the bed?

But the only sound from the living room was her humming the Britney Spears oldie, "Oops! ... I Did it Again."

Britney Spears? What kind of self-respecting hit woman would hum Britney Spears? I relaxed a little.

"Here you go, *Jane*," I said, returning to hand her a beer.

"Thanks." She clinked her bottle against mine, and then returned to studying the gator head on my coffee table. "How big was this thing anyway?"

"Ten feet."

I told her the *Reader's Digest* version of my sideline, and how my trapper cousin and I captured the alligator from a newcomer's pool.

She stuck a hand in the gator's mouth, felt the multitude of teeth. "Weren't you scared?"

I shook my head, deciding not to reveal she scared me a lot more than any alligator. With a gator, at least I knew what to expect.

She shuddered, gave me a nervous smile. "All those sharp teeth? I'd have been terrified."

Now she sounded more like a girlfriend at a pajama party than a hired killer. What was this woman's game?

When I said nothing, she swigged the beer, straightened in the chair, and got to the point of her visit. "How well do you know Anthony Ciancio?"

The flatness was back in her voice. It was hard to tell where she was headed. Was she a jealous girlfriend? Was she sent by a rival family to murder the Ciancio heir? Was she herself the rival?

"Why?" I hedged.

Leaning in, she put her elbows on her knees. "Look, I'm going to be straight with you, Mace. Carlos Martinez says you're good people."

She extracted a black wallet from her inside pocket, flipped it open, and revealed a badge. I was trying to read her agency's name when she flipped it shut again.

"We think Tony Ciancio committed a murder back in New Jersey."

A chill crawled down my spine. It had nothing to do with the open window.

"What makes you think Tony did it?"

"Evidence." She had the same terse cop tone I was used to hearing from Carlos. "It's possible he's linked to this killing here, too. Time frame makes sense."

"No. Tony didn't even get here until the day after Ronnie Hodges was killed."

She tilted her head, skeptical. "You sure about that?"

C'ndee had said her nephew drove all night to get to Himmarshee. But the snake-wary newcomer said she saw a green Lexus a day earlier. Was it Tony's? He said no. And I didn't know him well enough to say if he was lying.

Finally, I shook my head. "I'm not a hundred percent sure, no."

"That's what I figured." She rose from the chair. "Thanks for the beer."

She was just about to step through the front door when I called out, "How'd the New Jersey victim die?"

"Stabbed in the back. We found his body in his restaurant kitchen."

———

I didn't even wait for the sound of Ms. Sunglasses' motorcycle boots to cross my porch before I bolted and locked the front door. I slammed shut the living room window, and grabbed the spare key she'd left on my coffee table. I hid it in my purse and stashed the purse on the top shelf of my bedroom closet. I vowed to go shopping after the wedding for a hide-a-key that looks like a rock. I'd plant it at the third fencepost from the gate to the back pasture, where no one could find it.

The motorcycle roared to life from its hiding place in my back-yard. Peeking out the bedroom blinds, I wanted to make sure she was really leaving. I watched until her red taillight disappeared around the curve my drive took toward State Road 98.

"You can show yourself again, Wila. The coast is clear."

A Siamese nose poked out from beneath the bedspread close to the floor. Satisfied the intruder was gone, the cat slunk out of the bedroom and padded into the kitchen to be fed. I wished food was all it took for me to forget coming home to find a stranger in my living room.

While Wila ate, I checked and double-checked the locks on doors and windows. Kind of like putting up the shutters after the hurricane already hit. I straightened the picture on the wall that

"Jane Smith" had touched, and tossed her beer bottle into the kitchen recycling bin. Wila startled at the clatter.

"Sorry, girl." I stroked her sleek coat. "What do you make of somebody who breaks in—okay, uses a key—and makes themselves so at home like that? A lot of nerve, huh?"

The cat raised her head at the sound of my voice. I think I saw agreement in her expression.

"I mean she didn't let me examine that badge very closely. She could have bought it online for all I know."

Wila returned to her bowl.

"Yeah, you're right. Carlos wouldn't be taken in by somebody with a costume badge. And they seemed pretty chummy at the Speckled Perch. Collegial. She must be a fellow cop. Wait until I tell Mama."

Within fifteen minutes, I was ready for bed. Wila jumped up, too. I'm not normally a pet-on-the-pillow person, but tonight was an exception. I was grateful for the company, even if her breath did stink of salmon.

I fell asleep with the reassuring warmth of the cat's body beside me. That comfortable feeling vanished, though, once I began to dream.

Tony was in my living room, in the same chair where the Mystery Woman had sat just an hour or so before. He was studying a thick book, looking like the handsome college guy he'd once been. But when he smiled and beckoned me closer, I could see the book was stained with blood. A sharp knife was hidden within the pages.

I ran from him, but when I passed through the cottage's front door, the scene suddenly shifted. Dark woods surrounded me.

Vines and tree branches pressed close, scratching me. Suffocating me. When I tried to escape, a figure in a pig's head gave chase. No matter how fast I thought I was running, my feet wouldn't move. The huge head came closer and closer, until it loomed above me, eyes glittering with a murderous rage.

Then, the dream transported me to Lake Okeechobee, where I was on a boat again. I watched as Carlos stepped off the bow.

"Don't worry," I called to him. "It's shallow."

But when I leaned over to see where he went in, it wasn't the familiar dark water of Lake O after all. It was clear and turquoise blue, like the Caribbean Sea. I watched as Carlos fell, faster and faster, into the depths. My feet felt glued to the boat deck as he somersaulted out of my reach. Just before I awoke from the dream, I saw Carlos' hands, fingertips outstretched toward the water's surface and me.

My heart hammered. My T-shirt clung to my body, soaked with sweat. I felt a stab of fear and loss. Had I really watched him drown? I couldn't tell for a moment what was real and what was the dream.

When my mind cleared, I was struck by a single thought. I'd been a fool. Seeing Carlos sink out of sight wasn't real, but the emptiness I'd felt at losing him was. I loved him. All my flirting and playing and failing to commit couldn't change that simple fact.

Wila, awake now, blinked those Siamese-blue eyes at me. Ruffling her fur, I repeated the words I'd heard so many times from Mama.

"Sweetheart," I said. "How would you like to have a new daddy?"

FORTY

THE WEDDING DAY DAWNED sunny and clear. Not a dark cloud in the sky. I hoped it was an omen for the ceremony, and, even more, for the marriage beyond. Five just might be Mama's lucky number.

As I measured coffee into a paper filter, I glanced at my wall clock, a cut-and-varnished cypress knee, shaped like Lake Okeechobee. A largemouth bass leapt at twelve o'clock, and a speckled perch swam at six. It was an hour past the perch. I had all morning to think about getting to Hair Today, Dyed Tomorrow. What torture by teasing comb had Betty planned for me? Whatever, it was guaranteed to make me look like a big-haired contestant in a Deep South beauty pageant.

I could hardly wait.

I showered and dressed, poured some coffee, and caught up with a pile of *Himmarshee Times* newspapers I'd been neglecting. Lake Okeechobee was down a couple of feet due to the dry season and drought; some drunken high school kid hit and killed a cow while driving doughnuts in a pasture; and the cops busted a "grow house" for pot that was tucked away in the woods off Lofton Road.

I was bemoaning the fact that the big city was coming to little Himmarshee, when my phone rang. It seemed kind of early, but everyone who knows me knows I'm up with the roosters. Maybe it was Mama, calling off the wedding again. The upside would be I could skip that hair appointment. Perking up, I picked up the phone.

"I need to talk to you, Mace. I'm really in trouble."

Similar words on the telephone had never led to anything good. I should have hung up right then. But Tony sounded so desperate.

"Okay, talk. You can start by telling me if it's true you killed that restaurant owner in New Jersey."

There was a long silence. I could hear him breathing.

"I can't discuss this on the phone, Mace. Can I see you? Can I come over?"

Now, I've watched enough movies to know you don't throw open your door to a suspected murderer. "No way."

"Can I meet you somewhere, then?"

"How about Gladys' Diner?"

"No good. That place is crawling with cops drinking coffee and eating pie. I can't take the chance that some yahoo will try to make a name by bringing me down. An innocent customer could get hurt." He paused. "What about your nature park? We could meet where you held the walk the other day."

I thought of the park's wild spaces, all those hiding places. I remembered another meeting on an early morning before Himmarshee Park opened. That encounter nearly came to a tragic end.

"The park is closed," I said.

"I want to do the right thing, Mace. I'm going to turn myself in. But I need your help."

Tony had known me less than a week. But already he knew to push the button for my savior complex. Am I that transparent? Thinking fast, I came up with a plan.

"All right, you can come on out here. But give me an hour. I'm not even out of bed yet."

"Who says you have to get out of bed?" His voice took on a sexy growl. The man couldn't help himself.

"Look, I'm doing this as a friend. That's all we are, Tony."

"Sorry. I appreciate it, I do. Just don't call the cops. I'm going to hand myself over, I swear on my mother's life; but I have to do it on my terms. You know I'd never hurt you, right?"

No, I thought, I don't. "Sure," I said.

"So promise me you won't call Carlos. If I see the cops are there, all deals are off."

I waited for a beat. He needed to believe I was thinking about it.

"Okay, Tony. I swear I won't call Carlos."

The moment I hung up I did two things: I got Paw-Paw's shotgun from the closet, loaded it, and slid it under the couch in the living room within easy reach. And then I called Carlos.

———

"C'mon in. The door's open."

I could see Tony through the window. Eyes darting around nervously, he came through the screen door to the porch, and then on into my living room. Faint circles under his eyes were the only outward sign of the inner turmoil he claimed to be suffering. The collar on his pink-grapefruit polo shirt lay perfectly outside his navy blue blazer. His khakis were pressed and creased. The white smile was present, if a bit less luminescent than usual.

"No cops, right?"

"No cops," I said, failing to add the word *yet*. "We're alone. Now, I want to know: Did you kill that man up North?"

He heaved a huge sigh. Studied the cypress board floor. Finally, he nodded.

"You can't understand the pressure I was under, Mace. I'm the only son. Since I was born, everyone just assumed I'd take over for my father some day. It never mattered what I wanted."

His dark green eyes bored into mine. "It's my destiny."

"That doesn't explain how you could brutally murder someone. With a knife, no less."

"My father's terminally ill. He said our rivals were going to strike because everyone knew I didn't really want to run the business. I wasn't the man he was. No one feared me. I had to step up and show them I could be just as ruthless as my father."

"So you committed murder to send a message?"

He didn't answer. But I saw the truth in his eyes.

"Pretty extreme way to win your father's approval."

"Yeah. He got what he wanted. He even gave me the knife to do it. Now I'm just like him."

Shame and self-loathing filled his face. I almost felt sorry for him.

"That blond woman from the park was a cop, you know. She's looking for you," I said.

"I figured she was." He sank into a chair across from where I sat on the couch.

"They think you killed Ronnie Hodges, too."

He gasped, shaking his head. Could he truly be surprised?

"I had nothing to do with that."

"C'mon, Tony. A potential business rival? Stabbed to death? In a kitchen? Sounds like your M.O. to me, and I'm not even a cop."

"I swear I didn't kill him, Mace. I came down here to start a new life. I finally told my father I was out. I don't care if he's dying or not. I don't want to be part of his world. Why would I revert right back to what I hated about him? What I hated in me?"

"Because once you've killed the first time, the second time is easier."

Leaning toward me, he stared so deeply into my eyes that I feared he could see right through me to the floor beneath the couch, and the shotgun hidden there.

"You don't know a thing about me. My father forced me to do something against my will and against my nature…"

"Did he actually put the knife in your hand?"

Anger flickered across his face. "Killing a man is not easy. Not the first time. Not ever. I never want to do it again. That's why I'm running."

"Running? You said you were turning yourself in."

"When I thought about it, I realized I can't go to prison as Sam Ciancio's son. Every tough guy in there would want to prove himself by murdering me. I'd have to kill again to survive. It'd either be one of them, or me."

He collapsed back against the chair, sighed. "I'm going some-place where they don't even speak English. Nobody knows me. I can finally be free."

"Uhm," I said. "About that, Tony."

He tilted his head at me. God, he was good-looking. He was bound to have a tough time in prison, one way or another.

"I'm sorry, but I had to call the police. They're on their way as we speak."

Almost before I realized what I was seeing, Tony's hand jerked across his chest to the inside of his jacket. He pulled out a pistol. There was no smile now. Just green ice in his eyes and a gun aimed straight at me.

FORTY-ONE

THE CHARMING TONY FROM before had disappeared. A killer sat across from me, probably intent on making me his next victim.

"You won't get away. When I said the cops are coming, I meant now," I lied. "I just heard the first car turn onto my drive."

At the instant Tony whirled to look out the window, I doubled over and grabbed the shotgun from under the couch. Tony might be fast, but I am, too. The weapon was pumped and ready, almost before he had time to register the fact I was armed. The cops weren't outside.

He looked from the window to me, holding the gun. "You lied to me."

"Yeah, and you killed a man. Maybe you killed Ronnie Hodges, too. I wasn't taking any chances."

We stared at each other over the expanse of my coffee table; two Old West gunslingers ready to fire if the other so much as flinched. I don't know about Tony, but my heart was about to explode through my chest. I hoped he wouldn't notice the barrel of the shotgun shaking.

"I told you I had nothing to do with Ronnie. Why would I admit to one murder and lie about the other?"

"Because Florida has capital punishment. The murder here could get you the needle."

He shook his head. "I wasn't lying. I thought we were friends. I thought I could trust you."

"That was your first mistake."

He looked toward the yard again. "Did you really call the cops?"

I nodded. "Yeah, but I calculated some extra time because I wanted to talk to you first, see if you could explain. I wanted to find out before Mama's wedding if you killed Ronnie."

"Do you think I did?"

I looked into his eyes. I saw no cruelty there. No murderous rage. He seemed sad; wounded. I remembered how he jumped up to help the waitress at Gladys' Diner. How kind he was to the old couple at the Speckled Perch. How he rescued a turtle from the highway. Then I flashed on the Tony I'd witnessed in my living room, cursing into his cell phone, fully in command. Not to mention the Tony holding me at gunpoint right now.

Finally, I shrugged. "I can't say whether you killed him. I pray you didn't."

A spark of hope died in his eyes. His next move was unexpected. He stooped, slowly placing his handgun on the floor. Rising, he put up his hands in surrender.

"I'm unarmed. I'm going to walk out, get in my car, and go before the cops get here. Shoot me if you want. I'd rather die than go to prison."

As he turned and trudged to the door, time seemed frozen. My finger rested on the trigger. The stock of the gun weighed heavily against my shoulder. When he stepped through the door, I lowered the barrel.

There was no way I'd shoot an unarmed man in the back, and he knew it. Tony had outmaneuvered me.

I followed, calling to him from the porch. "You won't get far. The cops are probably speeding down State Road 98 right now. It'll go better for you if you stay here and let them arrest you. Face what you've done."

Still walking, he spoke over his shoulder. "Tell my aunt I'm sorry."

As Tony got in his car, I hurried inside to the house phone. I heard the engine start as I hit speed dial for Carlos. Phone to my ear, I crossed to the window. The Lexus sped from my yard, shock absorbers getting a workout over the bumps and ruts of the unpaved drive. As the number rang, I tried to figure out how to spin the morning's events so Carlos wouldn't be furious.

———

"You WHAT?"

I'd already recited the basics: What Tony was driving, when he'd left, and from what location so Carlos could relay the information over the police radio. Now, I was spinning; but he wasn't buying.

"When Tony got here early, I took the opportunity to talk to him. How was I supposed to know he'd be armed?"

Of course, I must have suspected. Why else would I have hidden the shotgun?

"We had to dot the legal *i's* and cross our jurisdictional *t's*, but you should have called immediately, Mace. I would've had someone on the scene. Now, we've lost the element of surprise. We may never find him. Even worse, you could have been hurt."

At least Carlos still thought my being hurt would be a negative. Would that still hold true if I confessed I'd built in the extra time so I could interrogate Tony?

"I'm sorry. I made a mistake. But I'm worried about Mama's wedding. I don't think Tony murdered Ronnie. That means whoever did is still out there. What if the killer has something awful planned for today?"

"Jane's pretty sure Tony did it," Carlos said.

"Who's Jane?"

"Jane Smith. The detective from New Jersey. She said you two had a nice chat last night."

"Jane Smith is her real name?"

"Of course. And she'd like to say hello. I'm putting you on speaker."

I heard a hollow echo, then a flat, toneless voice: "Thanks for screwing up my arrest."

I tried not to get my back up. I deserved that. "Hello, Detective Smith."

"Did Tony give you any information about where he might be headed?"

"Just that he was going someplace where they don't even speak English."

"That doesn't narrow it down much."

"Well, if he's dumping that rental car to head out by air, Orlando has more international options than the airport at West Palm Beach. So he'd be heading north. And if he wanted to stay off the Florida Turnpike and away from the state troopers who patrol it, then he'd want to take US Highway 441."

"Well, that's something to start with, at least," Jane said.

I could hear Carlos on the radio, relaying the information.

"Any other details you think we should know?" she asked.

I described Tony's clothing, and even told them about the leather seats in the Lexus and his country music CDs. As soon as the words left my mouth, I knew Carlos would wonder later how I was so familiar with the interior of the car of an alleged murderer, now a fugitive.

"Oh, yeah," I added. "He left his gun. He's unarmed."

"I doubt that." I heard the sneer in Jane's voice. "There's probably an arsenal and a suitcase of knives in that car."

"I don't think so. Tony said his father pressured him to kill that restaurant guy. It seems like he's running more from his family's expectations than from the law."

Aside from the whine of the speaker, their end of the phone was silent. Then they both burst out laughing.

"Please, Mace. You can't be that gullible," Carlos said.

I heard my peeved sniff, magnified over the damned speaker phone.

"Did he make big, sad, puppy dog eyes when he sold you that story?" Jane asked. "I bet he said he did this Himmarshee murder because his aunt held a gun to his head, too."

"I'm just telling you the impression I got." I bit my tongue before I added *bitch*. "Why do you think he'd admit to one murder and deny the other?"

"Oh, gee whiz, I don't know." Jane's voice was mocking, all naïve schoolgirl. "Maybe because he's a lying sack of crap?"

"All righty, then. As much as I enjoy hearing what an idiot I am, I have to get to town to get my hair and nails done."

"Oh, that's priceless." Jane snorted. "Gullible *and* vain."

Carlos chuckled, but quickly redeemed himself. "Mace is normally a pretty good judge of character, Jane. And the only reason she's getting dolled up is because she's in her mother's wedding today."

"*Mazel tov* to your mother," Jane said. "Maybe the wedding will keep you and the other civilians busy enough not to meddle in any more murder investigations."

Carlos laughed out loud. Redemption cancelled.

"Okay," I said, my voice as sweet as Marty's. "Y'all have a nice day."

I wasn't going to sink to their level. On second thought, what the hell?

"By the way, Detective Smith, you might want to ask Carlos about out-of-town cops who think they know everything. Ask him about the time he tossed my sweet little mama in jail when everybody in town tried to tell him there was no way a Sunday-school-teaching, sherbet-pantsuit-wearing senior citizen had committed a murder."

I slammed down the receiver, hoping for a speaker screech that would rattle their eardrums.

FORTY-TWO

"Ringlets, Mama? Really?" Even Marty, the first victim, was rebelling at this latest excess.

Maddie and I stood behind her, staring in horror into the mirror at Hair Today, Dyed Tomorrow. Marty may have looked as adorable as an antebellum doll in her corkscrew curls. But the two of us knew: We are not cut out for cute. With my shoulders, I'd look like a line-backer channeling his inner Scarlett O'Hara. And Maddie feared a picture of her in ruffles and ringlets would get out on YouTube, compromising her ability to scare her students.

Betty gave one of the curls a final pat with her purple styling comb. The curl jiggled like a coiled spring next to Marty's smooth cheek.

"Well, I think your hair looks splendid, honey. Betty, you've done a wonderful job." Mama turned to me. "Mace, climb up in that chair. You're next."

As one, Maddie and I started backing toward the door.

"Oh, no you don't!" She grabbed each of us by an arm. "Now, I don't ask much of you girls ..."

Catching Marty's gaze in the mirror, we all rolled our eyes.

"... I saw that. But this is just one little thing I'm asking you to do on My Special Day. Mace, I promise I'll never make you dress up again."

"Can I get that in writing?"

"And Maddie, you'll hear no more comments from me about your weight. Although there is one last diet I clipped out from *Woman's World* I'd love you to take a look at ..."

Maddie shook off Mama's hand. "I'm outta here."

"Sorry, honey." She mimed zipping her lip. "You are perfect exactly as you are. Beautiful, in fact, just like your sisters."

Linking elbows with us, Mama pleaded into the mirror. "Please, girls? It's only for today. You can brush them out the minute Sal and I drive away with our *Just Married* sign."

Sometimes, it's easier to go along than to argue with Mama. Besides, with five pounds of ruffles, parasols, and a Pomeranian in a satin top hat leading the bridal procession, how much tackier could the ringlets really make things?

"Whatever." Sighing, I took my place in the chair Marty vacated.

She leaned over and whispered, "Just close your eyes and think happy thoughts, Mace. It'll be over before you know it."

The bells jangled on the salon door, and D'Vora rushed in, late as usual. She quickly got Maddie into a chair, tossed a purple drape over her shoulders, and started brushing out her hair. D'Vora had come a long way since the unfortunate peroxide incident she inflicted upon Mama, back when she was a beautician-trainee. She'd since built a following among younger women and some of Him-marshee's affluent newcomers. She may even be in line to buy the shop from Betty some day.

But for now, D'Vora's boss aimed a pointed look at the salon's wall clock, shaped like a lady wearing a bouffant hairdo.

"You know, the little hand is supposed to be on the ten, not near the eleven, when you report to work."

"Sorry, Betty."

D'Vora divided Maddie's red hair with a clip, and then coated a one-inch section with setting lotion.

My sister wrinkled her nose. "That smells like bananas left in the fruit bowl too long." Ignoring her, D'Vora wound her hair onto a Marcel curling iron, held it, released, and then sprayed again from a can that said Maximum Hold.

D'Vora said, "Something big was happening at the police de-partment. There were a bunch of cop cars, and they had Main Street completely blocked."

I swiveled toward her, causing Betty to nearly yank out the hank of hair she was preparing to twirl.

"Ouch!"

"Mace, anyone with a passing familiarity with beauty parlor etiquette knows to keep still in the stylist's chair," Betty said.

"I'll remember that." I put up a knuckle to rub my temple. "What was happening with the police, D'Vora?"

"No idea. They wouldn't let me past to see. They just made me detour with all the other traffic. Since I was going that way anyway, I stopped at the drive-thru for some coffee. Linda-Ann asked me about those coveralls you found at Himmarshee Park, Mace."

My antenna went up. "What'd she say?"

"That she remembered Ronnie always wearing coveralls for work at the feed store. She bought a pair just like them from the store for Trevor. She says he thinks they're ironic, whatever that means."

My eyes met my sisters' in the mirror. " 'Ironic' isn't the word I'd choose. More like suspicious. Can we take a break so I can make a quick phone call, Betty?"

She glared at me in the mirror. "Would you ask your surgeon to put down his scalpel in the middle of an operation? I'm working here!"

Maddie shook her head at me. "Even if you did call Carlos, he won't tell you anything."

Marty nodded, her ringlets bouncing. "What's that line he uses? 'This is an *active* investigation.' "

"Don't worry, honey." Mama patted my hand. "Somebody will come into the shop and tell us all about it before long."

As Betty worked on my hair, questions flew through my mind: Had the police found Tony, barreling north for the airport in his rented Lexus? Had those coveralls linked Trevor to Ronnie's murder? Or, had Rabe managed to collect some damning evidence to point the cops to his sleazeball stepfather?

Whatever had happened, I hoped no one else had been hurt. And I hoped none of it spilled over to Mama's Special Day.

Her voice interrupted my thoughts. Something about those awful dresses.

"Beg your pardon, Mama?"

"I said I stopped by Fran's and got your beautiful gowns. The back of my car looks like a sherbet-colored rainbow."

"I'll bet it does," Maddie said.

Mama went on, "Betty's offered to do any touch-ups we might need before we pose for pictures, so we'll go ahead and dress for the wedding here."

It was either the hair salon, or the VFW bathrooms, so Mama's plan made sense to me.

"I'm as busy today as a one-legged man in a butt-kicking contest," Betty said. "Rosalee, you won't believe who's coming in to get her hair done for your wedding."

Mama lit an aromatherapy candle, releasing a lemon grass scent to war with all the other fruit and flower smells in the shop. "C'ndee?"

Betty pulled, spritzed, and rolled "No."

"Dab Holt? I still can't get over how she threw herself at that stripper."

"Could we call him an entertainer, Rosalee?" D'Vora asked. "I didn't mention anything about a half-naked cowboy to my mama."

Betty said, "Don't tell me you invited Dab!"

"Absolutely not! But that wouldn't stop her from showing up. She's got more nerve than a planeload of New Yorkers. Is it Charlene from Gladys' Diner getting her hair done?"

Betty shook her head, the purple comb in her mouth indicating no.

"Oh, for heaven's sake, Betty," Maddie finally interrupted. "Just tell us who has the hair appointment."

"Alice Hodges."

We all fell quiet. Marty broke the silence. "Poor thing."

"I thought Alice decided not to come to your wedding," I said.

"Me, too. But I'm glad she changed her mind." Mama tapped her chin the way she does when she's thinking. "Betty, I want to pay for Alice's hair today. Give her the works."

"Great idea, Mama. We'll all chip in, and get her face done, too." Maddie raised her eyebrows in the mirror at D'Vora. "Do you have time to do her make-up?"

"Sure. I'll juggle to fit her in."

"Good! It's settled, then." Mama started to clap her hands, but she frowned instead. "I just hope the wedding doesn't make Alice dwell on all she's lost. My happiness shouldn't make her sad."

———

"A purse *and* a parasol, Mama? Really?"

The over-the-top implication was clear, even in Marty's mild tone. We regarded ourselves in the mirror: Maddie and I were the cotton-candy-pink and lime-green bookends to Marty's orange-sherbet confection. At the last minute, Mama had asked Fran to stitch up some drawstring purses in fabric to match our dresses. They now dangled from each of our left wrists; the parasols swung from straps on our right. Together, the two accessories upped our ruffle quotient by at least thirty percent.

I was ready to make a smart remark, until I glanced over at Mama, standing off to the side. Her hands were clasped over her heart; her eyes shone with tears. I nudged my sisters to look.

"You girls are like a heavenly vision." Mama sniffled. "You're angels, that's what you are. And I just know the Lord will be smiling down on us today."

———

Traffic flowed again on Main Street by the time I gathered up my hoop skirt and climbed into my Jeep. Sitting in the driver's seat, swathed in fabric, I wondered whether suffocation by ruffles was a common cause of death.

I'd tried Carlos' number a couple of times, and went straight to voicemail. For a change, not a single one of Betty's clients was able to report anything on the police goings-on, either. If Tony was involved, Jane Smith had probably scared any officers prone to gossip by threatening to stick her motorcycle helmet where the sun never shines.

I stayed in second gear, cruising slowly past the police department. From the front, nothing looked out of the ordinary. But when I pulled into the lot and circled to the back, I saw a thick knot of uniformed and plainclothes cops. At least a dozen cruisers and unmarked sedans were parked haphazardly, as if their drivers had been in a hurry. Along with Himmarshee's familiar blue-and-whites, there were a couple of marked cars from the county sheriff's department, and three dark SUVs. I didn't recognize the big vehicles, but they bellowed *Police*.

Something was definitely up.

Jane's blond mane shone from the middle of the crowd. Carlos stood right beside her. Grins and high-fives were exchanged; laughter echoed out across the parking lot. As I got closer, I saw the silhouette of a suspect in the back seat of one of the sheriff's cars. Even from a distance and in the shadow, I could tell the handsome profile was Tony Ciancio's. Unbidden, a surge of sympathy washed over me.

I parked, and tried to extricate myself and my billowing skirt from the Jeep without showing off my ruffled pantaloons. By now, all eyes were on me, except for Tony's. Head bowed, he stared at the floor in the back of the cruiser. I could only imagine what was running through his mind. Whatever it was, it was far more serious than the picture I must have made, mincing across the parking lot in lime-hued ruffles from bonnet to matching high heels.

Somebody began to hum "Dixie." Snickers rippled through the crowd. One of the sheriff's deputies doffed his uniform hat and performed a courtly—if smirking—bow. "How 'do, Miz Scarlett?"

"Very funny." I pointed my parasol at the sheriff's car. "I see y'all caught your man."

Himmarshee Police Officer Donnie Bailey, my former babysitting charge, stepped forward. "You wouldn't believe it, Mace." His words tumbled out. "One of the county deputies was pulled off along 441, clocking speeders, when the BOLO came over the radio about the Lexus ..."

Jane's eyes burned holes into Donnie. Maybe he smelled the singe coming off his uniform, because he clamped his mouth shut so fast he surely bit his tongue. I looked around at some of the other familiar faces in the crowd. Most of them stole nervous glances at a glowering Jane. Lips were zipped; chins aimed to the ground.

The fact that testosterone apparently provided no vaccine against fear of Detective Smith made me feel a little better about my earlier reactions to her. She looked me up and down, an amused smile tugging at her lips. "Nice parasol. What would you call that color? Minty green?"

I ignored her.

"I'd say it's more like unripe banana. A little yellow in the green." Carlos winked.

"But pastel, right?" Jane said.

"Oh, yes." He winked again. "Definitely pastel."

"Carlos, you ought to see somebody about that twitch in your eye," I said. "And the dress is lime sherbet, as any fool can plainly see. Now, if you two are finished with the fashion commentary and the Two Stooges comedy routine, maybe you can tell me: Did Tony confess to killing Ronnie?"

"He hasn't said jack," Carlos said.

"Waiting for his mob lawyer," Jane added.

"Be sure and ask him why he didn't come armed with his own knife to kill Ronnie, the way he did with that man back in New Jersey."

"What a surprise. Another civilian who watches *Law & Order*," Jane said.

"Thanks for the advice, Mace." Maybe Carlos noticed the steam coming out of my ears because he managed to keep his mocking tone to a minimum. Jane didn't even try.

"Don't you have some cotton to hoe or corn pone to eat, Scarlett? You can run along now. We'll be sure to take your concerns under advisement."

"You do that," I said.

I could almost see the headline: *Southern Belle Batters Jersey Cop.* But I knew Mama would kill me for ruining my bridesmaid gown, so I gave Jane Smith a long, mean glare instead.

And then I flounced away, ruffles rustling, ringlets jiggling, parasol swinging.

FORTY-THREE

"Oh, for Gawd's sake! The flowers need to go at the *ends* of the serving table, not in the middle. That's where the prime rib carving station goes! Do I have to show you people how to do *everything*?"

Foghorn voice blasting, C'ndee stalked by me as I entered the foyer of the VFW hall. She snatched a floral arrangement from a cowering brunette, who wore the white blouse and black slacks of a catering staffer. If C'ndee knew about her nephew's arrest, it wasn't apparent from her screeching, typically abrasive manner.

The stop at the police department had made me late. But we still had nearly two hours before the wedding. The VFW bustled with activity. A black-and-white clad army shook out tablecloths, set up chairs, and created a path for the bridal party from the back of the hall to the stage at the front. That's where the ceremony would take place, with the Reverend Delilah Dixon from Abundant Forgiveness officiating.

I was just about to pull C'ndee aside to tell her about Tony, when I spotted Mama across the room. Her eyes were wild as she frantically waved me over. Please, Lord, not the on-again-off-again wedding, off again.

"What is it Mama?" I grabbed her shoulders. "You look like you've seen a ghost!"

She heaved a shuddery sigh. Tears were imminent. "It's Husband No. 2, Mace. He's here."

And I'd been worried about something as minor as a murderer maybe showing up.

"C'ndee hired him with all these other servers out of Orlando. He's supposed to be the bartender tonight." Her voice shook. "He swears the names in the wedding party were never mentioned. He didn't realize it was me getting married until he walked in the door."

"What are you going to do?"

She blew her nose into a length of toilet paper, and the first tear rolled down her cheek.

"I meant, what are you going to do besides cry?"

"I can't help it, Mace." She dabbed under each eye, trying to catch the tears before they mussed her mascara. "This is horrible. Marty ran off as soon as she saw him. I don't think she ever got over witnessing all those awful fights we had."

Marty wasn't the only one.

"Your big sister's on the telephone right now with the Speckled Perch, trying to see if one of their bartenders is available to work the wedding."

"Where's the VFW's usual bartender?"

"C'ndee said something about him having emergency surgery." She wrung her hands. "Oh, Mace, why does everything happen to me?"

I could have mentioned that the VFW bartender might quibble with Mama's assessment of misfortune's victim. If he survived his surgery, that is. But I gave her a pass owing to how upset she was over the sudden reappearance of No. 2.

"If Sal finds out who he is, he'll kill him. We exchanged our stories when we first started dating. Sal knows all about how Two did me wrong." Mama raked a hand through her hair, unsettling her perfect 'do. "Please, Mace. You have to do something."

"Don't worry, Mama. I'll go have a talk with him."

I found No. 2 in the back parking lot, smoking a filterless cigarette and leaning against a gleaming white convertible. The man never had a dollar in the bank, but he always drove a new convertible.

"I see those cigarettes haven't killed you yet."

"Hello, Mace." He took a long drag, coughed as he exhaled. "Nice dress."

He was still a handsome man, though thinner than I remembered. His full head of hair was mostly gray; a few more lines marked his forehead. His eyes were the same: small, dark, and mean.

"You know you can't work the wedding, right?"

"Hell, yes. I've been to a few of your family's shindigs. I want to stay as far away from this one as I can." He tapped a long ash onto the ground. "I'm just waiting to make sure they can get someone to replace me."

"That's nice of you."

"I figure I owe it to Rosalee."

"That and a lot more."

He sucked hard on the cigarette. Blew out a big cloud of smoke. "I've always regretted it, you know? Rosalee was the best thing that ever happened to me. I'm sorry for the way I treated her."

"You should be."

"Cut me a break, would you Mace? You always were too tough for your own good, even as a kid. I just wanted to tell you I'm sorry for the way I did your mama. And I'm sorry for all the heartache I brought into you girls' lives, too. Y'all sure didn't need that, not so soon after your real daddy died."

I could feel a hard lump of tears at the back of my throat. All of a sudden, the years since we lost Daddy disappeared. It seemed like just yesterday that this man, with his drinking, his cheating, and his fists, moved in to replace him. I hoped I wouldn't cry. With all the goop D'Vora had slathered on, I'd have a mudslide of makeup to deal with.

I breathed deeply; waited until I knew my voice would come out steady. "Are you sick or something? Are you trying to set things right?"

He took a last puff, then held up the cigarette between his thumb and forefinger and stared at it.

"Yeah, as a matter of fact I am sick." He flicked the butt out into the lot. "Cancer. The doctor says it'll get a lot worse."

I tried, but I felt nothing. I wasn't sorry. Would a more forgiving soul, like Marty, feel bad? I knew Maddie would happily start measuring for his coffin.

"Maybe you should give up smoking."

"Doesn't make much difference now." He coughed again, a hacking, pained sound. "See what I mean?"

He gave me a weak smile.

C'ndee stuck her head out of the kitchen door and shouted, "Jimmy, you can go. We got somebody else to come in. Don't worry. I'll hire you again. It's nothing personal."

Nothing personal? C'ndee couldn't know how wrong she was.

"Will you tell Rosalee what I said, Mace? Will you tell her I'm sorry?"

I looked closely into his face, saw the yellow pallor behind the tan; the dull cast to those beady eyes. In a year, maybe two, he'd be dead. And we'd still be here, the Lord willing. We'd still be a family.

"Sure," I said. "I'll tell her."

"What about this guy she's marrying? He okay?"

"Better than okay. Sal adores Mama."

"I'm glad. She deserves to be happy."

C'ndee's head popped out the door again. She bellowed, "Mace, pictures! We need you inside. Now!"

Jimmy grinned. "Man, she sounds like a piece of work. I wouldn't want to get on her bad side."

I thought about that. How bad *was* C'ndee's bad side?

I stuck out my hand to Husband No. 2. "Take care, Jimmy."

His eyes widened in surprise, but he shook. "You, too. See you around."

"Not if I see you first." I actually meant that, but I smiled a little when I said it.

What's that people say about the burden of hate? It's harder on the hater than the hated. I was finally ready to be a little less burdened.

FORTY-FOUR

I whispered to Maddie from the side of my mouth as we sisters posed for pre-wedding pictures. "So C'ndee knows about Tony?"

"No talking, Mace!" C'ndee barked. "Everybody look to the left. Big smiles. Say 'cannoli.'"

Grouped on the steps of the VFW stage according to height, we rested our open parasols across our right shoulders. We smiled out to the left. As the photographer snapped, Maddie spoke under her breath: "C'ndee told *us* as soon as we got here. Tony phoned her first thing, and she called in the family's lawyer."

"Oh, for Gawd's sake! Can't you two keep your mouths shut for one minute?" She stepped closer to the stage, lowered her voice. "Since you're curious, some would say nosy, Yes, I know Tony was arrested. No, he didn't kill Ronnie. And he didn't do that murder back home, either."

She waved a hand through the air, blood-red nails flashing. "Everything's going to come out in court. You'll see."

I knew what Tony had told me, but I wasn't going to argue. Maybe C'ndee wanted to believe the best about her nephew. Or maybe she was just accustomed to juries failing to return guilty verdicts against members of her family.

After the photographer had shot what seemed like a thousand pictures of the three of us, C'ndee left to help Mama repair her face after the tearful encounter with No. 2. Fortunately, there would be no posed pictures of the bridal couple until after the ceremony. Mama had insisted Sal stay away until just before the wedding began.

"It's bad luck for the groom to see the bride before she walks down the aisle, girls," she'd said. "And I'm not going to do anything to jinx this marriage."

We sat, skirts as full as open parachutes, waiting to assess the extent of Mama's makeup damage. When she returned, leaning just a bit on C'ndee for support, Marty let out a sigh of relief.

"She looks beautiful," my little sister said.

"Thank God," Maddie added.

Mama's lips shone with Apricot Ice. Her eyes were clear. Her rosy cheeks glowed. A faint dusting of powder hid her red nose.

"Amazing," I said to C'ndee.

"An ice pack cures many ills." She cupped Mama's chin and aimed her face to the light. "You can't tell you spilled a single tear over that S.O.B."

Her voice turned serious. "I'm really sorry for hiring him, Rosalee. I had no idea there was any history between you. I've been trying so hard to make this day perfect, and then I completely screwed it up."

The surprise on my sisters' faces surely mirrored my own. We all stared at C'ndee, whose eyes were cast to the floor. I wouldn't have believed she had a bit of doubt about her own abilities. It made her seem a step beyond tolerable.

Mama patted C'ndee's cheek. "Honey, just forget about it. I already have. And you've accomplished miracles with this wedding on short notice. You have nothing to apologize about."

C'ndee, seeming to stand a bit taller, clapped her hands together.

"Places everybody!" she blared, but at a less-obnoxious decibel than usual. "Veil shot's next."

She moved us this way and that, choreographing Mama's girls helping her put on her veil. I had to admit, it probably made a beautiful photograph, posed in front of a huge vase with calla lilies, white roses, and carnations. Delicate ferns and baby's breath filled out the display.

My sisters and I plucked our lilies from the vase. We each were to hold one elegant stem as we walked down the aisle. It was the single understated element in our ridiculous wedding getups. Then again, if we were to try to juggle purses, parasols, and a traditional fat bouquet, bridesmaid accessories would be dropping like horse patties along the bridal path.

———

The wedding was scheduled to begin in fifteen minutes. Mama's earlier nerves had disappeared, along with her ex-husband. Now, she truly was a beaming bride. Her radiant glow might have owed something to the generous glass of wine C'ndee had poured her from the bar.

Engulfed in our big skirts, Mama and my sisters and I crowded around a table at the edge of the hall. The VFW was transformed: Celadon tulle draped in graceful swags from the ceiling, softening the fluorescent lights. White china sparkled on linen tablecloths. Boughs of white flowers gave off a delicate scent. I even noticed sprigs of orange blossom with glossy green leaves in the arrangements—traditional for brides, and also a nod to our Florida family's roots.

"I have to say it, sisters. C'ndee completely got it." I pointed my parasol at the room's four corners. "This place looks amazing."

Mama stood and did a model's twirl. "And how about me? Not bad for an old lady of sixty, right?"

"Sixty-two," Maddie corrected, and then flinched as Marty kicked her under the table.

"You look beautiful, Mama." Marty placated. "Not a day over fifty."

Mama lovingly cradled one of Marty's ringlets. "Now, *that's* how you make your mama's day, girls."

She glanced at her watch. "Sal should be here any minute, with Teensy. I have to run back to the office and hide."

She held up her empty glass. "Wonder if I could get just a splash more of that wine?"

My sisters and I exchanged looks. "I'm not sure that's a good idea, Mama. Remember, that dress has a four-foot train," I said. "You don't want to stumble and end up flat on your face."

She shuddered. "I'd never live it down. Your Aunt Ida is just itching for something gossip-worthy to happen. Well, she won't find a thing. This day will be perfect. My wedding will be perfect."

Moments later, Teensy skittered into the hall. He gave an excited yelp when he spotted Mama, and vice-versa. "My stars and garters, girls, Sal's here!"

She jumped to her feet. "Mace! Help me with my train. Maddie! Run out and tell him not to come in yet. Marty! Scoop up Teensy and follow me into the office. I don't want that dog wandering around and lifting a leg on one of the silk trees. They're rentals."

We rushed around, trying to obey Mama's orders, which she continued barking out like a four-star general. On second thought, maybe the woman *could* use a little more wine.

———

Mama's white-suited groom looked a little green. He swallowed, took a deep breath, and pulled out his handkerchief for the fourth or fifth time to mop his brow.

The audience was seated. The members of the bridal troupe were amassed on stage, waiting for the featured player's big entrance. In addition to the three of us in our hideous ruffles, Sal's younger brother and two golf buddies stood up for him. They looked like extras from the double-wedding scene in *Gone with the Wind*. I'd finally broken down and watched it, since Mama would give me no peace until I did. I'm embarrassed to admit I cried when Rhett left Scarlett.

Sal wore a white suit and black string tie. Mama had insisted upon it, even though it wasn't accurate wedding attire from the movie's historical period. Maybe she'd mixed up Rhett Butler with Col. Sanders from Kentucky Fried Chicken. But considering how she'd been acting all *Bridezilla* in the weeks leading up to the wedding, none of us wanted to broach the topic.

Now, Sal seemed to be swaying a bit on his feet. "Are you all right?" I asked in a hushed voice.

He nodded weakly. I wasn't convinced. Seeing the Big Man go down like a pallet of fertilizer before the *I do's* would definitely give Aunt Ida something gossip-worthy.

I crooked a finger at C'ndee, who climbed up in a flash to join us on stage. My opinion of her was improving by the moment. Maybe she was brash and loud and a pain in the butt, but she was top-of-the-game when it came to planning and executing a wedding.

"Sal looks like he's about to toss his lunch," I whispered. "Why don't you ..."

"Bitters and soda water," she finished. "And I keep a pocket fan in my purse."

She was back from the bar in moments, handing him a glass of the stomach-calming drink. On the pretense of straightening Sal's white rose boutonniere, she stood in front of him and whipped out a battery powered fan. As he downed the drink, she aimed the cooling draft into his face.

Just as the music minister from Abundant Forgiveness struck the first note on his electric organ, C'ndee stepped off the stage. Sal's green was nearly gone as he stooped and called out to Teensy, as rehearsed. The little dog tottered down the aisle, satin top hat slightly askew.

"C'mere, boy!"

Teensy launched himself straight into Sal's arms. The wedding guests *oohed* and *aahed*. Untying the wedding rings from a white ribbon on the dog's celadon-colored saddle, Sal held them up for all to see. Laughter and applause rippled through the hall. Even Maddie wore a big smile.

"Teensy's a hit," Marty whispered.

I nodded. "Having him as the ring bearer wasn't as idiotic as I thought."

Next came the flower girl, D'Vora's four-year-old, L'Donna. She scattered white rose petals by the fistful, tossing them so energetically that some of the guests in aisle seats ducked. A constellation of camera flashes captured the adorable sight.

And then, the processional music fell silent. A hush came over the crowd. There was a dramatic pause. Just as Mama entered the hall, the familiar strains of "Here Comes the Bride" resounded. Heads turned. A collective gasp ensued. People stood and craned their necks to get a better view.

Mama looked like a fairy tale princess. And if her prince was a fast-talking, three-hundred-pound tough guy from the Bronx, so what? The moment was perfect. Until Aunt Ida hissed to her son from the second row: "You did not tell me Rosalee intended to wear white, Henry. That takes some nerve."

There were snickers, amid a *shush* or two. Mama bobbled the slightest bit. Sal blew her a kiss, covering a burp at the same time. Then she threw back her shoulders, held her veiled head high, and climbed the steps to the stage.

"Ida's going to pay for that," Maddie said between clenched teeth.

"I might toss the witch into a vat of potato salad myself," Marty vowed under her breath.

But there'd be no potato salad at Mama's wedding. C'ndee put together a menu of fingerling potatoes and roasted asparagus to go with the prime rib. *Very* classy! Of course, Mama insisted that fried catfish with hush puppies be the alternative selection to red meat. We weren't going to stray too far from our Himmarshee roots.

The music ended. The Reverend Delilah started in with preaching. Mercifully, she was moving right along, holding to her promise to keep the service short. My feet already felt like somebody cut them in half with a circular saw and stuffed them into two lime-green sausage casings. Trying to distract myself from excruciating high-heel pain, I looked out into the crowd.

I saw Linda-Ann, looking pretty in a hot pink dress. Where was Trevor? Rabe sat beside Linda-Ann. He'd changed out of his overalls, and cleaned up surprisingly well. His stepfather, Darryl, was nowhere in sight. Just before Delilah got to the vows, Alice Hodges slipped in near the rear of the hall, wearing pink pastel. I nudged each of my sisters with an elbow.

"Pssst, look at Alice."

"Wow!" Marty breathed.

"Like a new woman," Maddie agreed.

Glaring at us from a chair at the side wall, C'ndee lifted a scolding finger to her lips.

I returned my attention to the ceremony, and heard Delilah wrapping up with a verse from Ephesians: "And be ye kind to one another, tender-hearted, forgiving one another..."

Then it was Sal's turn to recite the lines he'd been rehearsing for weeks:

Rosalee, I knew from the second I saw you I wanted to spend the rest of my life with you. You inspire me. You challenge me to be the best man I can be. I promise to love you forever, to respect you and honor you. This is my solemn vow.

His Bronx honk was so loud, a few guests put discreet fingers to their ears. We suspected he downloaded his vows off the Internet, but that didn't lessen my appreciation of his enthusiasm.

Next, it was Mama's turn:

Sal, you make me feel special. You treat me like gold. And, best of all, you put up with me. She was interrupted here by knowing chuckles. *You've embraced my friends and family, and my hometown. You even love Teensy*—the dog barked as he heard his name, eliciting more laughter. *I promise to cherish you eternally, to love, honor and respect you. This is my solemn vow.*

After the ring exchange, Delilah linked hands with Mama and her groom. "I now pronounce you husband and wife. Sal, you may kiss the bride."

As the minister stepped away, Sal lifted Mama's veil. She offered her cheek for a chaste peck. Instead, Sal grabbed her and bent her backward into a deep dip. Very Rhett of him. He planted a long, wet kiss on his beloved's lips. When they finally came up for air, the VFW erupted in whistles and cheers.

As Mr. and Mrs. Sal Provenza stepped to the edge of the stage to take their bows, I saw only a few members of the audience who were not fully engaged. Aunt Ida sat forward primly, wearing a lemon-sucking frown. Linda-Ann seemed distracted, turning her head repeatedly to check the back door. And instead of watching the bride and groom on stage, Alice Hodges directed a gaze full of spite at the side of the room.

Her eyes were on C'ndee, who was standing now, clapping and whooping.

FORTY-FIVE

"ARE YOU ANGRY AT me?"

Arriving late, Carlos had snuck up behind me. His lips were so close to my ear, I felt his breath hot on my neck. It ignited images in my traitorous mind of us tumbling together on the bed at Darryl's Fish Camp.

"Not just angry. Totally pissed off." I didn't turn around. "Where's your blond sidekick? I thought maybe y'all would come to the wedding together and heckle Mama as she took her first dance with Sal. Or maybe it'd be funny to toss rotten tomatoes at them as they cut their pretty cake."

"Mace, I'm sorry." When I still didn't turn my head, he stroked a ringlet that lay next to my cheek. My skin burned where his finger brushed it. "As a target, you and your *Gone with the Wind* get-up were far too easy. I should have shown more restraint."

"Restraint would have been nice."

"I'll make it up to you, *niña*." He stepped in front of my chair. "How about you let me uncurl your hair? I'll brush it out, nice and slow. *Nice* and slow. Then I'll give you the best shampoo you've ever had. I'll make it last as long as you want."

Black eyes. Sexy smile. A snazzy dark suit that draped perfectly across his broad chest. My treacherous will was weakening.

"You wouldn't want to wash my hair in that suit. It looks expensive. You might get it wet."

He trailed a finger from my cheek, down my neck, and under the ruffled strap of my lime-green gown. My skin tingled.

"Oh, don't worry. I won't wear the suit. That way I won't have to concern myself about it getting wet." He gave my strap a little tug. "But you'll have to take off all your clothes, too. We wouldn't want to ruin this beautiful dress."

My desire for him was about to betray me. Again. I wondered if the warm feeling spreading through my lower regions was making the ruffles on my skirt quiver. And I wondered if anyone was using that manager's office in the back of the hall.

"Well?" He leaned in close, his lips just inches from mine. "What do you say about that shower?"

"My shower?" Mama stood beside us, seemingly clueless about the conversation she'd walked in on. "My shower was perfect, Carlos. We had a singing cowboy."

He straightened and took a step away. I looked up from my chair at Mama. A worried frown creased her brow.

"Have you seen Sal? I can't find him anywhere."

I took what I hoped was a steadying breath. I was still conscious of the heat from Carlos' body beside me. "Sal wasn't feeling well before the ceremony, Mama."

"Nerves," she announced knowingly. "They always hit him right in the bowels."

307

"Too much information, Mama."

"Well, they do, darlin.' He's probably sitting on the pot in the bathroom right now."

She peered more closely at Carlos and me; seemed to notice for the first time the flush on my face, and his hands stuck deep in his pockets. The DJ played Sinatra's "Fly Me to the Moon." Mama's matchmaking mode kicked in.

"My, my," she said. "You look like a million dollars in that suit, Carlos. Doesn't he, Mace?"

"No, Mama."

He lifted an eyebrow at me.

I smiled. "He looks like *two* million dollars."

Encouraged, Mama said, "We'll be opening the champagne soon. This would be the perfect time for the two of you to have a dance." She gave him a little push toward me. "And Carlos, make sure you stick right beside Mace. You won't want to go *anywhere* near that men's room for at least fifteen minutes after you see Sal step out."

"Thanks for the tip."

"You're welcome, honey. I heard y'all arrested Tony. I'd never have believed it. He had such good manners." Waving at someone across the room, Mama began to glide away. "Go dance!" she said over her shoulder.

"What do you say, *niña*? Shall we do like your mother says?"

His eyes smoldered. His voice was low and caressing. I had a better plan: tear off that suit, sweep away the place settings, and have my way with him right there on the table for eight. But a dance would have to do. I gave him my hand.

"I have to do what she says. This is Mama's Special Day."

As we spun onto the floor, I nestled comfortably into his arms. This, at least, felt right. We might scrap and argue, but I couldn't deny the physical attraction. It was like a drug. And what about the rest of it, the more complicated aspects of our relationship?

To borrow a line from Scarlett O'Hara: *I'll think about that tomorrow.*

I kissed him on the cheek.

"What was that for?"

"Just for being here," I said.

We continued dancing to the next song, too. "At Last," the classic Etta James version. I was acutely aware of Carlos' delicious, spicy scent; his body pressed against mine. I figured I'd better get my mind on something else, or those china place settings on the table weren't safe.

I looked out the window, where the sun was beginning its downward trek through the sky. It wouldn't be long now before Sal and Mama made their exit as husband and wife. I saw his Cadillac, fully decorated and tied with tin cans, courtesy of his groomsmen. A gleaming, vintage muscle car was parked just beyond the Caddy. Could that possibly be the rusting hulk from the fish camp? If so, Rabe had worked wonders in record time.

Then, a scene next to the Camaro caught my eye.

Linda-Ann stood there in her hot pink party dress. Trevor towered over her, wearing beige coveralls. Shaking her head, she backed away. Trevor, his face red and contorted, waved his arms wildly. He looked like he was shouting, but I didn't hear the words since the hall's windows were closed, the AC was cranked on high, and the music was loud.

He grabbed her arm; she pulled it away. That seemed to antagonize him even more. He raised a clenched fist, like he was going to hit her. But Linda-Ann stood up to him. Her face was inches from his as she shook her finger and gave him hell. Now, Trevor was the one backing up, surprise written all over his face. She turned and stalked back toward the VFW. He stared after her, his mouth hanging open.

I was about to ask Carlos what he thought about Trevor, and his potential for violence, when we spun away from the window. My gaze settled on Ronnie's widow, solitary in that cone of sorrow again. She sat at an otherwise empty table, staring into a full glass of what looked like bourbon. Was it grief and loneliness she was trying to drink away? Or was it something else?

Another turn, and I saw C'ndee and Rabe, huddled together in a far corner of the dining room. Maybe they were cooking up something that would focus suspicion on Darryl for Ronnie's murder. I was almost certain Tony didn't kill the caterer. Which left the question: Who did?

The song ended. Sliding his hand to the small of my back, Carlos pressed me close. "A *peso* for your thoughts, Mace."

"I was just thinking about Ronnie..."

Before I got the chance to finish, Mama took the microphone from the DJ at the foot of the stage. As she *tap-tap-tapped*, people covered their ears at the noise pain.

"Listen up, everybody. We're going to serve the champagne now. But before we do, I just want to say how grateful I am that all of you could be here with us." Her eyes found my sisters and me in the crowd. She blew us each a kiss. "All my favorite people in the world are here, and it's only fitting that y'all will share Sal's and my Special Day."

She dabbed her eyes with a cornflower-colored handkerchief she carried as the bride's "something blue." Sniffling a little, she cleared her throat.

"Now, C'ndee's going to start opening bottles and the servers will pour and pass." She raised her voice, aiming it toward the bathrooms way back in the far reaches of the hall. "I surely hope by that time, my new husband will be here to join me on stage."

A muffled bellow issued from behind the closed door of the Men's: "Don't worry! I'll be there, Rosie."

Amid laughter, the first *pop* of a champagne bottle sounded. The crowd cheered. And then *pop, pop, pop.* The servers quickly loaded glasses onto trays and began making a circuit of the room. They handed out sparkling wine, pink of course, until all the guests held a glass. "Don't forget the bride and groom," Mama said into the microphone.

With a flourish, C'ndee draped a white linen napkin across her arm and pulled out a final bottle. It was festooned with a showy bow of celadon tulle and white satin ribbons. She wiggled and worked at the plastic cork. Everyone watched. She hammed it up, raising the bottle, smiling.

"Best wishes to the married couple, from the best caterer in Himmarshee," she shouted.

Then C'ndee gave a mighty pull, and finally: *Pop!*

Almost at the instant I registered that this bottle popped more loudly than the rest, C'ndee flinched and clutched at her side. She slumped over. The bottle clattered to the floor, its contents spilling out in a fizzy pink stream.

And slowly a red stain blossomed across the white linen napkin that still hung on C'ndee's arm.

FORTY-SIX

"CALL AN AMBULANCE," SOMEONE shouted. "C'ndee's been shot!"

Women screamed. Teensy howled. Chairs overturned. Guests scrambled for the door or ducked for cover under tables. The DJ sailed off the stage, knocking the pastor's lectern onto the dance floor. Gun drawn, Carlos guided me as we crouched behind it. His eyes scanned the room. So did mine.

I'd lost sight of Mama and my sisters. Several tables had been flipped onto their sides. I prayed they'd have the good sense to hide behind one of them.

"Everyone remain calm. I'm with the police." Carlos' voice was loud, carrying over the strains of "YMCA" on the sound system. Someone wisely yanked the plug on the Village People. "Stay down and stay safe. Nobody move."

I heard some sobs. A few whimpers. A muffled bark.

And then I saw a flash of pink, the only upright body in the place, moving toward the kitchen door and the exit beyond. "Back of the room by the prime rib," I whispered to Carlos. "Eleven o'clock."

"Stop!" He spun toward the moving figure, his voice crackling with authority. "Police!"

Alice Hodges hesitated for a second. And then she reached behind a fake silk dogwood and hauled out the hiding bride. Gun held now against Mama's head, Alice dragged her backward into the center of the room. Oddly, what I noticed was Mama's four-foot train, trailing through pieces of prime rib and *jus* that had spilled onto the floor from the carving table. If Mama got out of this mess, she'd be mad about that. But at this moment, terrified was all she was. Her eyes were huge; her face as white as her gown. If, as Mama had said, the Lord was going to smile down on her wedding today, I prayed he'd get started soon.

Alice waved the gun around the room, getting everyone's attention. "If anybody tries to stop me from leaving, I'll kill Rosalee."

None of us doubted she would.

Time seemed to have stopped. But in reality, only a few moments had passed since the gunshot sounded. I hoped someone had dialed 911 before Alice showed herself. I glanced toward C'ndee, who sat slumped against Rabe on the floor behind one of the tables. His arm was around her, holding her up. The red stain was growing on the napkin.

The hall was as hushed as a church. Whoever had Teensy must have muzzled him. All eyes focused on Mama, but surely not in the way she would have wanted. Suddenly, she squared her shoulders. Then she turned, ever so slowly, to look into the face of the woman who threatened to shoot her.

"You can't do this, Alice." I was proud of Mama. Her voice barely shook. "We've been neighbors. Friends. You've worshipped beside me. The Bible says one burdened with the guilt of murder will be a fugitive down to the grave. You know what the Lord wants you to do. Put down that gun."

Alice shook her head. "It's too late, Rosalee. Things have gotten out of hand."

Carlos motioned for me to stay; then he started inching his way across the floor toward Alice. Of course, I followed right behind him, crawling on my belly, and hoping my giant skirt stayed hidden behind a row of overturned tables. Fleetingly, I realized slithering through spilled wine and food and who knows what else on the floor would ruin the Scarlett gown forever. I had no idea why, but I felt sad about that.

With a plea in her voice, Mama continued, "It's never too late to do the right thing."

"You're wrong, Rosalee. At this point, I have nothing to lose. All I wanted to do was protect our livelihood. That fool husband of mine was finally starting to make a go of it, when *she* entered the scene."

Face flushed with rage, Alice pointed the gun to where C'ndee had fallen.

"*She* made him happy, Ronnie said. That fool thought the Yankee bitch loved him." Alice shook her head, incredulous. "That morning in the VFW's kitchen, he told me he wasn't too old to want happiness. He was going to leave me and share our business with her." She shrugged. "I couldn't let that happen. The knife was right there. It was like a sign."

"So you killed Ronnie because you were jealous of C'ndee?"

Alice's laugh was a harsh cackle. "Not in the way you think, Rosalee. I couldn't have cared less about the fornicating. I was jealous about them going into business together. And, then, once the deed was done with Ronnie, once he was out of the way, I knew I didn't want her as my business rival." She glanced in C'ndee's direction. "You heard her crowing just now, bragging about how good she is. I had to shoot her. You eliminate the competition, by whatever means necessary. That's the most basic rule of commerce."

I wondered if that's the way they teach it at Harvard Business School.

"Well I'm sorry about all that, Alice. I truly am."

Uh-oh. I recognized that fed-up tone in Mama's voice. It told me we'd better hurry.

"Still and all, none of that gives you the right to ruin My Special Day." Like Bridezilla in full tantrum, Mama stomped a white satin heel on top of Alice's big toe. Howling in pain, Alice instinctively reached down to grab her sandaled foot. In the process, she dropped the gun.

Carlos and I leaped into action. He tackled Alice, who went down like a tin shed in a hurricane. I grabbed Mama, and pulled her behind an upended table.

"Watch the train, honey!"

I didn't have the heart to tell her it already had bits of rib fat and bloody juice permanently embedded. Why ruin her Special Day?

Teensy must have escaped, because the little dog scrabbled across the floor, sailed above the overturned table, and landed with a yelp on Mama's head. A big voice boomed from the bathroom hallway.

"Hold on for the toast, Rosie! I'm on my way!" The shock on Sal's still-green face was almost comical as he rounded the corner into the dismantled dining room. "What the hell?"

An ambulance siren sounded in the distance. Rabe was helping C'ndee stretch out on the floor. Linda-Ann sat beside her, holding her hand. C'ndee grimaced with every move, but her color wasn't bad. That was a good sign.

Guests emerged from under tables, dusting off their fancy duds. My sisters found Mama and me. Carlos kept a firm hold on Alice while he scooped her gun off the floor. He pointed Sal toward his wounded cousin-in-law.

"Could you check on C'ndee's condition so you can brief the paramedics when they arrive?"

"I'll live," C'ndee called out, her voice surprisingly strong.

Sal's years of experience kicked in. Seeming to appraise the situation in seconds, he started shouting commands. "All right, everybody move back. Give her some room." He knelt beside C'ndee. "The authorities are on their way."

Carlos started toward the door with Alice in custody. I touched his arm. "You saved Mama's life. I don't know how I'll ever repay you."

"I have a couple of ideas." He gave me half a grin, and then turned serious. "You were right there with me, even though I warned you to stay behind. We did it together."

"I guess we make a pretty good team."

"That's what I've been trying to tell you, *niña*."

FORTY-SEVEN

With Mama's bare feet in his lap, Sal tenderly probed the big toe on her right foot.

"I don't care what that paramedic said, Sally. I think it's broken!"

"You just jammed it when you stomped on Alice's foot, Rosie. It'll feel better in a few days."

An ambulance crew had come for C'ndee. After they established her wound wasn't as serious as we feared, Mama sought medical advice for her aching toe. I admired the paramedic's restraint in not telling Mama what she could do with her toe as he loaded C'ndee into the back of the vehicle.

A surprising number of guests stayed after the excitement was over. Chairs and tables were straightened; broken glass swept up; ruined food thrown in the trash. The DJ retook the stage. Linda-Ann slow-danced past us on the dance floor, entangled with Rabe.

"I guess Mr. Animal Rights is history," I said. "I saw the two of them screaming at each other outside in the parking lot just before Alice shot C'ndee."

Marty said, "Linda-Ann broke if off. She told me in the Ladies she suspected Trevor put that dead hog's head on Alice's porch. She said between that and those awful pig costumes, she couldn't love a man like him."

Something about that wild pig on the porch had been bothering me. Finally, I had it: "Does anyone else remember Alice saying she grew up on a hog farm?" I asked. "I wouldn't put it past her to have butchered that poor creature herself."

"Makes sense." Maddie nodded. "Based on how she killed Ronnie, she knows her way around a knife."

Images of that bloody scene in the kitchen pushed their way into my mind. I wondered if I'd ever stop reliving the morning I discovered Ronnie's body.

"Hey, Mama," I said. "Did any of those bottles of wine survive the mess in here? I could use a little glass of something alcoholic."

She slapped her forehead. "Sal and I missed our good luck toast. We can't start married life without it!"

She motioned to the DJ to bring her the microphone. She limped to the stage to speak to her guests.

"Well, y'all, this isn't exactly how I planned things. But I am grateful we survived. Let's scare up whatever glasses weren't broken, and bring in some booze from the bar. My groom and I are going to have us that toast!"

The DJ cranked up the perfect song, "We Are Family."

"I wouldn't turn down a piece of prime rib, either," Mama added. "I haven't eaten a bite."

Raising her voice over the music, she struck a Scarlett pose: "*As God is my witness, I'll never be hungry again!*"

It was late. The toast had been made. The wedding was almost over. Mama and Sal were about to take off. But there was still one thing to do before they left.

Mama stood on the stage, her back to the hall, her bridal bouquet raised high over her head. The remaining guests counted down. *One. Two. Three.*

Toss!

She gave a mighty heave. The flowers soared above the heads of the short girls in the front row. They floated past the divorcees and Mama's widowed bingo buddies in the middle. And, as if guided by invisible wires or my mama's brain waves, they plopped smack into the reluctant grasp of a tall single gal hiding behind everyone else.

Mama spun, and then squealed with joy when she saw who caught the bouquet. Me.

"See, Mace? I told you the Lord was going to smile down on my wedding today."

THE END

If you enjoyed reading *Mama Gets Hitched*, read an excerpt from the next Mace Bauer Mystery

Mama Sees Stars

ONE

I WAITED OUT OF camera range, holding the bridle on a saddled horse. Bright lights bathed the scene. The movie set was pin-drop quiet.

"Action," the assistant director said.

I let go of the bridle, slapped the horse's rump, and stood back so the camera could capture him racing past. Just as the horse with no rider entered a clearing, gathering speed to a gallop, a voice rang out into the silence.

"My stars and garters! Somebody's let a horse get loose. Don't just stand there, Mace! Come help me catch him."

An orange blur dashed into the animal's path, waving arms and yelling.

"Cut!" The assistant director put his fingers to his temples and massaged. I could tell him it's not so easy to rub away this kind of headache.

A short, elderly bald man in a bright red shirt kicked over a chair. "Security!" The word exploded from his mouth. "Would somebody grab the stupid hillbilly?"

A muscled guy in a baseball cap started toward The Hillbilly, a.k.a. my mama. Cringing, I stepped forward and admitted it. "She's with me."

The short man leveled a glare. "And who the hell are *you*?"

"Mace Bauer." I offered my hand. He looked at it like it was bathed, palm to pinky, in horse manure. "I'm the animal wrangler."

"And I am not impressed." His leathery face scrunched up like he smelled something bad.

As I slipped my unshaken hand into the pocket of my jeans, Mama marched to my side. She smoothed her orange-sherbet pantsuit, fluffed her platinum-hued hair, and straightened to her full four foot, eleven inches. The jerk in the red shirt may have had a few inches on her, but she had the Mama Glare. And it was set right now at stun.

"Well, who the blue blazes are *you*? All we know so far is you're a rude little man who has no idea how to talk to a lady. And by the way, Florida is as flat as a frying pan, so I can hardly be a hillbilly, can I?"

Whispers and a few snickers traveled around the set. His beady eyes met her glare. "I'm the boss here. The top dog. Let me put it in terms you'll understand. If this movie set was a hoe-down, I'd be the top hoe. If it was a barbecue joint, I'd own the building. I'd own the chairs and tables. I'd even own the pigs. And I'd get to say who gets to sit down for dinner, and who doesn't."

Mama, brows knit, glanced at me. "Is he saying I can't come to his rib joint?"

I shrugged.

"Well, I wouldn't want to go there anyway," she said. "I can tell you it'll never be as popular as the Pork Pit, which has been in Himmarshee forever. Not only do they have ribs to die for, they make the best peach cobbler, too. Besides, the folks at the Pork Pit know how to treat their customers. I'd say you have a lot to learn about how to treat people…"

As Mama went on, I tried to pretend I was somewhere else. The assistant director massaged his head so hard, I thought he'd rub the hair right off his temples. Meanwhile, the old guy's face was getting purple. Jabbing his cigar at Mama, he looked mad enough to pick her up and toss her off the set himself.

Just then, a woman stepped up to him with a cell phone in one hand and a sandwich in the other. She whispered in his ear. He traded his cigar for the phone, jammed half the sandwich in his mouth, and began shouting into the cell.

"What kind of idiot do you think I am? I'll have your ass in the courtroom faster than you can say breach of contract…"

He stomped away, Mama's transgression seemingly forgotten. As he left, little missiles of what looked like roast beef launched themselves from his lips. I pitied the person on the other end of the call. The woman who brought him the phone was almost a head taller than he was, but she had to run to keep up with him.

The behemoth in the ball cap still loomed next to Mama. "It's her first time on a movie," I apologized to him. "Don't worry. I'll explain everything, and make sure she understands the concept of Quiet on the Set."

The three of us watched the departing loudmouth. "Who is he, anyway?" I asked the security man.

"You mean besides being a First Class Asshole?"

"Language, son," Mama said, but she was smiling.

"Norman Sydney. He's the movie's producer, but he thinks he's God."

———

"How was I supposed to know you let the horse go on purpose?"

"We're shooting a movie here, Mama. The scene is supposed to look like something bad happened to one of the kids in the family. The horse is spooked, so it races off alone."

Mama's bottom lip was set in a pout. The horse, in contrast, plodded along with no whining at the end of a lead rope. He seemed happy to be heading back to the movie's corral.

The Hollywood folks were in Himmarshee doing a film about the early days of cattle-ranching in Florida. It was supposed to be based on Patrick Smith's book *A Land Remembered*. But I'd peeked at a script, and the cows were the only characters that hadn't been changed. Supposedly, the new working title was *Fierce Fury Past*. Hired to handle the horses, I was using vacation time from my real job at a nature park to make some extra cash.

After Mama's embarrassing interruption, we'd done five or six more takes of the galloping horse. Bored, she'd wandered off to find a place where she wouldn't get yelled at for talking.

Now, we'd met up again, and were about to have lunch. But first I had to return the horse, and check on the rest of the animals.

Still smarting over being dressed down by the producer, Mama was uncharacteristically quiet.

Saddle leather creaked as we walked through a pasture. The horse's hooves thudded on a sandy path cut through a blanket of Bahia grass. A mockingbird sang from an oak branch.

Curiosity finally triumphed over Mama's bad mood: "Have you seen any of the Hollywood stars yet? Is that Kelly Conover as pretty in person as she is on the screen?"

"It's just my first day. I'm sure I will see some stars, unless one of my family members manages to get me fired from the movie."

She narrowed her eyes. "Why would any of us want to do that?"

"Just try to stay out of trouble, would you, Mama?"

"Me? I thought *you* were in trouble. I thought you needed my help with that horse. What kind of mother would I be if I saw you in a jam and didn't step in? Besides, it was that awful man's fault for jumping all over me. He's wound up tighter than granny's girdle."

I chuckled. "That security guard pegged him, that's for sure."

A loud whinny sounded from the corral. The horse behind us gave a pitiful whicker.

"Well, that didn't seem very enthusiastic,'" I said. "What's wrong, Rebel? Not the right someone waiting for you back at the ranch? Not that pretty little mare?"

I did a half-turn to pat the horse's neck, and run a hand under his mane. Turning back, I plowed smack into Mama, who had stopped in her tracks. Rebel's big head hit me between my shoulders. I heard Mama take a sharp gasp.

"Oh, my! It's that horrible producer, Mace. I can see his bright red shirt. Your eyes are younger than mine. Isn't that him, leaning against the corral gate?"

I stepped around her to get a better view.

"I hope he hasn't come to fire you," she said.

"It's him, Mama. But he's not leaning against the corral."

I took my cell phone from my pocket and hit speed dial for Carlos Martinez, my boyfriend and a detective with the Him-marshee police department.

Somebody had tossed Norman Sydney over the fence like drying laundry. The white, sandy ground beneath his body was stained, as red as his tomato-colored shirt.

Charles Trainor, Jr.

ABOUT THE AUTHOR

Like Mace Bauer's, Deborah Sharp's family roots were set in Florida long before Disney and *Miami Vice* came to define the state. She does some writing at a getaway overlooking the Kissimmee River in the wilds north of Okeechobee, and some at Starbucks in Fort Lauderdale. As a Florida native and a longtime reporter for *USA Today*, she knows every burg and back road, including some not found on maps. Here's what she has to say about Himmarshee:

> Home to cowboys and church suppers, Himmarshee is hot and swarming with mosquitoes. A throwback to the ways of long-ago southern Florida, it bears some resemblance to the present-day ranching town of Okeechobee. The best thing about Mace and Mama's hometown: it will always be threatened, but never spoiled, by suburban sprawl.